THE CHOW
MANIAC

THE CHOW

MANIAC

A NOODLE SHOP MYSTERY

VIVIEN CHIEN

St. Martin's Paperbacks

This is a work of fiction. All of the characters, organizations, and events portrayed in this novel are either products of the author's imagination or are used fictitiously.

First published in the United States by St. Martin's Paperbacks, an imprint of St. Martin's Publishing Group.

THE CHOW MANIAC

For information, address St. Martin's Publishing Group, 120 Broadway, New York, NY 10271.

www.stmartins.com

ISBN: 978-1-250-33883-9

Our books may be purchased in bulk for promotional, educational, or business use. Please contact your local bookseller or the Macmillan Corporate and Premium Sales Department at 1-800-221-7945, ext. 5442, or by email at MacmillanSpecialMarkets@macmillan.com.

St. Martin's Paperbacks edition / April 2025

Printed in the United States of America

10 9 8 7 6 5 4 3 2 1

For my mother, Chin Mei
aka Carol:

Thank you for teaching me the history and
folklore of our culture.
(And for making me watch all those Taiwanese
soap operas I grew to love so much.)
我爱你

ACKNOWLEDGMENTS

This book, like my others, would not be possible without the extraordinary people that I find myself lucky enough to be surrounded by:

Lots of hugs and gratitude go to my agent, Gail Fortune. Lady, you keep me in line and looking toward a bright horizon. I'd be lost without your encouragement and pep talks. Thank you for caring about me "beyond the page."

Many, many thanks to my editor, Lily Cronig. It's truly a pleasure to create these stories alongside your skilled editing capabilities. You get me, you really get me. Thank you for making the fine-tuning process an enjoyable one.

Shout out to "my gals" at St. Martin's Press: fantabulous publicist, Kayla Janas, and phenomenal marketer, Allison Ziegler. Not only are both of you terrific humans, but you excel at what you do. I am beyond fortunate to have the opportunity to work with you. Thank you for caring about this series as much as I do.

To one of my fave behind-the-scenes peeps, my copy editor: John Simko. You save me time and time again with your eagle eyes. I commend you for putting up with my echoes and incredibly specific references. You are a gem.

To Mary Ann Lasher, the artistic genius behind the Noodle Shop covers. Thank you for making these beautiful covers. I already love the next one and I haven't even seen it yet. (That's how good you are!)

Really and truly, my gratitude extends to all of St. Martin's Press/Minotaur. I thank my lucky stars every day that Lana and I get to be a part of your family.

Much admiration goes to my friends and family. We have journeyed this tremendously winding road together and there is no other group of people I'd rather navigate it with.

A special shout-out to my parents: To my dad, Paul: Thank you for being there throughout the roller coaster that has been my life. I'll never be able to say it enough . . . your support has carried me through some of the most difficult times and I am forever grateful for that. To my mother, Chin Mei, to whom this book is dedicated: Thank you for teaching me the hard lessons, the importance of laughing at yourself, and for sharing a fantastical world of fairy tales and folklore with me. These stories I grew up listening to helped shape me into the daydream believer I am today.

To my sister, Shu-hui, I appreciate you more than words can say. Thank you for sharing your life wisdoms with me and setting the example of what a strong woman should look like.

And never to be forgotten: my fabulous readers. I am sending you so much love. I am grateful to all of you for allowing me to fill some of your free time with my stories. On top of that, the encouragement and support that I continue to receive from you lot leaves me speechless. (And we all know that is no easy feat!) Keep being the wonderful humans that you are, and don't forget, if no one told you today, you look absolutely amazing!

八仙过海，各显神通

Bā xiān guò hǎi, gè xiǎn shén tōng.

The Eight Immortals cross the sea,
each revealing their divine power.

HISTORICAL NOTE

—————————————

While the characters in this story are purely figments of my imagination, some of the historical context, events, and noted figures are very real. The references to the Chinese Masonic Lodge, Wan Lee Yew, and Sing Ki are kindly borrowed from moments dating near the turn of the twentieth century—a tumultuous time for many cultures as the proverbial melting pot kicked into high gear.

Inspiration was also drawn from the legend of the Eight Immortals, but the modern-day representation is strictly fictional . . . or is it? Just kidding! It totally is.

PROLOGUE

--- --- --- --- --- --- --- ---

Cleveland, Ohio—October 1901

Yunhao Zhang stood before his seven closest confidantes in one of the secluded meeting rooms on the third floor of the Chinese Masonic Lodge on West 3rd Street. For safety purposes, a password—which he was in charge of changing every thirty days—was needed to gain access to the second and third floors of the building.

His eyes slid toward the silk scroll painting of the Eight Immortals that hung to his left. Depicted were eight travelers highly regarded in Chinese culture as symbols of what could be achieved, even by the common man—all eight having been commoners themselves. In one of the most famous tales written about their adventures, they were said to have navigated the harsh seas to celebrate the Queen Mother of the West, Xi Wang Mu—the goddess of immortality. They were determined to achieve their shared goal of reaching her annual celebration by traversing the turbulent seas together as a group, while contributing to their journey's success in each of their own unique ways. Perhaps he'd stared at this painting for too many days, and perhaps it had filled his head with fanciful thinking. After all, it was no coincidence that he had specifically asked to meet with seven other individuals.

Clutched in his hands, behind his back, were old, rolled-up articles from two of the city's local newspapers: the *Plain Dealer* and the *Cleveland Leader*. Both contained stories about the Chinese community, and not all of what was written was entirely in their favor. He'd brought the old articles as examples. Some of his friends were not able to read what the papers said, so he planned to reference them directly if called to do so.

Yunhao had immigrated from China a handful of years ago, originally settling in the city of San Francisco. Unfortunately, the time he'd spent there had not gone as he would have liked. When the Chinese Exclusion Act was introduced, he found it increasingly difficult to find suitable work, and even if he'd had the money to own property, there were legal restrictions set in place that stopped him from purchasing land.

His initial hope, like many in his position, had been to escape the hardships and lack of opportunity that surrounded him and his family. The promise of the United States and all it had to offer were more than enough incentive to leave his country of birth, something no one in his family had ever done before. But as he had quickly learned in his short thirty years of life, not everything came as advertised. This situation was apparently no different. The seven men who sat before him were just a few who'd arrived in northern Ohio at the same time as he had, and he knew that if there was anyone to be trusted, it was them. *They* would understand.

He cleared his throat, holding his chin high as he

began to speak. He addressed his friends in Mandarin since they would better understand him in their native language. "Thank you for agreeing to meet with me on such short notice."

"What is this about?" The question came from the oldest man in their group, Chun Ming Wong. He was a firm man with little patience, but Yunhao knew that he was one of the smartest and most experienced of anyone in town. If Chun Ming followed, the rest would surely join him without much convincing.

Yunhao held up the papers he'd been concealing behind his back. "Have any of you read what they say about us in the newspapers?" He knew they hadn't but wanted to give them the benefit of the doubt he felt they deserved.

Chun Ming answered for the rest. "Who has time to read the newspapers? Who has time to learn *how* to read when we must work ourselves to death simply to live?"

The others nodded. A wave of unhappiness lingered throughout the room. The trials they had faced were wearing them down, and not being able to read was a reminder that they had more struggles than they cared to recognize.

Muchen Yeh, a quiet man who spent his days practicing and teaching the arts of meditation and Qigong, said in a calm tone, "Don't listen to his complaints, he is bitter because you have surpassed all of us in your studies—a commendable endeavor, my young friend."

Chun Ming mumbled something under his breath.

Yunhao gathered that it was something unpleasant and chose to ignore it, continuing on with his intended purpose. First he held up the story from the *Plain Dealer.* "Do you all remember Wan Lee Yew?"

There were a mix of responses from all seven. Some

nodded, others shrugged, and Chun Ming remained un-enthused, refusing to even look at the pages that Yunhao waved at them.

Muchen lifted his hand. "Is he not the man who married an Irish woman?"

Yunhao nodded. "The very one."

Chun Ming folded his arms across his chest, his face turned away from the others. "What does this matter? That was six years ago. It is old news."

Muchen clucked his tongue. "Are you simple? That man and his new wife were stoned right on Ontario Street. How can you say it doesn't matter?"

Chun Ming clenched his jaw but said nothing further.

What Muchen said was true, and it was a devastating moment for their small community of less than one hundred. Because their numbers were low, most everyone knew one another, and though some pretended not to remember the incident, Yunhao knew better than to believe them.

As of last year's census, there were only eight recorded Chinese women living within the city. Yunhao imagined there were close to none when Wan Lee Yew had married outside of his culture—something that was not widely accepted. Interracial marriages were considered taboo even in this more progressive region. On the day of their wedding, many an angry man who opposed their legal union littered the street where the couple took their ceremonial stroll. It was customary that those of their culture walk down the street of where the marriage had taken place.

Yunhao reminded his friends of these exact details, ignoring the grumbles from Chun Ming. He also wanted them to know that the name of the courageous bride was Mary and she had proudly told the *Plain Dealer* reporter who interviewed her after the awful incident that she did not regret her choice in marriage. Her words were a small comfort and perhaps a tiny piece of victory after such a horrendous public display of violence.

Yunhao moved on to the next article from the *Cleveland Leader* and alerted his friends of the negative details that had been written about them. That while they were touted to have "incredible work ethic" and known to be "mild-mannered," the article also said they were "dull" and "undemonstrative." He was not familiar with this second word, and when he used his dictionary to find the meaning, he was upset to discover that it meant their learned mannerisms left them appearing unfeeling and cold to others.

The article also suggested that they had failed to adapt to this society's ways since the time they—the Chinese—had first arrived in the United States.

But those examples weren't what had caused Yunhao to call this particular meeting. Yes, they weighed heavily on his mind, but the most recent incident—the death . . . no, the *murder* of Sing Ki—had sparked him to take action. He told his listeners as much, his voice deepening with every heavy word.

Chun Ming was the first to speak. "The restaurant owner who was found dead by his bartender? This is not proven to be murder. He was seen arguing with one of his waitresses the night before he was found dead. Surely, he knew he had dishonored himself and his family name."

Honghua Kang, who was known to assist newcomers in finding suitable places to live, had not spoken during the entire meeting. But the previous comment had perturbed him. He shifted to the edge of his seat, leaned forward, and rested his elbow on his knee. "Eh, come now, Chun Ming, are you implying that Sing Ki took his own life over something like this? It is despicable of you to say such words."

Chun Ming flared his nostrils. "I am not the only one who thinks this."

Yunhao took a step closer toward the group. "Yes, I have heard this as well. I have also heard rumors that it was a highbinder. But you mustn't believe everything that you hear."

The group gawked in unison, but it was Honghua who commented. "A highbinder? What convenient timing for one to appear," he said, narrowing his eyes. "There is no doubt in my mind that Sing Ki was murdered, but I do not believe it to be the work of highbinders."

Highbinders, as they were called, were assassins who resided in China but visited many Chinese business owners in the United States. They demanded payment for their own nefarious purposes, and if they did not receive what they requested there were consequences.

Chun Ming waved a hand to dismiss the idea. "I have heard enough. What does it matter? It is best to not make a fuss. Keep our heads down, do our work, and pray for an easy life. This is all we can do for ourselves. We mustn't dream too big, for we see that others do not approve and the more success we create for ourselves, the more attention we gain. Look at these stories you speak of . . . these men did no favors for themselves."

Yunhao held up a finger. "But that is exactly why I have called you here. I have a plan that I think will benefit all of us and secure our successes."

It was plain to see by the downward curve of his mouth that Chun Ming was ready to interject with another disapproving remark, but Muchen nudged him with an elbow. "Quiet, Chun Ming. Let Yunhao continue. I would like to hear what he has to say."

Yunhao felt encouraged by Muchen's words and, puffing out his chest, began explaining what he proposed they do. "We know that we can only trust ourselves. We have made the journey across an ocean to seek our futures . . . our destiny." His eyes slid back in the direction of the painting that inspired him. "I do not pretend to know what truly happened to Sing Ki, but it is clear to all we fear that even those from our native country would try to oppose us. We must rely on each other and create a brotherhood to pave the way to triumph. To help us live comfortably, find wives to create families, and perhaps even to send money home to our less fortunate relatives. This is *why* we came. We are here for a better life, and that is what I intend to achieve. Therefore, I propose we begin a network of trusted persons to build this collective success. All of us have businesses with different specialties. Imagine if we were to combine our knowledge and resources to help others who need assistance. If a few of us succeed, we all prosper."

Honghua nodded along. "It is true that we all possess different skills."

Muchen straightened in his seat. "And we do know people from various walks of life. I have met several interesting individuals who seek the path of enlightenment and inner peace. Such endeavors do not discriminate. We could bring these different people together . . . a network as you say. This could help many of them find jobs or learn new skills with those they trust."

Chun Ming snorted. "This thinking belongs in a fairy tale. We will be met by sabotage, just as you described in your story about Wan Lee Yew. He dared venture outside of what was made available to him and look what happened. He was fortunate to escape with his life that day."

Yunhao replied. "Yes, I agree. That is why I said we must have only trusted members involved. This element is key to our victory. The eight in this room will be the only ones who are aware of this project to its fullest extent. We must be in agreement before we propose to alert anyone outside this group to our existence. Only when all of us are in agreement can we then offer our assistance to the person who requires it."

Muchen tilted his head. "You suggest a voting system?"

Yunhao nodded. "Yes. I feel that is the fairest way to proceed. We must have checks and balances in place to protect the interests of everyone involved."

Chun Ming's jaw softened from its stiff position. It was evident that he was beginning to warm to the idea. He said, "If we were to do this, we should also have passcodes much like this meeting ground possesses. And perhaps something to signify to others that we are who we say we are."

Yunhao beamed with delight. "I have thought the same thing, my friend. Especially if we want our group to branch out farther than just this city. If we are successful in our efforts, my hope is to spread this idea back to San Francisco to some of those we had to leave behind. After all, others in our position will need a way to find us."

Honghua clapped his hands together. "Okay, then it is settled. We will need an identifying object to serve as the passcode. But how will people know the objects are not fake? Won't others learn of our group's symbols and pretend to be us?"

Muchen pursed his lips. "What do you think of this, Yunhao? He has a point. Surely there will be infiltrators who attempt to control the members of our secret society or to overtake it for their own selfish purposes."

Yunhao took a few moments to think this matter through. "Perhaps then, leaders of the eight will possess a logbook of the current participants in their respective cities. *And* it will be the leader who distributes the objects to identify that each person is in fact a member. This will act as a passcode and we shall display these objects within plain sight as a beacon for others to find us."

Honghua held up his hand. "But what will these objects be? And should one of us fall ill, who will be our replacement?"

Yunhao gave Honghua a reassuring smile. "Worry not about such things. I have thought it through for many days now. We will pass our positions to our children. And their children's children." Though he had yet to find a wife, Yunhao felt confident that he would obtain one and have many children. He paused, looking again to the painting on his left. "As far as what objects we will possess . . . I will take care of procuring those items."

"Shall you be our leader then?" Chun Ming asked. "It seems fitting that you should lead us as this is your idea. Are you ready to accept what this will command?"

Yunhao was caught off guard by Chun Ming's suggestion. Though he had secretly hoped to lead the group, he assumed that Chun Ming would argue the point and choose to secure the lead position for himself. He, after all, was the eldest. But Yunhao chose not to remind anyone of this fact. Instead, he smiled and gave a respectful bow to the older man. "It would be my honor to lead our group into victorious futures."

Muchen nodded. "I second the idea. You will make a fine leader, Yunhao. But tell us, Yunhao, what do you think about a name? How will we be known?"

Yunhao consulted the painting a final time. The very

painting that stirred his thoughts and inspired him to achieve greatness at all costs. He inhaled deeply, his eyes traveling over the seven men that sat now looking to him for guidance. "From this day forward, we will be known as the Eight Immortals."

CHAPTER
1

Of all the noodle shops in all the towns, in all the world, she had to walk into mine. "She" being Lydia Shepard— private investigator. The location? Ho-Lee Noodle House in Fairview Park, Ohio—one of the many suburbs making up the great city of Cleveland. The noodle shop referenced belongs to my family and is also the place that provides my weekly paycheck. Albeit a smaller one than I'd like, but I was back to managing my credit card debt with a bit more ease, so who was I to complain?

Speaking of who I am, I'm Lana Lee, restaurant manager, dog mom, homicide detective's girlfriend, noodle fanatic, and doughnut enthusiast. I like my hair cut at sharp angles and multi-colored. No shade of the rainbow is exempt. Well, maybe lime green . . . I have yet to go there. Currently, my hair is dyed jet black with peek-a-boo strands of smokey lavender, but that's not really the topic at hand now is it?

No, the topic is Lydia Shepard. I'd made friends with the local PI months back during an investigation I had helped with in a very unofficial capacity. I do that sort of thing on occasion. Some people like it, some people don't.

It just so happened that Lydia was on the side of liking it, she being a rule breaker much like me.

And, if we're going to do this whole telling-a-story thing, I have to set the scene properly. Because honestly, it's a day I never thought would come to pass. Even though Lydia had made me shake hands and swear I'd be ready, willing, and able to assist her with a called-in favor of her choosing, I hadn't actually believed her. But the thirty-something professional had kept her word and sought out the "amateur" after all. Shows how much I know.

Picture this:

It was a crisp Monday morning, my least favorite time of day *and* week. I'd dragged myself out of bed, pried my eyes open, and battled to stay awake. The way I physically felt was a stark contrast to the world that waited for me on the other side of my apartment door. While I was steeped in sluggishness, spring was valiantly trying to break free from the icy claws of a long Cleveland winter. The sun was making more of an appearance with each passing day, encouraging the trees and flowers to blossom and bloom. Traffic moved at a snail's pace as I trudged through the onslaught of rush hour down Center Ridge Road . . .

Okay, who I am kidding? I don't talk like that. Here's the reality of it: I woke up late and, of course, hit every red light on the way to work. The sun was blinding me, and it was one of those mornings where you have to put your sun visor at an angle where you almost can't even see the road—much less the car in front of you. Even with sunglasses on, I found myself squinting the entire east-bound drive—and seeing as the sun rises in the east . . . well, okay, you get it.

I like to get to Asia Village—the indoor shopping plaza

that Ho-Lee Noodle House resides in—at least a half hour before our head chef and one of my best friends, Peter Huang, arrives for his shift. Getting situated in the dark and empty restaurant has become somewhat of a ritual for me. It's how I gather my zen for the day. So, I don't like when that routine is disturbed. Especially on a Monday when I need it most.

As I arrived through the Chinese-dragon-covered wrought iron gates painted a deep shade of red, I waved hello to my two mythical friends—which always produced a laugh from anyone in the car with me. I hadn't gone so far as to name them, but who's to say I wouldn't at some point?

It felt like any other day, and I thought nothing out of the ordinary while parking in my usual space in the employee lot. With my travel mug in hand, I made my way to the main entrance, noticing a black Mustang with a dent in the fender parked in the first row near the double doors. It didn't fully register who it might belong to, but the familiarity must have clicked somewhere in my mind because I looked at it a little longer than one normally looks at something that's of no consequence. A tingle of electricity zipped down the backs of my arms and spine. Chalking it up to the crisp breeze blowing by, I shrugged off the sensation that something was slightly off. Sometimes when you've been through the kinds of things I've been through, your mind starts to play tricks on you.

Letting myself into the plaza, my shoulders relaxed and I realized just how stiff my body language had become on my short walk in.

I was so busy trying to untangle the restaurant key from my Hello Kitty keychain that I hadn't been looking at where I was going or noticed the figure standing a few feet away from me.

But I got that sense—you know the one: that change in energy, that feeling that someone else is present. I froze, hand outstretched with my fingers wrapped around Hello Kitty's head, my index finger pressing on the red plastic bow attached to her ear. My eyes rose to acknowledge the person standing in front of me. I recognized her immediately.

Her cinnamon brown hair with tints of burgundy looked freshly cut, and the angled bob—a little shorter than my own—was the perfect complement to her oval face. The olive of her skin and the deep brown of her eyes suggested she might be Italian. I already knew that she was, but anyone would easily come to the same conclusion. She was a little taller than me but petite all the same. And though her features were delicate and feminine, she held herself in a way that said she wasn't someone to be trifled with.

She was posed—almost like a model at a fashion shoot advertising rocker chic—next to the double doors of Ho-Lee Noodle House. Her arms were comfortably crossed over her chest, one foot propped up on the wall she leaned against. I noted her combat boots looked more like they'd come from Macy's than an Army surplus store. Under her form-fitting, black leather jacket, she wore a distressed gray T-shirt, dark sunglasses hanging from the collar.

As I neared and our eyes locked on each other, she pushed off the wall, standing straight. Her hands slipped into the pockets of her skinny jeans. An amused smile danced on her raisin-tinted, glossed lips. "As I live and breathe . . ." she said, sizing me up, her gaze landing on my Hello Kitty keychain.

"Hi Lydia," I said while internally reminding myself not to fidget.

I hadn't seen her in months, despite the offer for free meals we'd negotiated during our less than conventional terms of agreement. I had commissioned her help for a messy business involving Asia Village's proprietor, Donna Feng. The whole thing was a long story, but the basic gist is that Lydia and I had successfully solved a murder case that had been stumping the authorities, and we'd made a pretty decent team while doing it. However, due to some of the circumstances—one of them being that she didn't work side by side with people off the street—we'd made an informal contract of our own. She did me a few favors by letting me work on the case alongside her, and in turn, I offered free Asian food for a month and my consulting services should she need something only I could offer. "It's good to see you . . . I think."

She chuckled. "Let the jury be out on that one. At least until you hear what I have to say."

"Which is . . . ?"

Her eyes darted around the plaza. "I need your expertise. Have you ever heard of a group called the Eight Immortals?"

"The who?"

"I'll take that as a no then." She tilted her head in the direction of the restaurant. "Let's talk where we have a little privacy." In a lower voice, she said, "I've got a couple of dead bodies on my hands, and I could really use your help."

CHAPTER
2

My head was spinning as Lydia and I walked into the darkened restaurant, which was not a problem for me. It never had been. Seeing as I'd grown up playing and galivanting through the establishment, I could manage the entire area blindfolded.

Lydia stood waiting near the entrance while I wove through the tables to reach the switch on the wall just outside the kitchen. I flipped it on, and she squinted as the room filled with light. "Sorry to drop in like this, but I'm at my wit's end. Plus, I thought you'd process the information better hearing about it from me in person."

I rejoined her at the front of the restaurant. "Maybe we better sit down for this." Gesturing to what had become my regular consultation table, I chose the seat facing the door so I could keep an eye out for Peter. He'd be here soon, and I had no idea what he'd think about Lydia's presence. There was no time to wonder about that at the moment though.

"What is this about exactly?"

Lydia huffed. "I was contacted by someone who I will

keep confidential for the time being. They had this insane story about a secret organization that operates in Cleveland, maybe other places too . . . they wouldn't really say for sure. Anyhow, they call themselves the Eight Immortals and a few of them have proved to be *otherwise* in recent history."

"Meaning they are the dead bodies you mentioned earlier?"

"Exactly. To date, there are three alleged victims. Though outwardly, none of the deaths look connected and they haven't even been confirmed as anything other than regular passings. The first deceased party suffered a heart attack but didn't have a history of correlating health problems, and the second took a severe tumble down a flight of basement stairs. However, my client claims that they *are* related and very intentional. They were reluctant to tell me the existence of this secret organization but realized it was their best bet to getting some help."

"So, the police aren't actively involved in any of these cases?"

"No. Well, the first two are not being investigated at the moment. The third one is pretty fresh and is under consideration for suspicious circumstances. He was found in his garage, in his car, asphyxiated by exhaust fumes. I'll get into that more later on. You still dating that cop?"

I nodded.

"He probably is handling the most recent case right now seeing as it took place in Fairview Park just a few days ago. The other ones fall out of his jurisdiction. They happened in Cleveland and Westlake. Thankfully I have a friend on the Cleveland police force that might be willing to play nice, so that solves one problem."

I noted the corner of her lips curve up as she said the

word "friend." I tucked that away for another time when I felt like it was appropriate to ask. "What exactly is it that you need from me?"

"Well, according to my sources, you have direct connections with some of the people involved."

My stomach sank. "I do?" It wasn't exactly something you'd want to hear first thing in the morning . . . or ever.

"Yes. Plus you're good at this and you owe me that favor," she added as an afterthought.

"Who are your sources?" My tongue felt like sandpaper. I sipped my coffee.

"I'm not at liberty to say." She smirked. "You know the rules."

"Okay, who are the direct connections then?" I held my stomach with my free hand while the other clutched my travel mug.

Lydia leaned forward, tapping the table with her index finger. "You know I can't say that either. Not unless you agree to work with me. If you have no intention of doing so, then I'm afraid that information walks right out the door with me."

The sinking feeling in my stomach upgraded into a fiery pit, and a dull ache formed as I processed what she was saying. Was it my own family? Was my mother the ring master of some elaborate underground group? Did my dad know? A burst of laughter escaped as I realized how ridiculous that sounded and a visual of my petite mother in one of her floral blouses and penny loafers flashed in my mind.

Then again, catch her at the wrong moment and she was fiercer than a dragon . . . so . . .

Lydia studied my face. "Time's tickin' . . ."

"How long do I have to think about it?"

"You have until sundown," Lydia said, the smile from her lips fading, her eyes going cold as her eyebrows dropped.

"Sundown? Are you serious?"

Lydia erupted into laughter. "Nah, I just always wanted to say that. You have until I walk out that door, Sunshine. It's gotta be now. I have things to do and people to interrogate. My client seems to think he knows the next person who will be targeted and he's concerned it's going to happen fairly soon."

"Who's the next supposed target?" I asked.

"They haven't told me that much yet."

I didn't know how to respond to any of this.

She cleared her throat. "I may remind you again that you owe me. Now would be a better time than any to pay up."

My chest was tightening. I already knew the answer I would give her. Why pretend that it would be anything different? "Yes!" I said, a little on the forceful side. "Yes, okay? Now tell me, who are the connections?"

She didn't waste any time. "You're close with Wei Zhang, correct?"

That caused me to pause. I'd never heard anyone other than my grandmother say Mr. Zhang's first name before. Like ever. He'd always been, well . . . Mr. Zhang. Out of respect for his age, no one called him anything outside of his surname. At least that's what I had gathered was the reason.

Lydia snapped her fingers in front of my face. "Hello Lana . . . bring it back, chickadee. You're close with him, yes? He's dating your grandmother?"

I felt sick but tried to brush it away. "Yeah . . . I've known him for most of my life. And yes, he is dating my grandmother. I don't know much about his personal life though."

"I would think your grandmother does." She leaned in even closer. "Has she ever suggested that she suspects anything? Or has she ever mentioned strange behavior on his end?"

I shook my head. "No, she knows about five words of English. Her unofficial tutoring with my parents hasn't gone very well."

"What can you tell me about this Wei Zhang character?"

I began to open my mouth . . . to tell her that this whole thing was ridiculous and she must have it all wrong . . . or her client was sending her on a wild-goose chase.

Mr. Zhang was older than time itself. Not to mention, more innocent than a floating leaf. I mean, he peddled herbs and natural remedies for a living. He walked with a hunch and on rainy days he had a slight limp. It was hard to believe that he'd be involved with anything wayward.

Of course I was assuming that Lydia was implying this secret organization was something wayward in nature. Especially since there were three pending murders that all involved supposed members. And the fact that she had to question what their intentions might be based on the folklore of the actual Eight Immortals.

Or had she been insinuating that someone was trying to hurt Mr. Zhang? I needed more clarity before I went jumping to any more conclusions.

Before I could relay my thought process to Lydia, Peter's face popped up in the window of the restaurant. His attention automatically gravitated to the back of Lydia's head. His eyes narrowed and he pursed his lips as he directed his focus back on me.

"We probably have to take this conversation into my office."

Lydia twisted in her chair, following my gaze to where

Peter waited, looking openly unhappy. He wasn't one to hide his true feelings despite the fact that he used minimal words to communicate them. "Sure, no problem," she said.

I jogged over to the doors and twisted the brass lock to let Peter in. His dull acknowledgment consisted of a slight nod and stiff smile. The black baseball cap he never left home without was low over his eyes.

My cheeks were warm, and I silently thanked my full-coverage makeup foundation for masking any indications of the blush that was likely to form. Peter was one of my best friends, and he'd become more like a big brother in recent months, worrying about my welfare and all that mushy jazz. So, he didn't take too kindly to my detective-like practices. Matter of fact, since my last run-in with a psycho who needed a shiny pair of bracelets courtesy of the police department, Peter had doubled down on his continuing position that I had no business involving myself in anything related to the law.

"Morning, Peter," I said, trying to sound chipper and as though I weren't a bundle of nerves. "How was traffic?" I locked the door behind him.

"What's *she* doing here?" He fidgeted with the straps of the backpack he always carried with him to work. The contents usually contained at least two books—mostly science fiction—a sketch pad for his pencil drawings, a variety of pencils and erasers, plus random snacks he couldn't live without.

Lydia rose from her seat. "Peter! It's been a minute, hasn't it?" She extended her hand. "Thought it wouldn't hurt to get some of the best noodles in Cleveland while I'm on this side of town."

The muscles in his jaw relaxed a little bit. He was a sucker for cooking compliments. He grabbed her hand, shaking it firmly, which Lydia equally matched. "Don't take my question personally," he said. "My beef is with Lana."

"Nonsense," Lydia blew a raspberry and batted the idea away as if he had it all wrong. "Just catchin' up with our gal here."

Peter snorted. "No offense, but I don't believe that for a minute."

She held her hands up, palms forward as if in surrender. "Okay, you caught me. But I do need her expertise on a certain matter. I'm sure you know I wouldn't burden her with something if it wasn't totally necessary."

The former look of dissatisfaction returned to his face. "I just want to remind everybody," he said, widening his eyes directly at me, "that *Lana* is not a professional."

"Well, that's Lana's choice really, isn't it?" Lydia replied. "She had a job offer waiting for her. A very generous offer, I might add."

Peter lowered his brows at me. "Dude, what is she talking about?"

My gratitude for my makeup turned into a prayer of hoping it could hold up with the redness that now surely had encompassed my whole face. "Lydia, would you mind waiting in my office for a minute?"

"No problem, but keep in mind that I don't have all day, Miss Lee."

"I'll be right there, promise. Go through the double doors, past the kitchen. My office is on the left."

Lydia disappeared through the swinging kitchen doors. For a moment, all that could be heard was the swishing of the rubber guards as the doors brushed against each other.

"Peter," I said, folding my arms across my chest. "You're being kind of rude, ya know?"

He shrugged and began walking toward the kitchen.

"Hello. I'm talking to you." I trailed after him.

He stopped and spun on his heel. "What job offer, Lana? Are you leaving the restaurant?"

"No." I blurted out a laugh. "Don't be ridiculous. Lydia's boss offered me a job at their agency *months* ago. I said no immediately. Besides, if I was planning to leave, you don't think I'd tell you in advance? Come on, I thought we were closer than that."

Peter rolled his shoulders. "So why's she here then? Is it to convince you to take the job after all this time?"

"No." I took a deep breath, thinking about the best way to approach the topic. "All she really wants me to do is field some questions about Chinese mythology."

"Hmm" was all he said, and continued on toward the kitchen.

His lack of approval bothered me to no end. I didn't know what I expected because on the one hand, I completely understood his reservations. But I guess it felt a whole lot like he didn't trust my judgment or that I was capable of handling myself. Instead of admitting my feelings on the subject, I said, "I've got it under control. This probably won't be that involved anyways."

I didn't know either way if that statement was true. It sure felt like a lie. Another sentiment I would keep to myself.

Peter nudged the swinging door to the kitchen open with his elbow. I expected him to give me a final lecture before I met up with Lydia, but all he said was, "Let's hope so."

CHAPTER
3

When I reached my office, Lydia was in one of my guest chairs, typing at what appeared to be the speed of light. Her thumbs danced across the screen of her phone with precision. She didn't even look up when I entered the room and shut the door. Still focused on the screen in front of her, she said, "Your office might be smaller than mine."

I chuckled. "Thanks for waiting. I have to apologize for Peter's behavior." I shimmied around my oversized desk and pulled out my weathered swivel chair. I really needed to get a new one sooner rather than later.

"Don't worry about it. I get it." Lydia tucked her phone away in her back pocket. She tilted her head to the side, cracking her neck. "In this job, you get used to people giving you a lot of stink eye. I know it's not personal . . . preconceived notions and all that. Plus, I'm sure he's worried about your safety."

Sitting down, I grimaced, which might have been confused with actual physical pain. But it stemmed from the situation with Peter. I know he meant well, but it still irked me. "So, back to Mr. Zhang," I said, not wanting to waste another minute. The restaurant would be opening soon, and if possible, I wanted Lydia outta here before the Mahjong Matrons showed up.

My most regular customers, the four widowed women were how I started every day in the restaurant. They were also the eyes and ears of Asia Village, and I suspected they would take a lot of interest in Lydia Shepard's guest appearance.

Lydia leaned forward, resting her elbows on her knees. "According to my client, this Mr. Zhang of yours is the leader of their group."

I snorted. "Is this person trying to insinuate that Mr. Zhang is calling out hits?"

"Not necessarily, though he didn't completely rule it out when I asked him that very same question."

I noted this was the first time she'd intimated that her client was a "he." I'd noticed how careful she'd been about omitting that detail from what she'd told me thus far.

"Then what exactly is your client trying to get at?"

"That's where things get tricky, I'm afraid." She shifted in her seat. "Up until recently, he had a feeling that it had something to do with Mr. Zhang's interactions with the first two victims. Both were seen arguing with him shortly before their deaths. However, with the last incident, his opinion changed. Now the theory is that someone is after their artifacts, and he thinks he might know who it is."

"Huh?" I reached for my travel mug. Perhaps it was that I needed more caffeine to comprehend what she was telling me. That's when I realized I'd left my mug out in the dining room. "Their artifacts?"

"Yeah, a concept taken from the original folklore. I guess in the stories each immortal had an object that symbolized their power. Currently, in this supposed secret group, each member holds a corresponding object to identify them as one of the honored eight. The items are meant to be passed down ceremoniously from the previous generation. And my client thinks that whoever is doing the killing is possibly trying to secure the full set for themselves."

"To do what?" I asked.

"I'm assuming to gain total control of the group. I haven't figured that out just yet and my client hasn't been totally forthcoming."

"But . . . they're just . . . objects."

"And so are crowns and medals, but we still give those items relevance in the modern world."

"Yeah, but . . ."

Lydia leaned back in her seat, holding up a palm. "Hey, I get it. The whole thing is wackadoo for sure, but we're not killers, so naturally we don't get it. Logical or not, if my client is right, that means there are up to five more potential victims, and that's what I would like to stop."

I stared at the calendar blotter that covered my desk. It had become a doodle pad of sorts. I liked to draw hearts on things while chatting on the phone. "Okay, you have a point. But let's go back to the tricky part. I'm not following it," I said. "If anything, it sounds like Mr. Zhang could be in danger."

Lydia cleared her throat. "Well, that's where the other theory comes into play. It is possible that Mr. Zhang is the one trying to collect the other artifacts for himself."

"He's masterminding a diabolic scheme to take everybody down? At his age?"

Lydia tsked, wagging her finger. "Never underestimate an elderly person, Lana. This could be his crowning moment, after all these years. Maybe he feels wronged somehow. Or maybe he's sick of the other people involved . . . Who knows. Either way, I can't rule him out until I feel satisfied he doesn't have some hand in it. Could even be that he has a lackey of sorts. He's pulling the strings while the other person does the dirty work."

"I have a hard time imagining any of this. It sounds laughable."

She stood up, adjusting her jeans at the waist. "Look, I'd rather not continue without you. I know you would be a really valuable asset to this case. Especially helping me to get face time with some of these people. You're an insider, and a lot of people in the Asian community trust you. Are you able to put aside your personal feelings to help me find the truth of what's going on?"

It was a good question. Could I? I'd done it in the past, though it often came as a struggle. However, can the observer ever be completely removed from the observed? According to the observer effect, no. But I doubted that Lydia wanted to hear about quantum mechanics.

She pulled her phone out of her back pocket, checking the time. "I gotta get going. We definitely have more to talk about, but for right now, I need you to answer my question. Can you do this without showing favoritism?"

I rose from my seat, inhaling deeply. I gave her a firm nod. "Yes. When I said I was in, I'm in. I'll do my best to remain objective."

Lydia extended her hand. "Then it would appear that we have ourselves a deal."

I grabbed her hand and gave it a hearty shake.

"That's how I knew I liked you from the beginning, Lana. You have a solid handshake. A sure sign of a woman I can respect."

We walked through the kitchen in silence, Lydia giving a casual wave to Peter as she passed. He did the curt head nod thing he's so fond of before turning his attention back to prepping the grill.

At the restaurant doors, Lydia turned to me. "I don't think I have to tell you I need your absolute discretion with this whole thing. Paid clients have rights. Meredith, our agency secretary, has some forms for you to fill out. Stop by Price Investigations when you have a minute and sign whatever she gives you. Once you've done that, I'll share my client's information with you and we'll get started. We're open until six tonight, so if you can make your way there after work . . . well, the sooner we can get started on this, the better."

"Sure," I said, already visualizing rush hour traffic on Euclid Avenue where Price Investigations was located. The thought of I-90 at rush hour made me cringe.

Just as Lydia went to turn and walk out the doors, four faces appeared on the other side. Along with those four faces came four sets of raised eyebrows.

Heat rose from my neck into my face. I was busted.

Lydia pulled on the door handle, but it was locked. She disengaged the dead bolt, tried again, and then stood to the side, holding the door open for the Mahjong Matrons. While she did that, my mind went into story mode. What would I say was Lydia's purpose here? Would they even remember her? Even if they didn't, surely they would wonder why this random woman was in the restaurant with me before opening—a rare, if nonexistent occurrence.

Helen, the leader of the pack, honorary mother hen, and loudest of them all, stood in front of the other three women. "Good morning." She said it slow and with an air of apprehension. As if she wasn't totally sure she wanted to wish Lydia an actual good morning.

"Good morning, ma'am," Lydia replied. "Ladies." She tipped her head at the other three, who all returned her gesture with half smiles before continuing on into the restaurant.

The Matrons never waited to be seated. They had their own table and sat themselves upon arrival. And even though they ordered the same items—off-menu—I still brought them a menu to look at . . . just in case they tried to throw me for a loop one day. You have to stay on your toes around this place.

Lydia smirked. "All four of them ladies are trouble dressed up as innocence. I can smell it in the air," she said in a low voice.

"You're not wrong," I replied, taking a quick glance over my shoulder.

"Talk to ya soon, chickadee." She gave me a salute and then headed in the direction of the plaza entrance. I stood in the doorway, watching her leave. I wasn't sure why I felt frozen in place. Maybe it was all that she'd told me. My mind was trying really hard to catch up with the things she'd divulged. And just imagine, she hadn't even told me everything there was to know yet.

As I was about to head back into the restaurant, something in my peripheral vision caught my attention. It was Mr. Zhang coming out of his shop, the Wild Sage. He was watching Lydia leave just as I had.

CHAPTER
4

I greeted the Mahjong Matrons with a menu and an overexaggerated smile. My facial muscles were really getting a workout. Some part of me felt like if I smiled hard enough they would forget anything related to Lydia Shepard.

Aside from Helen, you have Pearl and Opal, two sisters who couldn't be any more of a contrast to each other. In all the ways that Pearl is loud and outspoken, Opal is soft and demure. Pearl, the eldest of the group, is more to the point and calls things how she sees them. While her younger sister is more about what she feels and senses in the air, Opal is an expert at reading between the lines and spends more time watching versus commenting.

And the final matron, Wendy, is usually the voice of logic in the group. She thinks about the sensibility and practicality of most matters, trying to put her personal feelings to the side. Often, she is the last to speak because she is busy taking in all accounts and viewpoints before she's willing to share her own assessment.

All having lost their husbands at early ages, they'd first bonded over their grief and later, their love of mahjong. Whether there was a mahjong tournament or some other event taking place, they still spent all of their days together in one another's company.

Helen looked me over, much in the way that my mother does when she's getting ready to critique me on whether or not I'm underweight, had enough sleep, or taking proper care of my skin.

"Good morning, ladies. It's a beautiful day out there, isn't it?" I always resorted to weather talk when trying to avoid a specific topic. I placed the menu down in front of Helen.

She pushed it away, fixing her gaze on my face. "When I woke up this morning, I assumed the excitement would be about the new store opening today. But it seems as if I was mistaken. Who was that woman you were speaking with? We have seen her before, yes?"

The other ladies exchanged glances and nodded in unison.

In all the hubbub, I'd almost forgotten that the shop across the way, Eastern Enchantments, would finally be opening today. There had been a few false starts and I had begun to wonder if the store would ever actually open.

The four women stared at me with expectation of an answer.

"An old friend of mine," I replied casually. "Stopped in for a quick chat. I'll get your usual breakfast order put in and grab some tea."

Helen tilted her head. "Yes, that will be fine."

I spun on my heel and hurried off to the kitchen before they could interject. Despite my easy getaway, I had a feeling I wasn't quite off the hook.

In the kitchen, I informed Peter that the Matrons had arrived and he gave me a thumbs up as he began preparing their morning meal. We didn't have to communicate on what those specific items were, seeing as they always wanted rice porridge, century eggs, pickled cucumbers, and scallion omelets.

When I returned to their table, the Matrons were whispering amongst themselves. Noting that I was within earshot, Helen shushed the others.

I placed their teapot on the table and considered running away at lightning speed.

"Lana," Helen said as she turned over her cup and reached for the teapot, "we have decided that we do not believe this woman who came here today is an old friend."

"Oh?" I flipped the tray on its side and rested it under my arm.

Opal was the one to respond. "I sensed there was a certain tension that you both felt when we arrived. Why would that be the case if she were merely an old friend?"

I hadn't noticed that Lydia tensed up when they arrived. "The topic we were discussing was a little intense is all. Nothing to worry about."

"Yes, but who *is* she?" Wendy asked. "The way you spoke with her didn't seem as though she is an old friend. Perhaps you were a bit formal?"

Helen nodded. "We have ways to find out other than you. You know this."

I sighed, knowing that was one hundred percent fact. "Lydia really is an old friend of mine . . . sort of. She's a PI that I—"

Pearl clapped her hands together, her face lighting up.

"Ah yes, she was the one who helped you when Lady Feng was in trouble."

"Yes, that's her. She just came by to ask me some questions about someone who passed away in the Asian community and if I knew them personally."

The four women regarded each other before speaking. Then Helen asked, "Does this have anything to do with George Wong?

I felt my heartbeat quicken. "Who is that?"

They shared another momentary glimpse amongst each other, but their expressions didn't clue me in on what they were thinking or what untold information they possessed.

Finally, Helen replied for the group. "He is an old friend of ours."

I pursed my lips at her choice of words. "Come now, Helen. Fair is fair, I told you what you wanted to know."

Wendy smirked. "Yes, but still not the whole story, I assume."

Helen sipped her tea. "He is our old friend, but he is also someone very important in the community. He is a top lawyer and handles many legal matters for Chinese and Taiwanese immigrants. He passed away two days ago."

The bell in the kitchen rang and I excused myself from the Matrons to get their food. After I dropped off their meal, I went to hang out at the hostess station and collect my thoughts. Their mention of George Wong caused me to return to the spiraling thoughts I'd had while talking to Lydia.

This morning was definitely not going as planned.

I'd thought maybe I'd go properly introduce myself to

Talia, the new Asia Village resident, this morning, but I found myself having lost interest in the entire idea.

I guess finding out there's a secret organization within your community and that your grandmother's "boyfriend" is maybe involved in it will do that to you.

CHAPTER
5

"I still can't wrap my head around it," I said to Megan. As soon as the Mahjong Matrons had left, I'd called my best friend and roommate to fill her in on my unexpected morning encounter with Lydia. I sat on my perch, wrapping silverware, with my cell phone tucked between my ear and shoulder.

"It sounds like something out of a thriller movie or something," she said. "But what I really want to know is, does this mean that I can't help you work on the case?"

"I'm not sure. I hadn't really thought about that."

Megan Riley, for all intents and purposes, is my right-hand gal. And usually the one I conducted my most ridiculous shenanigans with. Aside from the hassle I'd dealt with in Irvine helping my Aunt Grace figure out who'd murdered a close friend of hers, doing this sort of thing without Megan was uncharted territory.

It hadn't been too bad working with my aunt, and my sister, Anna May, had provided a few helpful moments, but in general, I'd struggled in California not having my best friend to rely on. Her most favorable trait being the internet snooping part. While I had a difficult time with my patience, or finding information on the first go-around, Megan always seemed to know exactly where to look.

Megan let out a heavy sigh. "Well, I can't sit on the sidelines twiddling my thumbs, Lana. Especially with something this huge. I mean, think about it . . . a secret organization running through the veins of Cleveland." Her voice raised an octave as she went on. "They could be paying off cops and councilmen. Ooh, I bet they have the mayor in their pocket, calling the shots on city decisions. And people say nothing exciting happens in this city. Pft."

"That's a bit dramatic, don't you think?" I didn't want to admit it, but I had thought similar things as well. Were these over-the-top insinuations a possibility? Lydia hadn't given me enough information to make heads or tails of what the secret organization stood for or how deep their connections ran.

"If you mean to tell me that none of these same theories ran through your mind at least once, Lana Lee, you are a straight-up liar."

"I plead the fifth."

"Uh-huh."

"We could be completely wrong," I said. "And besides, whoever her client is could be lying about the whole thing."

"Well, are you going to go there after work and fill out the paperwork or what? Diving into this is the only way to find out."

"I really don't want to deal with rush hour traffic. I was thinking I'd go tomorrow."

Megan clucked her tongue. "You're joking, right? You're going to delay this process because you don't want to be inconvenienced on the freeway? Also if you go in the morning, you're going to deal with the same thing in the opposite direction."

"I didn't say I would go first thing in the morning. You know I hate driving on I-90. It's like freakin' NASCAR."

"Don't make me come pick you up and take you there myself. I have to work, and Robin gets cranky if I'm not there for happy hour."

I groaned, extra theatrically for Megan's benefit. She knew I hated to inconvenience people. "Fine, I'll go after work."

"Good. The sooner we get this moving, the better."

"Yeah." The word came out deflated. I knew that Megan caught the evidence of lackluster sentiment in my voice. If there was one person who knew me better than anyone else, it was her. And perhaps the cause of my feelings was that, despite the fact I was willing to involve myself in the matter, deep down I really didn't want to know. It would shatter the fabric of my reality on some level. Just to think that people I knew might be involved in something like this right under my nose sent me spiraling.

If Mr. Zhang was involved, did that mean others in Asia Village were also involved? Again, I had to ask myself if my family was aware of this group's existence. I'm sure that it must have crossed Lydia's mind at least once or twice. What kind of PI would she be if she hadn't considered it herself?

I thought about my dad, the solo white guy in this equation. Would he be included in a secret Asian organization? Highly doubtful. Was my mom living a double life? Much like earlier, it all seemed utterly laughable to consider any of this as truth. Yet there I was, having similar thoughts to Megan and probably ones she hadn't even considered.

Megan had been lecturing me the entire time, but I hadn't heard a word she'd said. I must have failed to respond to a question, because she paused and barked my name. "Lana! Are you listening to me?"

"Sorry, I got distracted." I didn't want to admit what I'd just been thinking—to her or myself. At least not right now anyways. My eyes flitted up in the direction of the new shop. "That new shop, Eastern Enchantments, opened today. The one that's selling all the crystals and whatever."

Eastern Enchantments was what many would refer to as "metaphysical" in nature. The owner would be selling a wide variety of crystals, tarot and oracle cards, spiritual statues, and also some home goods like candles, blankets, and mugs.

"Oh?" Megan said, growing quiet.

"Yeah, I had been thinking I should officially go meet the new owner, Talia Sun. She's close to our age, I think. I've only said hi to her in passing while she was bringing in boxes of inventory. But after all this kerfuffle, I don't know if I'm feeling the social vibe."

"Well, okay. Hey, I gotta get going."

That caught my attention. "Huh? Are you mad at me now? I'm sorry I wasn't paying attention . . . it's just a lot is going on."

"No, no, I'm not mad. I just have to go." Megan said hurriedly. "I'll talk to you later. If you have time, stop in at the Zodiac."

Before I could say anything else, she hung up.

I looked down at the phone in confusion. I wasn't sure why she suddenly wanted to rush off the phone. I thought about calling her back, but two middle-aged women—a blonde and a brunette—carrying tote bags walked in with large smiles.

The blonde stepped up in front of her friend. She had long eyelashes and bright red lipstick, a shade I wish I could pull off. She cleared her throat. "We'd like a table for twelve, please."

My jaw dropped against my will. It wasn't often that we had such a large party in the midmorning hours. If I had been looking for a distraction from everything else going on, I'd just gotten it.

The brunette stepped up next to her. "It's for our book club. We're trying out an early hour meeting." She tilted her head to the side, looking past me, and noted the empty dining area. "That's not a problem, is it?"

"Not at all," I said. "We actually have a banquet area off to the side that's sectioned off from the rest of the dining room."

"Oh perfect, that'll give us a little privacy," the blonde said. "We can get a bit loud sometimes."

I counted out twelve menus. Peter was in for a big surprise.

The rest of my workday went much in the same fashion of keeping me busy. The book club group ended up staying for about two hours and, thankfully, Peter's mom, Nancy, one of my mother's closest friends and our split-shift server, had arrived at eleven to help out.

For a Monday it was rare to have an almost packed dining room. But I was thankful that something other than Lydia's news was keeping me preoccupied.

The book club ladies had racked up a large bill and left a generous tip, which Nancy and I split. They promised to be back next month, and I felt a dash of excitement that a book club had selected our restaurant as their meeting spot. Being a book lover myself, I enjoyed meeting fellow bibliophiles just as much as I loved meeting someone else with funky colored hair.

When my shift ended, I felt that familiar bubbling up of anxiety lodging itself into my throat. It was time to head to Price Investigations, and I didn't know if I was ready for what would come next: Prior to Lydia's unexpected visit, I'd begun to feel like things were just getting back to normal.

Thinking about it now, perhaps things had been too normal and that should have been a cause for suspicion. I'd gotten comfortable with the daily minutiae and a certain sense of peace that had come along with it. But much like Cleveland's fickle weather patterns, my life was carried wherever the wind would take it.

As anticipated, traffic was heavy as I neared downtown, and Progressive Field came into view from the I-90 bridge. I got off at the Ontario Street exit and made my way past the baseball stadium and then Rocket Mortgage Field House—which will always be the Gund Arena to me—and headed toward Public Square. Passing Jack Cleveland Casino, I remembered an instance when I tailed a suspect through the reinvented department store. The casino was housed in the infamous Higbee Building and the city's residents took great pride in the fact it had been featured in the classic Christmas movie *A Christmas Story*.

I'd seen it from a different perspective, however. I snickered thinking about how inexperienced I'd been at the time. Of course, that left me thinking about all that had happened since then—how it felt like I'd lived an entire lifetime.

A traffic light on the corner of Euclid Avenue and East 4th Street stopped me near the House of Blues. And that reminded me of a date that Adam and I had gone on toward the beginning of our relationship.

When I really thought about it, the city held a lot of memories for me—both good and bad. As the light turned green, I wondered what fresh life experiences I would accumulate on this new adventure with Lydia.

As they say, time will tell. Time always tells.

I pulled into the parking garage near Price Investigations and accepted the ticket the automated machine spit out. Since most people were leaving to head home, I was able to find a spot by the time I got to the second level of the garage.

My heartbeat quickened as I got out of the car and made my way onto the street, the agency within sight. Going through these steps made everything more official, and I knew once I signed the papers they had waiting for me, there was no turning back. Not that I ever dropped out of a case, but in the back of my mind it was always the last resort.

I inhaled deeply as I reached for the door of the office building. "Okay future, ready or not, here I come."

CHAPTER
6

Price Investigations is on the first floor of a rather large building. I wouldn't give it skyscraper status, but it was one of the bigger buildings that's been around maybe since the city was built. And though it was sizeable, it somehow still remained underwhelming in its appearance.

I felt transported back in time to the case I'd helped solve concerning Donna Feng. The small lobby area was exactly how I remembered it: dusty, stuffy, and quiet. The directory on the wall informed me that Price Investigations was in suite 102.

As I opened the door with its frosted glass window and entered the small reception area, I found their administrative assistant, Meredith Walker. Flashbacks washed over me as she came into view, sitting behind her old-fashioned oak desk that was surely older than yours truly.

Meredith did a double take as I shuffled hesitantly toward her desk. "Hey there, young lady, I've been expecting you."

I smiled, feeling the edges of my lips quiver. "Hi Ms. Walker, it's nice to see you again."

She batted a hand at my formality, a bemused grin forming. "Oh please, call me Meredith. The only person that calls me Ms. Walker is my husband."

I chuckled. "Well, Meredith, you know why I'm here then."

She nodded. "Got some forms for ya." Holding up an index finger, she began riffling through a stack of file folders on her desk. "They're around here somewhere."

A door behind her whipped open, and a man in a loosened tie and crumpled dress shirt emerged. "Woman, are you talkin' to yourself again?" He jerked his head back as he looked up, acknowledging my presence. "Oh, Miss Lee, it's you."

"Hi Mr. Price," I said, offering another shaky smile. I hadn't been this nervous since . . . well, since the last time I was this nervous. Was it hot in here?

Meredith snorted. "This one is big on the formalities," she said to him. Then to me, "Just call him, Eddie, honey."

"It's about time I got some respect around here," Eddie quipped.

"No it's not." Meredith found the folder she was looking for and handed it to me while keeping her eyes on her employer.

Eddie rolled his eyes, blowing a raspberry. "You're lucky my wife is your best friend. Otherwise you'd be standing in the unemployment line." Directing his attention to me, he said, "You know, since I caught ya, why don't you step into my office for a minute."

"Oh . . . uh . . ." My eyes slid toward the exit.

Eddie grinned. "Oh, no ya don't. You're not gettin' outta

here that easy. I promise not to bite. Besides, you still have to sign those forms ya got there."

He shut the door behind him and gestured to a chair opposite his desk. His office wasn't much bigger than Lydia's—or mine for that matter—but it was definitely an improvement.

The giant desk was covered with file folders, stacks of legal pads, pens and highlighters, along with a jumbo-sized Stanley thermos and an oversized mug that read Boss Man.

I sat down in the chair he'd offered, my grip tightening on the file folder.

As Eddie scooted his rolling chair in, I heard the wheels drag across the plastic mat that was below his desk. I knew the sound well from my own office seating. He folded his hands on the only empty space in front of him. "How ya been these days, Lana?"

I cleared my throat. "I'm okay, I suppose. Looking forward to spring." There I went again with the dreaded weather talk. "And yourself?"

"Just peachy keen . . . minus one particular situation I find myself in." He held my gaze.

"I'm one detective short. The last guy didn't work out and well, poor Lydia, she's just struggling to keep up with the overload. Seems that these current times we find ourselves in produce a little more work than usual."

"That must be tough," I said. "Good help is hard to find and all that."

"I read the paper quite a bit and happened to notice that you're still . . . participating in your extracurricular activities . . . That's what you've called them before, right?"

I silently cursed our local newspapers for their efficient reporting. How was I supposed to keep myself under the radar if they kept telling everybody what I was up to all the time?

Eddie continued. "I sure could use a shining star like yourself on our team. My original offer still stands. I thought you'd like to know that in case you decided to change your mind. Seeing as you're still flexing your detective muscles. Of course, there are some formalities to consider, like licensing. But I'd help you with all of that, of course. Take you under my proverbial wing."

He watched me expectantly while I squirmed in my seat. Deep down I'd known that when he asked to speak with me, it was most likely about his previous job offer, but I'd also assumed that after all this time, he'd moved on from the idea. "I appreciate the offer, but my answer is the same."

Eddie pursed his lips. "You realize you're offering services for free that you could be collecting payment on, don't you?"

I thought about the people I'd helped and whether they'd have the money to pay me for the help I provided them. Outside of Donna Feng, the answer would have been no. Then again, none of the people who I'd offered to help had wanted my assistance to begin with. "I don't do it for the money," I said.

Eddie laughed good-naturedly. "Ah, to be young and altruistic. I miss those days."

"If my refusal of your job offer means you don't want me to work on the case with Lydia—"

He held up his hand, shaking his head. "Not at all. Lydia requested your help and I'm not going to interfere with that. If your answer is still no, then it's no. But just keep in the back of your mind that my offer is on the table indefinitely. Even if I'm fully staffed, I'll make room for you."

The sincerity on his face was almost palpable. I had issues saying no—believe it or not—and the whole exchange left me feeling uncomfortable. I began to think of ways I could work for him *and* my parents at the same time. That thought caught me off guard. Was I actually considering this? No. No, just a fickle thought brought on by my unwillingness to disappoint.

"Is Lydia here?" I asked, completely avoiding the topic of employment all together.

"She had a meeting she got held up at but told me to pass along that she'd speak with you tomorrow. As long as the papers are signed."

"Do you have a pen?"

Eddie reached for his penholder and plucked out a ballpoint with their logo printed along the side.

After accepting the pen, I opened the manila folder to review the documents. Everything appeared standard and easy to read, completely void of legalese, which soothed the butterflies that were already having a dance party in my stomach.

I signed on the dotted lines to confirm that I understood the following:

- Should any harm come to THE CONSULTANT while working with Price Investigations, the company and anyone under its employ will not be held liable.
- The terms of the agreement are only applicable to the case/client at hand and do not solidify future employment with Price Investigations, nor would THE CONSULTANT be considered an employee while under contract.

- Payment is to be received after the case require-
  ments have been completed and closed to the satisfaction of the client and lead investigator (aka
  Lydia Shepard).
- Particulars of the case will not be discussed with
  anyone outside of the detective agency, including,
  but not limited to, law enforcement, legal repre-
  sentatives, and media outlets.
- THE CONSULTANT will be solely responsible
  for all tax filings and required payments to the
  IRS should such circumstances become necessary.

When I was finished, I reviewed the documents one
more time and wondered if I really knew what I was getting myself into. This was the most official I'd gotten
with anything I'd investigated, and signing my name on a
binding contract made everything seem more real . . . and
more serious.

I closed the folder, placed the pen on top, and handed it
to Eddie. "Do you need anything else from me?"

"Not at this moment," he said, taking the folder and
opening it to review the contents. He nodded as he flipped
through the pages, and then added his signature to each
page that I'd signed. "I'll leave these on Lydia's desk and
she'll be in contact with you tomorrow."

I had to admit I was a little disappointed that I wouldn't
get to talk to Lydia right away. After all, that was the whole
reason why I'd come in right after work. But there wasn't
much to be done about it. "Okay, well, I look forward to
it . . . I mean . . . the talking to her part, not the contents
of what we're going to talk about it."

Eddie chuckled. "Don't worry so much, kid. I know
what you're drivin' at."

I wished he hadn't pointed it out, but he was right: I was worried. The whole exchange was odd and somehow made me feel like I was in the principal's office and needed to be dismissed. Did I just say "Okay bye" and be on my way?

He seemed to notice my indecisiveness. "Is there anything else?"

"No, I guess not. Well, just this . . ." I dug in my back pocket and pulled out the garage ticket. "Do you validate parking?"

CHAPTER
7

I made a quick stop at home to let my pug, Kikkoman, out for a tinkle time before I headed to the bar where Megan works. She was a shift manager and served during the evenings. Her master plan was to open a bar of her own at some point, but every time I asked her about it, she changed the subject to something completely unrelated.

The Zodiac is a neighborhood bar that isn't too far from home. The place is all jazzed up with large murals of constellations, the drink names are themed around the twelve astrological signs, and they'd just recently painted the floor a glossy black with sparkly golden stars. If you stared too long, the whole experience was kind of trippy.

I found Megan behind the bar washing glasses in the sink below the counter, her long blonde hair secured with a metallic claw clip to keep it out of her face. I hopped on to my usual stool—at the end of the bar, nearest the door—and gave Megan my best whistle . . . which wasn't very good.

Still, she heard me above the music and noise, smiled,

wiped her hands on a dish towel, and headed over. "I was wondering if you'd show."

I removed my purse from my shoulder and placed it on the bar top. "I had to get out of the house, I could barely stand myself. By the time you get home tonight, I'll already be in bed. And this isn't really a texting conversation."

"So what happened?" She held up a finger while looking behind her. "Actually, hold that thought."

She zipped away and I watched her pick through various bottles of liquor, pouring a shot of each into a mixer. She shook it vigorously in that way that bartenders do and produced a bright blue drink along with one of their logoed napkins. "It's a Pisces Punch. Okay, now you may continue."

"You always make me these blue and green drinks. You know I hate them."

"Yet you drink them anyways," she smirked. "Now go."

I took a quick sip of the drink and found that it tasted like cotton candy. Surely a sign of trouble if you weren't paying attention to your limits. "Well first, Lydia wasn't even there. She had a meeting that held her up. Also, Eddie offered me a place on his team again."

Megan leaned against the bar. "Are you going to take it this time?"

"I declined." I shook my head while I stared into the drink. "It's . . . I don't know. I can't see myself doing it for a living. Plus, I can't leave my parents high and dry with the restaurant. Anna May is too busy with her lawyer path to be bothered, and I don't see them allowing non-family to run their pride and joy." I let out a long sigh. Being bound by family obligations was not my favorite thing. Especially when there were parts of me that at times longed to break free.

Megan drummed her acrylic nails on the bar top. I could tell she'd just gotten them done—a classic French manicure, but with black tips instead of white. "Maybe in another lifetime, Lana. I don't know if it would be right for you anyways. You'd feel it in your gut if it was."

"True."

"So what is it that you couldn't wait to tell me?"

I shrugged. "I don't know. I felt all wound up and couldn't stand the thought of sitting at home by myself massaging Kikko's ears."

"She hates when you do that."

"I know, but they're just so darn cute."

"Well, do you wanna know what I've been up to?"

"Yes, please. I need the distraction."

Megan pulled her cell phone out of her back pocket, tapped the screen a few times, and then asked, "Do you know anybody by the name of George Wong?"

I raised a brow. "The Mahjong Matrons mentioned that name. Who is he exactly?"

She turned her phone so I could see the article she'd been reading from. "Recently deceased, found dead in his home, and it's still being investigated under suspicious circumstances."

"You think this is one of the victims that Lydia is talking about?"

"I do." Megan replied with a firm nod. "And so I did a little digging on this guy. He was a lawyer. He did a lot of pro bono work for Asian Americans who didn't have the money to get legal representation."

"Lydia mentioned something about that." I thought about the way that had made me feel when she'd told me. It had struck a chord, but I couldn't explain why I felt the way I did.

"He had a clean record from what I could tell. Good

guy, divorced, no kids. Seemed really dedicated to his work."

"So why would someone want to hurt him?"

"Exactly what I was wondering." She turned her phone back around and her fingers flew across the screen once more. "Then there's this . . . Do you know Walter Kang or Theodore Yeh?"

"No clue."

"Also recently deceased . . . well, Theodore not quite as recent, but within the past year. And as far as I could tell, more Good Samaritans. Real pillars of the Asian community from the way it reads."

I took the phone from her hands, so I could see for myself.

"You look at that, I'm gonna do a lap around the bar and make sure everyone has what they need."

I nodded, too engrossed in what I was looking at to respond verbally. The phrase that Megan had used to get the results was populated in the search bar as "recent deaths in Asian community, Cleveland, OH."

The return on it had produced memorial services for the named parties, and below that were cover stories done by local papers talking about the contributions each person had made to their fellow citizens. And though none of their positions in society appeared to be affiliated with each other—just like Lydia had mentioned—they were all well-to-do and "upstanding" by any definition of the word.

This potential new spin about their below-the-radar secret society had me double guessing my original thoughts. They didn't appear to be villains or mobsters like I'd first considered. Which relieved me when it came to Mr. Zhang's involvement. But still, something was off, and why did it have to be so secretive?

If the murders were connected like Lydia's client insisted, why would a bunch of do-gooders be the victims? And were they for sure even murders? That had yet to be proven by anybody.

It made me wonder if perhaps the other two deceased parties were being used as a cover-up to get to someone specific.

Before I could delve in any further, I felt a hand rest on my shoulder, causing me to jump and almost drop Megan's phone. Thankfully, I'd caught it before it slipped through my fingers. As I turned to see who was invading my personal space, a feminine voice said, "I thought I'd find you here doing things you weren't supposed to be doing."

It was Lydia.

"What are you doing here?" I asked, turning off the screen of Megan's phone and placing it on the bar.

Lydia sidled onto the stool next to mine. "I stopped at the office after my meeting and Eddie was still there . . . filing paperwork of all things. He told me you stopped by and signed the contract. Which I might have you recall, says that you're not to discuss the case with anyone outside of the agency." She tapped the phone with her index finger.

I felt my cheeks getting warm. I'd had a feeling she caught sight of what I'd been looking at before I realized she was behind me. "It's not what you think . . . I—"

Megan returned just then, hearing the tail end of our conversation. "It's my fault. Lana didn't tell me anything other than you asked for her help. I did the rest on my own."

Lydia studied her, perhaps for telltale signs of lying. "I should have guessed this would happen. From what I know, you two are thick as thieves on any given day of the week."

I said, "She's really good at researching suspects. A lot of the time I end up needing her help digging up information."

Megan nodded. "It's true. I'm pretty sure that I was a spy in a former life."

Lydia chewed on her lip. "I don't know that Eddie would allow me to bring on another person. He was willing to let Lana assist on the case because of her affiliations in the Asian community. Plus, he seems to have a soft spot for you."

I blushed. "It could be an unofficial sort of thing. We won't tell anybody. Plus, Megan usually operates behind the scenes. Lots of internet snooping. No one would even know." Never mind that this wasn't completely true. There were many times that Megan had helped me out "in the field." In the present moment, Lydia didn't need to know about that.

Lydia still seemed skeptical, but after thirty grueling seconds of silence, she nodded in resolution and directed her attention at Megan. "I'll tell you what, I'm feeling generous today seeing as I had myself a good meeting, so I'll consider you an informant should anyone ask about the particulars. But I need you to keep this between the two of you, and it's best if you keep a low profile, Megan. Can I get your word on that?"

Megan used her index and middle finger. "Scout's honor."

Lydia snorted. "How's that for official?" She turned to me. "Lana, can you promise you're not going to involve anyone else?"

I held up my right hand. "I swear that I won't. Megan is the only person who knows everything I do anyways."

"What about that boyfriend of yours . . . Detective . . ."

her eyes slid in Megan's direction. "What did you call him that one time? Detective Hottie Pants?"

Megan laughed. "I can't believe you remembered that."

"Like a steel trap." Lydia tapped her temple.

I ignored the reference. "I'll keep him out of it the best I can. He's pretty good at catching on to things on his own."

Lydia smirked. "It's the detective in him. He can't help himself. I get it. Just don't go offering up confidential information and we'll be solid."

"So it's settled then?" I asked.

"Between you swearing, and Megan's oath, I guess we're good to go." Lydia replied. "Just don't make me regret it."

"Okay, so now what?" I asked. "Since we're here, should we talk about the case?"

"Nah, I've put in my time for the day, and frankly I'm exhausted." Lydia rested her elbows on the bar. "We'll get to it tomorrow. I set up a meeting with my client for noon. They've offered to take us out to lunch to discuss the particulars. Can you swing it?"

I agreed without hesitation and immediately began concocting reasons why I might be gone for lunch longer than normal. "Yeah, I'll make it work."

"Great," Lydia replied. "We'll start fresh with crisp minds tomorrow then. Now how about a drink?" she said, addressing Megan. "After all our negotiating, I'm feeling a little parched."

CHAPTER
8

I could hardly sleep that night. My mind kept going in circles about what the client lunch would be like. Most of the time I had to meet people under false pretenses so this was a little unusual for me.

After a while I tried focusing on Kikko's snoring, her rhythmic breathing almost becoming a sort of mantra. I must have fallen asleep around 3:47 a.m. It's the last time I could remember looking at the digital clock radio that sat on my nightstand right next to my head. Despite the fact that I had said alarm clock, plus three or four alarms set on my cell phone, I still managed to oversleep more days than not.

I believe that I was born a night person, though my sister often disagreed with me that such a creature even existed. According to her, we all had one internal clock and it rose and set with the corresponding movements of daylight. Well, of course, she would say that. That's totally what a *day* person would say, isn't it?

Yet, the whole thing was irrelevant considering I was

forced to live like a day person, my alarms normally set for the seven o'clock hour.

Despite the little sleep that I'd had, I managed to wake up to the sounds of my first alarm feeling completely awake but heavy as an anchor. As I swung my legs over the side of the bed and planted my feet firmly on the floor, I already knew that today was going to be a bear. Mass amounts of coffee would be needed for sure.

When I stepped into Asia Village, my eyes automatically went to Wild Sage, Mr. Zhang's herbal shop. He was standing near the entrance, looking at me almost as expectantly as Kikko does. If I didn't know any better, I would say that he'd been waiting for me to arrive.

I felt a lump form in my throat as I neared where he'd been standing. "Good morning, Mr. Zhang," I said, trying to sound cheerful and not at all leery. "It's a beautiful day out, isn't it?"

Mr. Zhang shuffled closer, his eyes narrowing as he studied my facial features. "Yes, good morning, Lana. You seem a bit troubled today. Is everything okay?"

"Oh yeah, me?" I said, a nervous laugh escaping. "I'm alright. Just a little tired." I held my travel mug. "Just needed more of this to get me going this morning."

His eyebrows bunched together and his line of sight moved back and forth from my mouth and my eyes. "Does this have anything to do with the woman who came to see you yesterday?"

I could feel my face getting hot, my palms beginning to sweat. "Oh, her? No, she's just an old friend who was in the neighborhood."

He pursed his lips. "I feel this is not the truth, but I will not push you to tell me anything. My only hope is that you are not in any kind of legal trouble."

"No, no," I said, shaking my head. "Everything is okay. I promise."

"I am here as your friend whenever my friendship is needed," Mr. Zhang whispered. "I care very much about your grandmother and your whole family. I only want the best for all of you. I wish you to know and understand this."

"I do," I said. I wanted to say more, but I didn't know what to say. The amount of guilt I felt for the thoughts I was harboring would be enough to secure my spot in therapy sessions until I was clear into my forties. "I better get going." My eyes drifted above his head into his shop. Above the sales counter, I noticed an old-fashioned sword secured to the wall resting on hooks that were surrounded by other pieces of art he had on display. There were scroll paintings of dragons, mountains, and mythical figures like Ma Gu—the deity of longevity.

But one particular painting stuck out to me. Next to the sword was a depiction of several characters sailing on a wooden boat that might as well have been a raft.

Mr. Zhang noticed that my attention had drifted and turned to see what it was that I'd been looking at. "Ah," he said with a slow nod as he turned back around. "That painting is one of my favorites. Do you like it?"

"Who are they supposed to be? I've seen paintings like this before, but I just assumed they were no one in particular."

Mr. Zhang chuckled. "I see your mother has not taught you much in the way of history."

"She's tried," I said, forgetting that I'd wanted to leave. "But I don't think I've always been the best student when it comes to things like that."

Mr. Zhang softened. "I was not eager to learn such

things as a young man myself. But to answer your questions, the painting is a tribute to a story written by Wu Yuantai during the Ming dynasty called *Journey to the East*. The people in this painting are thought to be the Eight Immortals and this is their famous voyage across the sea where they combined their individual powers to reach an annual birthday celebration for the Queen Mother of the West."

I nearly dropped my travel mug but balanced my grip on the handle before the contents went splattering all over the floor. I'd had a feeling that Mr. Zhang would answer as he did. I'd felt it in my gut, as Megan would say. "What's their purpose? In history, I mean." It felt necessary to add that specific detail, but probably because of that whole "guilt of me knowing something I wasn't supposed to know" thing.

Mr. Zhang turned back to the painting. "They are a symbol of prosperity and are said to hold the secrets of nature. It is also said to be a symbol of what is possible when you learn the mysteries of your own mind."

"I see" was all I could bring myself to reply with. I was preoccupied with finding it interesting that I'd never paid much attention to these details in his store before. And now, knowing that he was almost certainly affiliated with the Eight Immortals that Lydia had spoken of, I felt like maybe this painting was a beacon of some kind. Perhaps to let others know of his affiliation. I'd have to mention it to Lydia when we met for lunch.

"You are never too old to learn," he said with a smile. "I am willing to teach you anything you would like to know."

It might have been my paranoia, but it felt like there was a double meaning to what he was saying. "I appreciate your offer. Maybe another time. I better get going."

"Yes, you have a full day ahead of you, I'm sure." He patted my shoulder. "I hope it is wonderful."

"Thanks . . . same to you." I continued on toward Ho-Lee Noodle House berating myself for losing my cool right from the get-go. If I was going to work this case with Lydia, I had to strengthen my backbone and get my head in the game. There was no other option.

As I reached for the lock on the door to the restaurant, Mr. Zhang's innocent eyes flashed through my mind. I squeezed my own shut, shaking my head to remove the thought. I had to remain objective.

When I opened my eyes again, and thrust the key into the keyhole, I had that feeling again. That someone was there . . . watching. I twisted my head to scan the length of the plaza, and my gaze fell across the way to Eastern Enchantments. Talia Sun was standing at the front of her shop, staring at me.

I gave her a quick, half-hearted smile before turning back around and letting myself into the restaurant, shutting the door quickly behind me. As I engaged the lock, I let out a groan. "Doesn't anybody mind their own business around here?"

CHAPTER
9

- - - - - - - - - - - - - - -

The morning came and went with little activity. The Mah-jong Matrons had come in per usual but seemed to be pre-occupied with something they didn't care to share with me. Every time I showed up at their table they slipped into a silence and greeted me with superficial smiles.

It irked me a little that they always expected me to be extremely forthcoming but apparently had their own se-crets. If I'd had the time, it probably would have bothered me more than necessary, but I had my own problems to contend with.

At 11:25 I excused myself to stow away in my office and wait for Lydia's text saying that she'd arrived. We were going to drive together to an undisclosed location. I didn't understand why everything had to be so hush-hush, but it wasn't me calling the shots.

Promptly at 11:30, Lydia texted. *I'm here.*

I didn't bother with a reply, just grabbed my purse and the light jacket I'd brought with me to work. I sped through the kitchen, blubbering to Peter that I'd be back soon without giving him any time to comment or ask questions.

Nancy already knew that I would be leaving for lunch, so I just waved goodbye and went on my way.

I found Lydia in her black Mustang, parked right in front of the entrance. I did a quick check behind me to see if anyone was watching me leave with her, but no one was in sight. At least not that I could see.

Once I was in the car, Lydia shifted into drive. "Are you ready for this?"

"I'm not sure," I replied. "Are you going to tell me anything before we get there? I feel like I'm flying blind."

"I'll tell you about my client—our client actually," she said. She turned onto the side street connected to 210th Street and headed toward Center Ridge Road. "His name is Felix Hao. He's a local talent agent who focuses on Asian representation in entertainment."

"So like actors?" I asked.

"Actors, singers, performance artists; you name it, he covers it."

"Okay, and he claims to know that these murders are connected?"

"*And* he claims to know who is next on the chopping block," Lydia added.

"How would he know that?"

Lydia shrugged. "Beats me. He hasn't been very forthcoming with me. Dragging information out of him is worse than taking your dog to the vet."

I laughed. "I know that struggle."

"Oh, you have a dog?"

"Yeah, a little pug named Kikkoman."

Lydia chuckled. "Cute name. I have a toy fox terrier named Ashes. She's my little sidekick."

"But I don't get exactly what you need me for today."

No matter how much I loved talking about dogs, I wanted to make sure we stayed on topic.

Lydia cleared her throat. "Based on the things he's said, and his position on tradition . . . his preference to assist . . ."

"Lydia, spit it out." Normally she was very straight to the point. But I noticed a level of discomfort in her that I hadn't witnessed before.

She sighed. "It's like I was saying the other day, you're my 'in' to the Asian community. I think he's holding back on some things because he views me as an outsider and maybe doesn't want to tell me."

I snorted. "Do you really believe that? I mean he hired you after all."

She took a quick glimpse in my direction. "Are you offended that I think that?"

"No, not at all," I said. "It's just funny to hear someone say it out loud. I don't think about race all that much when I interact with people."

I looked down at my lap. It wasn't something I liked talking about generally. I'd been a target of cultural prejudice and racism a time or two myself. Either I wasn't white enough, or I wasn't Asian enough for some people. Most of the time it didn't get in the way, but it stung all the same.

And while those things had happened to me, it didn't change my viewpoint on others. I still form my opinions on people by the manner in which they conducted themselves.

"Sorry, if I brought up a sore subject. I meant no offense. That's why I didn't want to say it, but—"

"Well, we can't keep avoiding these topics. I think that's how we got to where we are in society. But regardless of what my feelings are on that subject, it still doesn't change the fact that he hired you. So some part of him has to trust you."

Lydia veered onto the freeway ramp going east on I-90, her eyes staying on the road in front of her. "I've concluded that he hired me to look into everything that's going on, and wanted me to find the answer, but then when it came to the particulars, he didn't think he'd have to tell me any of that. I tried explaining to him that I needed the full picture if he wanted a result of some kind. But like I mentioned, he gave me limited information. I thought your presence and maybe some background knowledge of your culture would help move things along. When I mentioned that you would be assisting me on the case, he seemed eager to meet again."

"I see. So what else can you tell me about him then?"

"I'd rather wait until after you meet him before I give you opinions or extra information. I like for people to make their own assessments if the opportunity presents itself. It helps create a more genuine reaction."

"Okay." I sighed. I was beginning to feel like I was being strung along and I couldn't figure out why. But I was confident that Lydia was good at what she did for a living, so I didn't press any further.

"You're a good sport," Lydia said.

"Outwardly," I replied. "Always outwardly."

Twenty minutes later, we arrived at YY Time, a newer restaurant located on Payne Avenue. There'd been rumblings in the foodie community about the former tire shop being renovated into a ten-thousand-square-foot Asian food hall. It was the first time I'd been there and even under the circumstances, I was excited to sample the menu, which I'd read about online when they'd first opened. There was an emphasis on street food that had caught my attention.

It wasn't often in recent history that I got the chance to try different Asian cuisine. I ate at Ho-Lee Noodle House so much that by the time I went home, I found myself craving pizza and burgers.

Lydia led us into the restaurant. "Don't forget, the cardinal rule is to say less, and ask open-ended questions. Never rush to respond . . ."

"I have done this before, you know."

Stepping inside the amply spaced venue, I took a moment to appreciate their modern, yet traditional, design. White scroll paintings with brush calligraphy adorned the black accent walls and provided a simple decorative element that was pleasing to the eyes. In contrast to the deep shade of paint, the prominent use of light wood for their table and chairs complemented the area nicely. And not to go unnoticed were the red fabric-covered light fixtures that hung above the tables and were reminiscent of Chinese lanterns.

In the far corner, near a window, sat an older Asian man with graying temples and the beginnings of a receding hair line. His skin was weathered from the sun, but as we got closer, I realized that he wasn't as old as I'd originally thought. I placed him somewhere in his late forties or early fifties.

He was thin and dressed in a well-fitted, black suit, white button-down shirt, and black dress shoes. If anything, he appeared professional and I got the impression that he took himself very seriously. When we approached him, he was staring into his teacup.

"Hello Felix," Lydia said.

He looked up. "Hello Ms. Shepard."

"I'd like to introduce you to my associate, Lana Lee." She turned to me. "Lana, this is Felix Hao."

"Nice to meet you, Mr. Hao." I said, extending my hand.

"You can call me Felix," he said, returning the gesture. His handshake was that of a businessman: firm grip and sharp, quick movements. "Thank you for coming. Please have a seat."

Lydia and I took our seats across from him with me sitting closest to the window.

"I took the liberty of ordering some appetizers. They should be out shortly," Felix said, sliding the extra menus across the table. "But feel free to order whatever you like."

As I skimmed the items on the menu, my stomach growled. There were more rice noodle soups than I could count, a variety of barbeque options, dumplings, grilled seafood platters, and a whole page dedicated solely to fruit and milk teas. I'd skipped breakfast and only nibbled on an almond cookie I confiscated from our kitchen. I was having a hard time picking just one thing as my lunch option. Was it unprofessional to eat my weight in noodles in front of our client?

We quickly placed our order and I opted to appear like I had some self-control. I chose the rice noodle soup with braised beef shank, deep fried spring rolls, brown sugar sticky rice—because I'd never had that before—pork fried dumplings to share with Lydia, a pork bao—because I hadn't had one in forever—and an oolong milk tea.

Okay, so clearly I was working on my definition of "self-control," but hey, a gal's gotta eat.

"Lana, I've heard of your reputation with solving these types of circumstances involving suspicious murders. Has Ms. Shepard discussed my situation with you?"

Before I could reply, Lydia answered. "I've told her very

little. I'd like her to hear everything from your point of view."

Felix narrowed his lips into a tight smile. "I had hoped that Lana would be better informed so we could move this whole thing along more quickly. Time is of the essence."

Lydia countered his smile with one of her own. "Yes, I understand that, Felix. However, there are critical details that you have yet to inform me of that I need in order to do my job properly."

He raised a brow. "I gave you all the necessary information you need to move forward, which is the simple fact that these deaths are related and, despite appearances, they are in fact, murders."

"Yes, but why?" Lydia asked. "I can't just take you on your word. I need a little more than that."

"You must take my word," he replied, slamming his fist on the table.

The impact caused the teacups and kettle to rattle against the table. It also caused me to jump.

Lydia doubled down in her stiffness, leaning her body forward as if to assert herself.

I took a deep breath. "Okay, Mr. Hao, uh, Felix . . . Why don't you start from the beginning so I can get a better idea of what's going on. Then we can go from there."

He closed his eyes, folding his hands in front of him. His thumb etching a pattern onto the table. "I belong to an exclusive organization that operates in secret: The Eight Immortals."

"Okay, this much Lydia has mentioned," I said. I didn't include that I knew his feelings toward Mr. Zhang—I thought it would be a good idea to let him tell me that on his own. Maybe Lydia had interpreted it wrong. I couldn't imagine anyone believing that Mr. Zhang, of all people, was capable of purposely doing harm to anyone.

"Lately, there has been some tension within our group." He sighed, reaching for his tea. Realizing it was empty, he picked up the kettle that was on the table and filled his cup to the brim. "This dissention has caused three people I care about to be murdered."

"Allegedly," Lydia added.

Felix scowled at her interjection but made no comment.

"What exactly is the nature of this group?" I asked. "And what caused all this tension?"

"It all began a few months ago when a woman by the name of Talia Sun entered our group."

My heartbeat quickened. The new shop owner at Asia Village. What did she have to do with this? I tried to keep the expression on my face level, so I didn't give away any concern I might be feeling.

He didn't seem to notice that I'd reacted in any way, so I mentally patted myself on the back while he continued on with his story. "Talia was the first to replace one of the Eight. She replaced Theodore Yeh at the request of Lois Fan, and the others all agreed that this was not appropriate.

"The two who proclaimed the loudest were Walter Kang and George Wong, my friends since childhood. George and I were the closest of friends. Both having lost our mothers at early ages, we bonded over this tragedy. And I know that he wouldn't harm himself. He had everything going for him."

I tried recalling the names that Megan had shown me the night before. George Wong was the lawyer who had been found dead in his garage, asphyxiated by exhaust fumes. It was undetermined whether foul play had been a factor or not. "I'm sorry for your loss," I said.

He nodded, his head hanging down as his shoulders sank. "Thank you. It has been difficult losing them, but

I do believe they were silenced and I want justice to be sought."

"I think we both can understand that," Lydia said, glancing in my direction.

Felix looked up, his eyes focusing on hers. "My only wish is that I would have acted sooner. I had suspected something before when Theodore was pronounced dead. He'd had a heart attack but had no prior heart problems. Truly he was healthier than most. But there was nothing to go on then besides my own suspicion."

"I don't understand the big deal with this Talia Sun person," I said. "Why was there such a disagreement about her being involved in your group?"

"Because everybody who represents one of the Eight Immortals is a descendent of an original member, passed down through lineage. We have never accepted an outsider before. However, Theodore didn't have children or any other family to succeed him, so Lois Fan recommended Talia Sun. You—"

Lydia stopped him before he could continue. "In the event there isn't a family member to replace the . . . open position . . . what is your protocol?"

Felix grimaced. "We have not come across this situation before, but some in our group have argued that a more extensive vetting process should be undergone."

"Who are these 'some'?" Lydia wanted to know.

Felix ignored her question and turned to me. "You know her, I presume? Talia Sun, that is." With a sneer, he added, "I'm aware she's just opened a *trinket* shop within Asia Village."

"I have yet to actually meet her more than to say a quick hello in passing," I admitted. "She just officially opened her shop yesterday."

"I don't know if she is directly involved or simply a

means to an end. Little is known about this young woman or what lies in her past—*or* why Lois saw fit to rush her into our ranks. But she is where the problems seemed to start. I fear that Lois Fan is behind all of this. Talia was a client of hers, and it would not be uncalled for to assume the young girl's presence could simply be to have someone around who's easy to manipulate. The young are so easily convinced, aren't they?"

Lydia looked up from her steno pad and I sensed she wondered if that was meant to be a dig at the two of us seeing as we were both younger than him. Whether she did or not, she chose to ignore it and continue with her line of questioning. "And what exactly is Lois's position in your group?"

"She is involved with arts and fashion. Talia was a contact from her modeling agency whom she had grown close to . . . or possibly groomed to her liking. One cannot say for sure. But once she found that Talia was involved with reiki and acupuncture and had a deep knowledge of crystals and natural medicine, the wheels began turning that she could transform this young lady into He Xiangu. In some ways she almost seemed to become obsessed with this idea. Which only furthers my concerns that she can mold Talia to be what and who she wants."

"I'm sorry, who?" I asked.

"He Xiangu is the name of the only woman who existed in the real group of historical persons. Though we have never held true to the specifics of male and female counterparts. The original group consisted of eight men. However, Lois felt that a woman should be in the position. I suspect she thinks that all of us should be replaced with women. Donna Feng as well . . ."

"Donna Feng?" I dropped my chopsticks.

"Yes, she took over the spot that belonged to her husband, Thomas Feng. I know this must be a lot for you to absorb. You had no prior knowledge of any of this, and here I am shattering your existence of the very community you surround yourself with."

I could worry about my shattered existence later. Right now, I wanted him to tell me about Donna Feng. "So Donna has said that she wants to replace everyone in the group with women?"

"Not directly, but since the beginning, once she was initiated into the group, she hasn't been shy about suggesting that we are old-fashioned and need to update the way we conduct ourselves."

Lydia held up a hand. "So wait, prior to Donna Feng becoming involved in your club, what other girls were allowed in the tree house?"

Felix shifted in his seat, looking everywhere but at Lydia. "Lois was the first."

Lydia and I exchanged a glance.

He studied us. "You must believe me. There is a conspiracy to remove certain members, and Lois is involved somehow. I just know it. If it's not her making the directives, well, there is also the matter of the missing artifacts . . ."

He'd trailed off most likely because he wanted to implicate Mr. Zhang, but this man knew enough about me and Mr. Zhang to know that he should tread lightly. I decided to skip over his insinuation and focus on the missing artifacts. "Yeah, explain that whole thing to me," I said. "What is the significance?"

"As I told you, we are descendants of the original members, the objects were given to them ceremoniously at their initiation and then passed down to each of us. Only the leader of the group may pass on these symbols of status to active members. They identify our standing and are a beacon for anyone searching for us. We don't carry them with us, but instead we have them prominently displayed in our places of business or our homes. Each object serves as a passcode that we use to gain access to other members and meeting locations."

"So are these artifacts worth money?"

Felix tilted his head back and forth. "I'm sure in this modern society, they would be worth something, but they are not genuine artifacts such as you may be assuming. They consisted of items that were brought over from China in the 1850s when our families first immigrated. No matter their cost, they are priceless to each of us. In all three instances, those items have gone missing."

"Hold up," Lydia said, scribbling furiously on her steno pad. "Then what does this Talia Sun person have . . . I'm assuming the object should have been passed down to her."

Felix nodded. "Yes, the object Theodore possessed was a golden spoon shaped as a lotus flower. But it was never found, so Wei Zhang presented Talia with a golden lotus flower instead."

"And it's okay to replace the original item like that?" I asked. "What stops anyone from replacing one of your objects and inserting themselves into your group?"

Felix replied, "Wei Zhang is the only one who can present a new member with any type of object. He holds the book of record, which states who the true members are and what item they have in their possession. If there is ever a question of legitimacy, Wei is the only one who can answer with true authority."

"So by someone stealing them, they could do what exactly?" Aside from their potential monetary value, I didn't see a good reason why anyone would want to take these items to begin with.

Felix scoffed as if this were the most unreasonable question I could ever dare to ask. "You must remember, Lana. I have specific people in mind."

"Okay . . ," I said. "So then what reason would *they* have to take these items?"

"To control our faction, of course. If my suspicions about the guilty parties are correct, then I would think it's to reset the board to their liking. Not to mention it sends a clear message to the other members, whether they want to acknowledge it or not, that there is dissention in the ranks."

"I see." I ran a hand through my hair, feeling almost as if I wanted to rip it out. This was a lot to take in and I still felt like I didn't have the whole story. Deciding I wouldn't look the best bald, I left my hair alone and continued on with my questions. I wanted to get them out while he was still in front of us. "Lydia mentioned to me that you think you know who's next to be replaced. Can I ask how it is that you think you know that?"

Felix took a few seconds to answer, his eyes traveling around the length of the dining area, fixating on the door for a few beats, and then finally, he turned his attention back to me. "I know who it is because . . ." He paused, scanning the dining area, then leaned forward and whispered, "It's going to be me."

CHAPTER
10

- - - - - - - - - - - - - - -

Lydia's mouth dropped. "Excuse me? And you failed to tell me this when we first met because why exactly?"

She'd gotten a little loud, and the table next to ours gawked at us as if she'd just sprouted another head.

"Keep your voice down, Ms. Shepard," Felix said while he covered the side of his face with his hand. "I didn't tell you this because I'm hoping to be wrong, and I didn't know if you would help me."

"You got that right," she said. "You should be going to the police with this, if you truly feel like your life is in danger. Then you need to come clean with what you know. I won't be held responsible if something were to happen to you. And I'm not exactly a bodyguard; I can't protect you."

"I can't go to the police with this," he replied. "Not only might they not believe me, but I would be exposing a century-old organization that involves many people. And if there is even a chance that I am wrong, then it will have all been for nothing. It could ruin people's lives."

I raised a brow. "I'm sorry, maybe I'm not understanding

things, but how would this ruin people's lives exactly? Unless you're involved in something illegal—"

"No! Because people will misunderstand our intentions and assume we are much like groups in history that have been accused of the same. But we are not. We only wish to help our community grow and be successful."

I wanted to ask him if he was referencing the Illuminati but didn't want to risk sounding like a conspiracy theorist. What other groups could he be talking about, though? It's not like people went around misunderstanding the 4-H Club. I decided to follow Lydia's advice on how to question him. Let him fill in the blanks. "Then, Felix, I think it would be in your best interest to tell us the nature of this secret group. In more detail, please. It could help us resolve this whole thing much quicker."

Felix wrung his hands together. "We help those who come to us get into certain positions they might not have been able to get into on their own. All eight of us have deep connections throughout the city and across the country. And while it may look to an outsider that some of these people received things they didn't earn, that is far from the truth."

"How exactly do people find out about you?" I asked.

"Mostly through word of mouth from trusted individuals," he replied.

"And who are these trusted individuals?"

Felix sighed, massaging his forehead. "Sometimes people we have helped in the past. On occasion we are the ones who deem someone in need of our assistance. If we come across someone in our community who we witness having a difficult time, we may step in to help as long as all of us are in agreement. There is an open discussion and we vote on whether the person in question can know of our existence. Sometimes we find it necessary to keep that person out of the equation but will assist them from behind the scenes."

"Meaning they have no idea that they'd gotten where they are with outside help?" I wanted to clarify the point because I could see how there would be people who wouldn't want that and some who probably would find it an unfair advantage.

"You are correct, Lana," Felix confirmed. "If we were exposed, it could cause problems for people in their current positions or fields of work."

Lydia tapped her pen against the table, having shoved away her plate of food. She'd scribbled down the entire conversation thus far, but I could tell she wasn't completely satisfied with his answer.

My own plate was empty and I was still hungry—being an "eat your feelings" type of person. I pushed the empty dish away and rested my elbows on the table, my gaze drifting out the window. As anxious as I'd been to get to this lunch meeting, I desperately wanted to be anywhere else.

Lydia broke the silence. "Let's get back to your previous statement, shall we?"

Felix sat back in his seat, straightening his back. "What are you referring to, Ms. Shepard?"

"You said that you think you're next. What gives you that impression? Or do you have a guilty conscience?"

Felix flinched. "I most certainly do not. I fear this because I am the odd man out. Now with the others gone, it is me against *them*." He'd said the word with such disdain, you could almost envision him spitting at their feet.

Lydia cleared her throat. "And by 'them,' you mean, Wei Zhang, Lois Fan, and Talia Sun?"

He nodded.

"But not Donna?" I asked.

Felix snorted. "She'd take their side over mine any day, but do I think she has a vested interest in getting rid of me specifically? No."

It provided a small amount of relief for him to say so. It was bad enough having to keep one person I cared about on the list of potential suspects. I didn't think I could handle Donna being on it too.

Yet, there was an implication he was making that Donna would easily go along with the idea of picking people off. I was just about to say that I thought it highly disrespectful to insinuate such a thing, but Lydia spoke up before I had the chance. "What about Douglas Chen?" she asked. "You don't suspect him of foul play?"

"Douglas is the money man," Felix replied. "He'd sooner buy everyone off than kill anyone. On top of that, he doesn't much concern himself with the politics of it all."

Lydia wrote this down, and I noted that she'd put a question mark next to his name.

Felix glanced between me and Lydia. He put his hands together in prayer. "Please, you must help me. I've answered all of your questions. I only ask that you look into their deaths to see that I am telling the truth, that these people didn't die naturally and that they are all connected. If you look into Lois Fan, I think you will find that she has some hand in it."

The way he spoke was almost as though Lydia hadn't completely accepted taking his case. And that wasn't the first time I'd felt that since sitting down with Felix Hao. I looked to Lydia expectantly, hoping she'd lead the conversation in some way to give me a clue. I felt it was important we appeared to be on the same page, a united front.

But all she did was stare at the soy sauce bottle that sat in the middle of the table. Her pen tapped rhythmically against the Formica tabletop, five quick taps and then a pause. I counted along with the sound, wondering what it meant to her.

I decided I couldn't take the silence any longer. And I wasn't going to leave without finding out why he thought Mr. Zhang might be involved or guilty somehow. It was time for me to be more assertive. I cleared my throat. "There's just one thing I want to know."

His hands dropped to the table. "Yes?"

"Why is it that you think Mr. Zhang is a part of this? If you're so sure that Lois Fan is guilty of something, how does this involve him?"

He looked down at his hands. I thought I noticed him squirming in his seat, and I watched as his eyes moved side to side almost as if he was calculating his next move. "I don't have proof of this, but I suspect that Lois Fan is his daughter."

I couldn't hold in my gasp. "His daughter?" I'd never thought Mr. Zhang had any children. He never spoke of them, nor had he ever mentioned a wife. Nothing. And no one else had ever said anything of him having family either. I'd been led to believe that's why he was so partial to Donna's deceased husband, Thomas, treating him as if he were his son.

Felix rubbed the back of his neck, his eyes darting every which way except at me. "I dislike telling any of these secrets, but I feel that they might be important. I fear that it's possible she is doing these things at his request."

I was having a hard time processing the information. Was this man telling the truth?

Before I could ask any more questions, Lydia set her pen on the table with a considerable amount of force, folded her arms across her chest, and rested her elbows on the table. "Look, Felix, this is all beginning to sound a little like *The Young and the Restless*, and I know there's something you're not telling us that would make all of this sound a little more reasonable. How about you tell us the real deal here?"

His jaw tensed. "I have been. And I will only say it one more time. I have told you everything you need to know to get to the truth. Now please, get started," he said. "Money is not an issue, so there is no reason for you to delay the process any further." Reaching into the inside pocket of his suit jacket, he pulled out an envelope, slapped it on the table, and slid it in her direction. "Here is the payment you asked me for at our last meeting—in cash—plus ten percent extra."

Her eyes widened as she accepted the envelope and peeked inside. From my angle next to her, I tried to peek into the envelope without it looking too conspicuous. But I couldn't see denominations. Only green. And there was a lot of it.

Lydia quickly tucked the envelope into her messenger bag. "I'll make sure this gets recorded and have a receipt mailed to you."

He leaned to one side, producing a wallet from his pants pocket. He threw three fifty-dollar bills on the table. "No need. Do what you must, just please do it fast." He returned his wallet to his pants pocket and rose from his seat. Acknowledging me, he said, "Lana, it was a pleasure meeting you. I feel confident that with you involved in this matter, we will get to the results more quickly."

He left without saying anything further to Lydia. She turned to me after he'd walked away. With a shrug, she said, "I guess our meeting's over."

Almost the entire car ride back to Asia Village was filled with silence. The conversation we'd had with Felix kept replaying in my mind, like a broken record. I kept hearing him say that Lois Fan was Mr. Zhang's daughter.

Was she an illegitimate child just as Peter had found himself to be? Or was she a long-lost daughter? Adopted, maybe? What proof did Felix have about this? Did all the members of their group have this knowledge? And if not, how did it come about that Felix would be the one with the keys to the skeleton closet?

More important, why would this even be a secret? I didn't understand any of it, and it sure seemed like I had more questions than I'd had to begin with.

As we got off the freeway exit, Lydia broke the silence. "Part of the reason I didn't want to tell you anything prior to meeting with Felix is not just so you could hear it for yourself. Though I do believe it's important and makes a difference."

I turned to her. "You wanted to see if he'd repeat the same information to me."

She nodded. "Yup, you got it, chickadee. I was hoping to catch him in some inconsistencies, but everything he told you today, he told me. Except the whole bit about him being the next victim."

"So you knew the part about Lois Fan supposedly being Mr. Zhang's daughter?"

"I know that Felix Hao claims it, but whether it's true or not remains to be seen. I haven't fact-checked it yet so I didn't want to say anything. Based on your reaction, I'm guessing this hasn't been something that's out there in the open."

"As far as I know," I replied. "I wasn't aware of him having any children at all . . . ever. No wife, he never speaks of family."

"What *do* you know about this man?" Lydia asked, studying my expression while we sat at a red light.

I shrugged. "I guess not as much as I thought. I mean . . . I didn't even know his first name until I heard my grandmother say it once. No one else says it, he's just Mr. Zhang. No one knows how old he is . . ." The more I thought about it, the more it bothered me. He'd largely been a mystery of his own, never questioned, I supposed out of respect for his age.

"Does anybody know anything about him?" As the light turned green, Lydia returned her focus to the road. "What about those elderly ladies that were in the restaurant yesterday?"

"If there's anybody who would know, it would be them," I said. "I just . . ."

"You're having a hard time believing that any of this is real."

"Yeah." I looked out the window. It was only a matter of minutes before we'd be back at the plaza. I'd gone over my allotted lunch time by a half hour and was hoping that Nancy wouldn't notice.

"I'm leaning toward skepticism myself. But in the meantime, I need you to work your magic at the plaza. It makes sense for you to be there seeing as you're there anyhow. I'm going to try and keep away as much as possible and work on getting us a meeting with Lois Fan. That way if Mr. Zhang is involved somehow, he won't get suspicious with me poking around."

I decided not to tell Lydia just yet that Mr. Zhang had noticed her presence in the plaza the previous day and asked about her. It might signify that he is already being paranoid or suspicious, and I didn't want her to get the wrong idea. I needed time to suss out the Mr. Zhang angle. Maybe it was loyalty because I'd known him since I was a little girl, but I couldn't believe he had anything to do with this.

Lydia pulled into the Asia Village parking lot, navigating herself toward the main entrance.

"Actually, drop me off at my car," I said, pointing to the employee parking area. "Just in case . . ."

"You got it." She wove through the lot, stopping near the area I'd shown her. "I also want you to learn what you can about this Talia Sun person. See if you can figure out what her deal is and what's so special about her."

I nodded as I took a quick scan of our surroundings, making sure that no one I knew was within sight. I didn't want to explain to anyone else who Lydia was. "I'll be in touch, then? I mean, is that what I do? Just report in to you?"

Lydia smirked. "Yeah, I suppose so."

"Okay, I'll contact you as soon as I find something worth finding out." I opened the door.

"Hey," she said before I exited the car.

I twisted in my seat to face her. "Yeah?"

"Don't worry. We don't even know if Felix is telling us the whole truth. Could be that this Mr. Zhang of yours isn't even part of the equation at all."

I got out of the car and leaned down so I was at eye level. "For the sake of everyone involved, I really hope that Felix Hao is lying through his teeth."

CHAPTER
11

- - - - - - - - - - - - - - - - -

I didn't see how I was going to concentrate on work for the rest of my shift. Especially when two of the people associated with this case were in my direct vicinity.

After Lydia had driven away, I'd stood in the parking lot for a few minutes, digging around in my car as if I was looking for something. Though I hadn't seen anyone around, I had that distinct feeling that someone was watching me again. I could only hope that it was my overactive imagination giving me grief.

My feet dragged as I trudged back into the plaza. My mood didn't match the day. It was a beautiful spring afternoon with a nearly clear blue sky. The air seemed as fresh, crisp, and lively as it often did when nature was taking bloom.

Yet, I felt bogged down, heavy and burdened like a fall sidewalk covered in wet leaves. It's not what I wanted for myself. Though I can't imagine anybody did.

The main entrance door seemed even heavier than normal, and as I entered the shopping plaza, I began to wonder whether if I checked above my head I'd find a thick rain cloud following me around. "Snap out of it, Lee," I mumbled to myself as I made my way to Ho-Lee Noodle House, my eyes completely averting any contact with Wild Sage. I could sense Mr. Zhang eyeing me as I passed.

When I walked by China Cinema and Song, I noticed a messy bun of hair bobbling down the opposite side of an aisle filled with kung fu movies. It approached me much like a shark's fin—the only telltale sign of advancement.

Moments later, my childhood friend Kimmy Tran came into view at the end of the aisle. A scowl rested on her round face, her balled-up fists rising to her hips. "Lana Lee, just one minute."

Knowing I wouldn't escape a full interrogation, I stepped off to the side of the main walkway to allow room for customers trying to get by, Kimmy sidestepping with me. "Hey, I gotta get back, what's up?"

She flashed an index finger in my face, almost poking my nose with a hot pink acrylic nail. "Don't give me that 'I gotta get back' BS. I know you're up to something . . . only I can't figure out what, and I want in. Everybody is talking about it. Who was the mysterious woman who came by yesterday? And thanks a lot for totally avoiding me by the way. Don't think I didn't notice."

Again, I felt that someone was watching me. I tried to nonchalantly check my peripheral vision to see if Talia Sun was standing at the entrance to her store just as she had been earlier in the morning, but too many people were walking by and I couldn't get a clear line of sight.

Kimmy clucked her tongue. "Lana, are you listening to me?"

I turned my attention back to my friend. "Yes, I'm listening. Sorry, things have been busy. Lydia Shepard came to see me yesterday. Just to ask a couple of questions."

"You mean the private detective chick?"

"Yeah, her."

Kimmy clapped her hands, rubbing them together. "Then this has got to be good. If a PI is involved, then it's probably juicy."

"There's no juice," I replied. "Just questions. Nothing else."

Kimmy returned my response with a sly smile. "Okay sure. If you want to waste time pretending like your hands are clean, then by all means, but I think we all know how this ends." Kimmy folded her arms over her chest, pushing her cleavage out of the top of her scoop neck blouse. "You'll need my help at some point, and when you do, we're going to waste a lot of time playing catchup. Might as well clue me in now."

I admired Kimmy's attitude more often than not. But I knew that her acts of bravado might be a detriment in this situation. Especially after Lydia specifically asked me not to involve anybody else in the matter. Still, I knew that Kimmy was right, and I might need to call in a favor at some point. After all, Lydia had her resources, and I had mine.

Kimmy inspected her manicure. Below her casual outward appearance of satisfaction, I knew she was waiting to see who would show their hand first, me or her. She knew I was hiding something, and despite not knowing what it was, she knew that I held the higher cards. Whatever I was keeping from her, she wanted, if only to simply be "in the know."

"Okay," I said. "How about this? I really do have to go. Why don't you let me figure some things out and we can meet up tomorrow after work for drinks."

Kimmy tilted her head to the side. "Hmm, I suppose that's fine." She raised her index finger to my nose again. "But don't think you're going to get out of it, missy. I know where you work *and* I know where you live." Then she smiled a big cheesy grin and shooed me in the direction of the noodle house. "Off you go."

With a smirk and a shake of my head, I went back on my way to the restaurant. Sometimes Kimmy was a bigger handful than some of my suspects.

Business in the restaurant had been slow while I was gone and neither Nancy nor Peter made any comment about my lengthy lunch time. I didn't offer up anything and stowed away in my office, claiming that I was doing paperwork.

But what I was really doing was searching the internet trying to find information on Felix Hao, Talia, and her former modeling agent, Lois Fan. It wasn't what Lydia had asked of me, but I wanted as much background information as I could get my hands on.

Felix and Lois had their own websites, both being the owners of their respective agencies. Linked on their sites were all their available social media handles and pertinent articles that had been featured in magazines and blogs.

Searching their names online didn't provide me with a ton of information outside of their careers and charitable work. When it came to Lois, however, I tried extra hard to dig for personal information. If she was born in the state of Ohio, I could try requesting a copy of her birth certificate as long as I had the right information, but Lydia was already doing that.

I wondered about the likelihood of her being born in Ohio. Her website bio didn't mention anything about where she came from outside of saying that she currently resided in Cleveland but split her time between Ohio and New York.

When I felt like I wasn't getting anywhere, I changed

my focus over to Talia. The first link that showed up was attached to Eastern Enchantments. It was an overview of the shop and listed out merchandise to purchase online.

Her bio was equally vague and didn't tell me anything I hadn't already learned about her at today's lunch. I planned on heading over to visit her shop, but I hadn't wanted to rush out as soon as I'd returned from my outing.

To fill up time, I decided it was best to tackle a few items on my to-do list. I needed to call in some supply orders and update info on our payroll service.

I was able to concentrate for about forty-five minutes before I could hardly stand waiting around anymore. After straightening up my clutter, I shuffled out from behind my desk and ambled through the kitchen trying not to call any attention to myself.

Peter was preoccupied with cutting up chicken and didn't seem to notice me walking by.

In the dining area, I found Nancy wiping down menus at the hostess booth. She looked up at me as I approached. "There you are. I have barely seen you today, Lana. Is everything okay?"

"Yeah, everything's okay." I forced a smile. "How are things going up here?" Seeing as there was only one table of two in the entire restaurant, I knew how things were going: slow.

"It is a nice, quiet day. I don't mind this. Yesterday was quite busy for us." Peter's mom, Nancy, was not only one of my mother's best friends, but she was also an honorary aunt to me and Anna May. When I was younger I still called her and my mother's other best friend "*A-yí*" which means "auntie."

But when I became an adult, they told me I could call them by their first names, especially at work so that we appeared more professional. Honestly though, it felt weird at times.

Nancy was always the gentle one, soft and nurturing, while my other "auntie" Esther was a bit more harsh, commanding me at an early age to stand up straight like a general and to cross my legs like a lady. Which is all fine and good, except when you're seven years old, you don't really care much about posture.

"Do you need help?" I asked.

"No, I am almost done cleaning up," she replied. "Are you sure everything is okay?"

"Oh yeah. I'm fine. Hey, have you been to see the new shop owner yet?"

She nodded. "Talia? Yes, I went to meet her yesterday. I bought this bracelet from her store." Nancy held up her wrist to show me a purple jade bangle. "You should stop by and see her if you have not done so already. Perhaps buy something to show you wish her well with her new business."

Relieved that she suggested it, I jumped on my opportunity to leave the restaurant without being questioned about my intentions. "You know, you're right. I probably should do that right now. I don't want her to think I'm rude."

"Yes, you go." She shooed me away. "I will handle everything here." She turned to check on the only two customers we had. "I should be able to manage." She gave me a playful pinch on my arm before she went to attend to their needs.

I headed out into the plaza, straight over the koi pond toward Eastern Enchantments. It was finally time to meet Talia Sun, face-to-face.

CHAPTER
12

The scent of sandalwood wafted in the air just outside Eastern Enchantments, along with a trail of soft instrumental music. The transformation of the former tea shop was most impressive.

The walls were painted a soft gray and brushed with a patina finish to give them an antique look. And the once-drab laminate floors had been replaced with glazed, octagon-shaped terra-cotta tiles. Every so often there would be a black tile engraved with a Chinese character painted in gold. Upon my initial inspection, I spotted the characters for water, fire, longevity, and double happiness. There were a few I didn't recognize without a little help, but I had a feeling I'd be committing them to memory in the near future.

I didn't know what would come from this initial meeting with Talia, if anything, but Nancy was right; I did, at the very least, have to introduce myself.

I think I'd been more excited about meeting the new shop owner prior to my lunch with Felix Hao and finding out that Talia was part of their secret club. Was she a plant? And if so, for what purpose and how deep did this whole thing go? Ian Sung, our property manager, was the one who had to approve bringing her on board—did that mean he had some kind of involvement? Plus, he was Donna's right-hand man.

I had to wonder if any of it even mattered. The murderous parts mattered, yes, but did it really affect my life as far as who belonged to the Eight Immortals? It was a difficult question to answer because Mr. Zhang was involved. So on some level it *did* affect my life . . . especially if Mr. Zhang had something to do with the aforementioned murderous parts.

Talia was nowhere in sight and there were no customers lingering around. I walked up to the checkout area to see if maybe she was bent behind a counter. In the showcase directly below the cash register were more expensive pieces of jewelry and large chunks of crystals that had price tags showing some of the items cost well into the hundreds.

I rested my hands on the glass top, feeling the heat coming off the display lamps inside the case. I felt mesmerized by a large piece of solid black stone. In front of it was a card with a few lines of information. I bent down closer to read the provided description.

"It's black tourmaline," a voice said from behind me.

My body jerked into an upright position, and I turned around to find Talia observing me with a pleasant smile on her face. As if appreciating my curiosity of her merchandise.

The tension that I'd been feeling seemed to melt away as she took a few steps toward me. There was something about her that was both calming and reassuring.

Sure, I'd seen her in passing, but I hadn't spent a lot of time assessing my initial take on her. The first thing that stuck out to me right away was her height. I put her to be around five ten, potentially one of the tallest Asian women I'd ever met. She was slender but not so much that she appeared lanky. Her loose linen pants didn't look baggy on her tall frame, and the soft blue billowy top she wore didn't take away from her figure. My own body would have been lost in an outfit like that.

"It's a great source of protection from negative energy." She extended a slender hand. "I'm Talia. It's so nice to finally meet you."

"I'm sorry?" I shook my head. She was talking about the black stone, not about herself, but I was so enthralled with her hair. It reminded me of raven feathers, so black they appear blue. I immediately wondered where she'd gotten it done. With an apologetic smile, I extended my own hand. "You'll have to excuse me, I'm a little sidetracked today. I'm Lana, it's nice to meet you as well."

"I was expecting to meet you yesterday, but it would seem that the Universe had other plans." Her eyes—the color of roasted chestnuts—flickered with amusement as she waited for my reaction.

I think because I was already on guard, I was able to hold back showing my proverbial hand. That poker face I kept working at was beginning to pay off. The only problem was that I couldn't figure out if she was being passive-aggressive or eccentric. I decided to take the flippant approach. "You know how Mondays can be," I said.

"Hmmm, yes," she replied, the pleasantness of her expression never faltering. "I would recommend this black tourmaline for you. You were drawn to it, yes?"

I had been, but I didn't want to admit it for some reason. Also, I couldn't spend that amount of money on something like that. Megan would put me in the financial time-out box if I came home with a hundred-dollar rock.

As if reading my mind, Talia said, "I was thinking of something less expensive and *much* smaller. Perhaps a palm stone, or a tumbled piece . . . something to keep in your pocket." Then she signaled for me to follow her. "I do have bracelets and other jewelry as well, but maybe try these first and see how you feel."

We walked over to a circular display of stones and crystals in clear acrylic bowls. Talia walked with the grace of a model and the perfect posture that Esther was always insisting I command at any given moment because a "true lady" never slouches. "Here, pick one." She pointed to a bowl that held smaller versions of the stone I'd been looking at in the case. "Feel the energy you want to connect with. Take your time with it."

I raised a brow. "I don't know what you mean." My eyes skimmed over the stones in the bowl. Aside from their natural differences they all appeared to be somewhat similar.

"I believe that objects from nature call to those that need their help." She picked up the bowl and held it closer to me. "You will sense a gravitation toward one stone specifically. Relax and focus on these, pick what you feel is best."

This whole thing felt weird, and I was beginning to regret coming to see Talia when I wasn't at the top of my game. I'd always had a hard time with this sort of stuff—the skeptic in me trying to enter logic into the equation.

Still, I didn't want to hurt her feelings. I inhaled slowly, trying to clear my mind as best I could, focusing my attention on the sounds of the instrumental music that had been playing unobtrusively in the background.

I noticed a stone sitting on the edge of the bowl that had small grooves throughout the surface, and an indentation in the center that appeared as if it was meant for my thumb to rest in, even though the dip was clearly natural. When I picked it up, I noticed that the other side of the stone was smooth and flat.

Talia's smile grew larger as she put the bowl back down on the shelf. "This stone is meant to be yours and will protect you as you need it. If it breaks, it has done its job and you may return it to the earth."

I rolled the stone over a few times in the palm of my hand. It did feel as if it was emitting some kind of energy, but I didn't know if that was a direct result caused by the power of suggestion. "How much do I owe you for it?" I asked, searching for a price tag on the display.

She put her hand over mine, closing my fingers around the stone. "This is a gift from me. If you were drawn to this stone, it means you need assistance with protecting your energy. Perhaps you will have some tribulations to conquer in the coming days."

"Um, okay," I said, pulling my hand away from hers. "Thank you."

"It was so nice meeting you, Lana. I hope we can talk more soon."

"Thanks, same here," I said, slipping the black tourmaline stone into my pants pocket. "Have a good rest of your day." I waved before turning to head out back into the plaza.

After I'd made my way back over the koi pond, I halted mid-step, almost causing a collision with the person who'd been walking behind me.

I mumbled an apology as I stepped off to the side of the bridge. It had taken this entire time to realize that I hadn't talked to Talia about anything I had originally planned on discussing with her. Somehow, she had dominated the direction of our conversation and made it all about the stone. Perhaps I was being dramatic, but did she put some kind of woo-woo spell on me or something? Or was she just an experienced con artist with the skill to work a room? Either way, I felt I'd been had.

When it was Nancy's turn to go on lunch, I set up camp at the hostess station to cover the dining room. I'd brought my travel mug that was somehow still filled with coffee, my cell phone, and a small bag of glazed doughnut holes I picked up on my way back from meeting Talia.

I'd asked Mama Wu her feelings on the new shop owner, and all she'd said was she thought Talia was a nice girl and would bring many customers to Asia Village. The customer part remained to be seen, but I knew part of me was looking for problems with Talia. It wasn't exactly fair of me to judge her business capabilities considering she hadn't been open that long.

I noticed that I had a missed call on my phone. Lydia. She didn't leave a message and I couldn't imagine what she'd be calling about this quickly.

I also noticed that I had received three text messages while I'd been away.

Megan: *hey girlfriend, just checking in. How'd lunch go with Lydia and the mysterious client?*
Kimmy: *I saw you over at the new store talking to that Talia girl . . . what's up with that?*
Adam: *Hey dollface, I'm finally free tonight. Dinner?*

The only message I responded to was Adam's to let him know that I was definitely available for dinner.

Since there were no customers at the moment, I decided to call Lydia back, just in case it was important.

While the phone rang, I glimpsed over my shoulder at the kitchen door to make sure Peter wasn't coming out into the dining room to talk with me. On occasion, when things were painfully slow, he'd come and hang out with me at the hostess station to help pass time. That's usually when we talked about all kinds of crazy things like government conspiracies or random topics that he'd taken an interest in—he's the one who'd originally taught me about the observer effect.

Lydia finally picked up the phone: "Shepard."

"Lydia, it's me . . . um, Lana. You called?"

"Oh hey, sorry, can you hang on a sec, I'm at Starbucks." She didn't wait to see if I could "hang on." I heard the phone getting shuffled around and muffled talking between two people.

About a minute went by before she came back on the line. "Sorry, they forgot to put whip cream on my macchiato and it's just not as good without it. Anyways, I called because I made copies of the client file for you and completely forgot to bring them to lunch. Do you mind if I swing by and drop them off? I need to get to another meeting for a different client, so can you meet me in the parking lot?"

"Yeah, pull up over by my car, I can put the files in my trunk. Probably shouldn't bring them in with me anyways."

"Great, see you in fifteen."

I checked the clock. Nancy would be coming back right around that time.

I figured I might as well sample some goodies from Shanghai Donuts while I texted Megan back. But by the time I opened the chat box—and the doughnut bag—six men in coordinating polos with the same logo came strutting into the restaurant.

Sigh. Megan and doughnut time would have to wait.

CHAPTER
13

- - - - - - - - -

The table of six men kept me busy while I waited for Nancy's return and Lydia's arrival. While I took their drink order, one of the men explained to me that they were in town on business from their corporate office in Santa Fe. They'd heard rave reviews about the food at Ho-Lee Noodle House from fellow co-workers and had to come see for themselves.

I usually appreciated meeting people from out of town. Especially when they said they'd heard about our restaurant and made a special trip in, but today I felt anxious and didn't feel much like participating in small talk.

After I finished serving their drinks and taking an appetizer order, Nancy returned. "I can take over the table if you have more paperwork to do," she offered.

"Actually, I just need to run out to my car really quick and grab something."

"No problem," she replied.

I hurried to get my car keys from the office. While I'd been taking their order, I'd felt my cell phone vibrating in my back pocket. I had a feeling that Lydia was waiting for me outside.

Peter was so busy preparing their appetizers that he didn't notice me running back and forth as I passed through the kitchen.

In the plaza, I tried not to appear as if I was scurrying along. Surely someone would notice. Kimmy, Mr. Zhang . . . the ladies at Asian Accents hair salon. I kept my pace at a brisk walk while checking my peripheral vision as casually as possible.

I caught sight of Kimmy ringing up a customer as I passed by and was relieved that she couldn't stop me again or ask me where I was off to.

I made it out to the parking lot without incident and found Lydia's black Mustang idling behind my car.

She must have seen me in her rearview mirror because she got out of the car as I approached, holding a manila envelope—the kind that seals with that strand of red string.

"I'd appreciate it if you didn't show it to anyone," she said, handing it over. "Including Megan. I know I said I don't mind if she helps with corralling some information, but documents . . . these are for your eyes only."

"You got it," I said, opening the trunk with my key fob. "I even have a hiding place to store it at home."

"Well aren't you fancy?" Lydia chuckled.

She'd probably laugh harder if she knew that the hiding place was beneath my mattress. Granted it wasn't the most secure location, but it did the job. "I finally met Talia, by the way. It was the strangest thing."

Lydia rested a hand on her hip, leaning her weight against the back of her car. "Oh yeah?"

"Yeah . . ." I closed my trunk and turned to face her.

"It's almost like she made me forget my purpose going over there. I didn't learn a damn thing about her."

Lydia's eyes narrowed. "We have a slippery one on our hands, don't we? That might be a telltale sign."

I massaged my forehead. "I felt like a real idiot after I realized it."

"That's okay, don't let it slow you down. Try again tomorrow. Now that you know she's slick, you'll be on guard."

"I guess you're right about that."

A car horn honked right behind us, causing both of us to jump.

Lydia clucked her tongue and waved her arm, signaling the driver to go around us. "Geez, they have plenty of room."

"Maybe they think this space is going to be opening up." I turned to look at the driver who had still failed to move on, but I couldn't see their face. The visor was down, and the glare from the sun obstructed my view.

"Ugh, who knows, I gotta run anyways," she said, tapping her wrist.

She wasn't wearing a watch, but I got the point. "Thanks for dropping this off." I patted my trunk.

She gave me a two-finger salute and hopped back into her car.

As she left, the car followed behind her. Guess they weren't waiting for my spot after all.

I turned to head back into the plaza, and as I directed my attention near the entrance, I noticed that Talia was standing at the edge of the parking lot.

When we made eye contact, she stepped off the curb and headed my way. She walked with such grace, it almost appeared as if she were floating along the pavement.

I wondered if she had witnessed my meeting with Lydia. How long had she been standing there? Had she followed me out into the parking lot?

As we approached each other, I offered my best customer-service smile. "Are you heading out for the day?" I was attempting to act natural, like I hadn't just been meeting with a private detective in the parking lot. Nope, that wasn't me putting confidential files in the trunk of my car either.

"No," she replied. "Just taking a walk and getting some fresh air." Her eyes drifted to where my car was parked.

I took another step toward the plaza, hoping to bring her attention along with me. "The sunshine has been great, hasn't it? Such a nice change from the gloomy weather we were having last week."

A smile spread across her lips. "Yes, spring is always a welcome visitor."

"It sure is," I said. "Well, I've gotta get back."

"See you later, Lana."

I chose now to do my scurrying. It felt appropriate in this scenario, before I started rambling on about the ten-day forecast or some such nonsense.

I couldn't figure out what it was about this woman that had me acting all wackadoo. Hopefully I'd come up with something before we had our next encounter. Like Lydia had said, I would need to try again tomorrow.

When I returned to the restaurant, thankfully not being stopped by anyone on my way back in, I found that the table of six had been served their meals and that a few more customers had come in.

Nancy was waiting on a table of four, and two young

women were standing at the hostess station waiting to be seated. I greeted them and showed them to a table, took their drink order—a Coke and an iced oolong tea—and made my way into the kitchen.

Peter was busy at the grill, bobbing his head up and down to whatever was playing in his headphones. When I walked in, he removed his earbud, set down his spatula, and walked over to join me at the ice dispenser. "Kimmy texted me."

I waited for further explanation, but he didn't offer any. "And?" I filled the two glasses with ice.

He crossed his arms over his chest. "She wanted to know what you were up to and if you'd left work for the day. I wonder what would give her that idea . . ."

I shrugged as I walked over to the refrigerator to pull out the iced tea pitcher. I made a fresh batch every morning when the weather started to get warmer.

"I knew you were up to something, Lana Lee," he said. "I knew that Lydia coming around meant that nothing good would follow."

I shut the refrigerator door with some force. "You shouldn't assume anything. Besides, I have everything under control."

"Famous last words," he replied. He returned to his post at the grill, flipping the strips of beef that he was sautéing. "If you don't want to tell me the truth, then whatever, but don't let Kimmy get involved in this one. You know how I feel about this kind of stuff. And if a PI is involved, I feel like there is extra shadiness to be found."

The first thing that sprang to mind was my need to tell him that he was judging something based on a stereotype. But I also wanted to tell him that I knew where he was coming from and that I understood. However, at the end of the day, Kimmy was her own person and there was nothing I could do about it. Especially when his girlfriend found her own way to get involved in things. And the only person I could control was myself.

But it all felt pointless. We had the same argument over and over again. And he already knew that I wasn't going to change who I was to make anybody else feel better.

I filled the other glass from the soda fountain and decided to just leave things as they were. No point in using my energy to convince him of anything different.

I left the kitchen without saying another word. As a matter of fact, we didn't speak for the rest of the afternoon. Nancy and I rotated between serving tables and standing guard at the hostess station.

When my shift was over, I grabbed my things from the office and left without saying goodbye to Peter. I wished Nancy a good evening and went on my way.

Checking my phone on the way to the parking lot, I saw that Adam had texted me again saying that he'd pick me up for dinner at seven. I replied, letting him know that I'd be ready and waiting for his arrival.

Thinking about dinner with Adam brought a sense of relief and excitement. It would be good to finally see him and enjoy a night out together.

Perhaps I was so preoccupied with wondering about what I was going to wear that night, that I didn't notice right off the bat that something was wrong with the picture in front of me.

I paused in between two cars, staring at my own car that was about fifteen feet away. My trunk was wide open.

The vein in my neck felt like it was going to consume my throat. I quickened my pace. Maybe that wasn't my car. Maybe I had it wrong. Yanking my keys out of my purse,

I pressed the fob . . . and my parking lights flashed. Dammit, it was my car.

As I neared it, I checked the windshield and the four passenger windows. Everything was intact. I swung around to the back of the car, looked in my trunk, and it was as I had feared. The files that Lydia had given me were gone.

CHAPTER
14

-   -   -   -   -   -   -   -   -

After shutting my trunk and doing a cursory scan of the parking lot—just in case I caught the thief trying to run away—I got into my car and locked the doors. I sat there for a few minutes with the car running, listening to the steady idle of the engine, trying to remember if I had shut my trunk properly. I had, hadn't I? And besides, whether I did or didn't, the fact still remained that the envelope Lydia had given me was gone. Everything else was in there: my jug of wiper fluid, my snow brush, that damn bag of clothes I'd been meaning to drop off at Salvation Army for over two months. It was all accounted for.

Next I pulled out my phone and opened the text thread with Lydia. What was I going to say? I began typing the scenario of what just happened. It sounded so ridiculous, I deleted it and attempted again. The blinking cursor taunted me. How would I explain that the files she'd just dropped off, not even four hours ago, had been stolen from my car? Would she think I was irresponsible? What if she didn't believe me? Then again, what reason would she have not to trust me? What would I even do with the files . . . Not having them wouldn't do me any favors.

When I became this indecisive about something, my usual tactic was to avoid addressing the problem. Granted, it wasn't the best course of action, but I needed time to marinate, aka mull it over. I decided to drive home and overthink the situation on the way there.

About seventeen minutes later, I pulled into my usual spot outside our apartment building. The complex was divided into eighteen separate buildings that each contained twelve apartments. Each building had its own parking lot, and most of us kept to the same spots even though they weren't assigned.

Before going inside to let Kikko out for her afternoon tinkle, I investigated my trunk more thoroughly, which I hadn't done at the plaza. I probably should have, but I'd also considered that maybe someone was still watching me. The thought caused me to inspect the surrounding area. I was probably being paranoid in thinking that someone had followed me home, but you could never be too safe.

I crouched down, running a hand over the outside of my trunk. There were no marks and nothing looked tampered with. There wasn't even a keyhole for anyone to pick open. This model only had a button tucked underneath the lip of the third brake light. The only way it could be activated was if the car was unlocked. "Ugh!" I couldn't remember locking my car after Lydia and I parted ways. "Wait a minute!" I smacked my forehead. I'd gotten distracted when I noticed Talia in the parking lot.

"Are you talking to me?" a husky voice said from behind me.

I jumped, almost falling onto my butt, but caught

myself with my hand. A few stray pieces of gravel clung to my palm as I hoisted myself up.

It was my neighbor, Mike. He was a nice older man who lived a few doors down.

I wiped my hands on my pants. "Oh hey, Mike, sorry. I was talking to myself and didn't realize anyone was there."

"Well, you know what they say . . . as long as you don't answer yourself in a different voice then you're A-OK." He gave me a thumbs-up. "You havin' some kind of car trouble? I could take a look if you need some help."

"Oh no, just making sure . . . um . . . I remembered to put my registration sticker on my license plate."

He squinted. "Yeah, you don't want to rock and roll without that on, they'll get ya for that. Eighty-dollar fine, I heard. But then again, you probably know that, dating a cop and all that."

"Yeah . . . no fines for *this* girl." I gave him an awkward smile. "I better get Kikko out here before she pees her pants. You have a good evening."

"You too, now. I'm heading for my afternoon stroll. They're doing some construction by the pool and I want to see what's going on. I'll let you know what I find out."

"Okay, see you later, Mike."

We waved and went in opposite directions. My thoughts returned to the subject at hand: realizing that Talia had distracted me in the parking lot. Not only that, but she'd had her eyes on my car.

Was she the thief? But how could she—or anyone else for that matter—know they'd be able to get into my trunk? Unless it was just dumb luck. It's not like anybody would know what I was up to or know that I had anything of worth in my trunk to begin with.

Probably what happened was she saw I'd put something

in my trunk and maybe she'd seen Lydia as well. Most likely she took the chance to see if she could get into my car, and seeing as I'd unknowingly left it open, it made things easier for her.

I grumbled all the way to the door, berating myself for the mistake that I'd made. After I finished walking Kikko, I'd make sure to text Lydia about the stolen files.

When I opened the door, Kikko came galloping toward me, snorting the whole way over. "Hey you," I said, kneeling down to pet her. "You're a sight for sore eyes."

She sniffed my kneecap; my pants probably smelled of the restaurant. After a few seconds of thorough investigation, she licked the area she'd been intrigued by, then looked up at me expectantly.

I stood and grabbed her leash that was hanging on the hook by the door. "Okay, let's go outside. Wait till I tell you about the day I've had."

Kikko hadn't been all that impressed with the story of my day and found that her favorite bushes and trees were much more interesting than anything I had to say. Despite her lack of interest, I continued talking with the hope that if I said everything out loud, it would all make sense. But by the end of our walk, I concluded I felt no better than when we had started.

Once Kikko was situated with a fresh bowl of water and a portioned scoop of food, I went back to the task of texting Lydia. I tried to keep it short: The envelope was stolen from my car, gasp, who would do such a thing. The end.

While I was rummaging through my closet, the phone rang. Checking the readout, I saw that it was Lydia. "Hello?"

"Lana . . . what the hell happened? Someone broke into your car?"

I relayed the chain of events to her, telling how I'd found my trunk wide open, the envelope nowhere to be found.

"They didn't break into your car first?" she asked.

"No, they went straight to the trunk. Funny thing, right after you left, I noticed Talia Sun in the parking lot."

"Ya don't say."

"How could someone get into my trunk without damaging anything?" I left out the part about potentially leaving my car unlocked.

"There are ways . . . There's this whole thing you can do with a magnet that I learned from Eddie. I don't know if it works with all cars, but I haven't had a need to do it personally. And I don't know if it's anything that Talia Sun would know how to do. The person would have come prepared and potentially had a tool kit of sorts for just such occasions."

Talia had been empty-handed as far as I'd noticed. Not to say she didn't have another way to get in. I contemplated asking Lydia if she would teach me some of the tricks she knew but decided against it. I didn't want to take the chance that it might open up conversations about me coming to work at the agency again. "Weird also, they left my trunk open. You'd think they would have at least closed it so I didn't know right away."

Lydia tsked. "Most likely that was on purpose. Whoever did it wanted you to know that your car had been tampered with, maybe to create some paranoia on your part. That's my guess anyways."

"What exactly was in that envelope?"

"Information I've collected on Felix Hao and the names he's mentioned so far. Plus anything I have on the murders that have already happened. Contact information . . . stuff like that. Thankfully they were copies, so we didn't lose anything. But now, whoever has it knows what I know."

"I'm sorry, Lydia. I thought they'd be safe in there."

"Don't sweat it, chickadee. I can make you new copies . . . I'm actually at my office now. Can you meet?"

I checked my watch. There wasn't enough time before Adam arrived. "Adam is on his way over—"

"Say no more, I'll prep another set and bring them to you first thing in the morning. Can you meet me at Asia Village before you guys open?"

"Yeah, how about we meet there at seven thirty," I suggested. "I don't think Mr. Zhang will be there yet." He was always the first to arrive in the mornings, but if I remembered correctly, he didn't get there until eight o'clock.

"Sounds good, I'll see you then."

We hung up and I let out a groan as I flung my phone onto my bed. Kikko, hearing my dissatisfaction, came scuttling into my room to see what my problem was. When she couldn't find the cause for my frustration, she snuffled and disappeared back into the living room. I heard some squeaking—probably her stuffed duck—and then she fell silent. Little dog had properly tuckered herself out with all that vigorous eating.

I'd finally gotten my outfit together—black blouse with sheer three-quarter sleeves and skinny jeans, which I would pair with wedged booties—hopped into the shower with lightning speed, freshened my makeup, and touched up my hair with five minutes to spare.

At seven o'clock on the dot, there was a knock on my door. Kikko sprang to action from her napping position on the couch. Her nose magnetized to the crack between the door and the floor, sniffing out our newcomer.

I always enjoyed the moment when Adam's familiar

scent registered in her memory and her squiggly tail wiggled with excitement. I opened the door, and Adam wrapped his arms around me, scooping me up. He closed the door with his foot, careful not to kick Kikko in the process, and then carried me into the living room.

"Put me down," I laughed into his neck, inhaling the scent of his cologne. "You're going to wrinkle my shirt."

Kikko barked a few playful yips. Adam set me down and gave me a kiss before bending down to pet my hyped-up pug. "How are my favorite two girls doing?"

"Oh you know, living the life," I said, spreading my arms out. After not seeing him for several days, the last thing I wanted to do was talk about my woes. Plus I didn't think he'd be too happy knowing I'd taken a case with Lydia. I wanted to enjoy our evening a little bit before the lectures came. Over time he'd become more understanding of my need to get involved in such things, but he still didn't like it and every instance came with a warning.

"You all ready to go?" he asked, standing up straight.

"Yeah, just gotta grab my purse."

I collected my purse from the kitchen table and then got a treat out of Kikko's stash. I always gave her something before I left the house as an incentive to be good while I was gone.

After we'd gotten in the car, I caught Adam watching me as I put on my seat belt. I'd known him long enough to know that he was struggling with something. "What?" I asked, looking him right in the eye. "Spit it out."

He flared his nostrils, then put the car in reverse. "I want to ask you something . . . This is kind of unprecedented, but I . . . well, you might be able to help me understand some things."

"Okay . . ." Immediately I felt on edge.

Adam shifted the car into drive and pulled forward to the edge of the driveway, leading to the road that wound through the property. "Do you happen to know anybody by the name of George Wong?"

CHAPTER
15

"Excuse me?" Since Adam was paying attention to the road, he had the advantage of avoiding eye contact. I studied the profile of his face, searching for any sign of intention. "You just said George Wong?"

"Yeah." He looked at me out the corner of his eye. "Why, you know him?"

"I know of him . . ."

"Obviously I wouldn't normally discuss a case with you," he replied. "And there's nothing saying that I'm going to start now, but I did want to at least ask what you know about George Wong."

I tugged on the strap of my seat belt. "He was a lawyer. Did some pro bono work . . . A decent human being from what I gather."

His head turned briefly in my direction. "Is that *all* you know?"

"Yeah, that's it," I replied with clarity. It was nice to actually mean it for once. Usually I did have other information that I was withholding for an opportune moment, but as of now, that information was sorely lacking. "Why are you asking anyways?"

"I thought this case would be open and shut, an obvious suicide . . . or maybe even an accidental death. The guy gets drunk, leaves his engine running, and shuts the garage door without thinking twice about it." He shook his head. "But his tox screen showed something me and Higgins weren't expecting to find, and it complicates the situation."

"And that was what exactly?" A shiver went up both my arms, causing goose pimples to appear.

"Aconite alkaloids," he said without elaborating.

"What is that?"

"Aconite is a plant. Higgins said it can be used medicinally, but it's extremely poisonous and can become volatile pretty quickly. George Wong had considerable levels in his body at the time of his death . . . Too much to be helpful."

"Is it possible that George took it on purpose?" I asked. "Maybe he didn't realize the amount he'd taken . . . or, maybe he had and that was the point." Even though it's what I'd chosen to say out loud, I had the information from Felix swimming around in the back of my mind that George's death was not accidental in the least.

Adam shrugged. "He might have taken it intentionally, but it doesn't sit well with me . . . or Higgins, in case you're curious on his take. We both agree it's almost overkill. If he wanted to harm himself, the aconite would have done the job. The consumption of toxic fumes wouldn't be necessary . . . so why stage it in this way?"

"So what you're saying is, he died from poisoning and it was covered up to look like asphyxiation?"

"Well, it's more likely that he died from the asphyxiation and that was used to cover up the poisoning.

Higgins has a running theory that the poison was slipped into something George ingested to be used as a way to weaken and overpower him. It was staged in the man's own home, a space he knows well. Poisoning him would be an advantage to his attacker."

I shivered. The idea of that scenario creeped me out. It meant that George had more than likely known his killer. Without any signs of a disturbance in the house, it also meant the person had taken their time.

"I hope I didn't upset you," Adam said, resting a hand on my leg. "You've been through your share of grisly situations, so I didn't think this would get to you."

I covered his hand with my own. "No, I mean, it does weird me out, but I was thinking about something else. While we're on the topic, I do want to tell you about a certain situation that has presented itself."

"Oh?"

"Lydia Shepard came by to see me yesterday and asked for help with a case she's working on."

His hand stiffened. "Lydia Shepard, as in that PI who helped with Donna's case?"

I nodded. "That's the one."

"Are you going to tell me her case is associated with the one I'm currently working on?"

"It is and I am," I replied. I didn't know how much else I should tell him, but I felt I owed him something considering all the times he'd helped me despite his conflicting feelings about me being in harm's way. But, I also had to walk a fine line because I *was* working with Lydia.

Our own investigation would benefit from knowing about this aconite detail. At least, I assumed that Lydia would find it interesting.

"Lana?" Adam exited the freeway ramp and headed in the direction of Crocker Park. It was one of our favorite shopping complexes to have dinner out that wasn't too far from home. "What is going on in that head of yours?"

I huffed. "You didn't hear it from me, okay? I had to sign papers and everything saying I'm going to keep my big mouth shut, and so far, I'm not really doing that great of a job. But let's just say that Lydia's client suggested that foul play was involved with George's death and that there were others . . . that the deaths are linked."

He stopped at a red light, turning all of his attention to me. "What deaths?"

"There were two other deaths in recent times, both Asian men . . . and their deaths looked natural so they weren't investigated. This man—Lydia's client—is claiming that all three deaths were actually murders."

"Who is this man?"

"The light's green." I said, pointing at the traffic light.

The car behind us gave a friendly beep of their horn. The quick burst of sound that—at least in my head—equates to *Hey, look lively!*

Adam gave them an apologetic wave in the rearview mirror. "Who's the man, Lana?"

"I'm not at liberty to say," I replied, taking a page out of Lydia's book. It felt odd to say something like that to Adam, of all people, but one thing I could do for the moment was protect the client.

"He could be involved somehow," Adam said. "Maybe an accomplice trying to get ahead of the story before trouble finds him. How does he know for a fact that the murders are related?"

"They were all close friends . . . and he doesn't believe any of the circumstances regarding their deaths." I decided for the time being that I would leave out any details about the Eight Immortals. It didn't seem like the right time to explain the operation of this secret organization until I had more facts and knew for sure Felix Hao wasn't telling us a series of lies.

Of course, based on the art displayed in Mr. Zhang's shop, I was starting to believe that the things Felix was telling us were true . . . or at least plausible.

Adam drummed the steering wheel with his thumbs. "I might know about one of the potential incidents . . . an Asian realtor who died at one of his listed properties. Took a nosedive down the basement steps and cracked his neck. But there was no evidence of any foul play involved. As far as anyone could tell, he was in the house alone; the people who found him were the potential buyers."

"His name was Walter Kang. Did they do a toxicology screening on him?" I asked.

Adam clenched his jaw. "I don't think so. I know one of the cops who was on scene and everyone was chalking it up to an unfortunate accident."

"The other person . . . it was a while back, Theodore Yeh . . . I can't remember how long ago, six months maybe? But he had a heart attack and, according to our client, Mr. Yeh didn't have any pre-existing heart conditions."

"Something about this doesn't sit right with me," Adam replied.

"What do you mean?"

"I can't put my finger on it just yet, but this whole case stinks of something. Why would this client of Lydia's just now be coming forward? If the first victim had a heart attack and had no previous medical condition, what steps did this guy take, if any? And then his next friend goes sailing down a staircase and he doesn't have anything to say about that either? Just now he's wanting answers?"

"He said he wasn't positive that things were adding

up or not. Just had his suspicions, and this recent tragedy with George Wong really solidified it for him," I replied.

"It's still odd though. There's a giant piece missing and I want to know what the hell it is." He stopped for a light, his attention drifting out the driver's side window. "By the way, we're not releasing to the public that the aconite was found in George Wong's system, so try and keep that under your hat as much as possible. I'm assuming you're going to tell Lydia. At least . . . that's what I would do if I were in your shoes."

I couldn't get a solid read on his tone. I felt like there was a bit of disappointment laced in with what he'd said. But I wasn't sure what the disappointment was pertaining to.

Adam fell into a silence for the remainder of the drive, which wasn't really that much longer. We arrived at Crocker Park within the next few minutes and parked in front of a Nordstrom Rack. The sun had already set and the temperature had dropped considerably since we'd left my apartment.

We held hands as we strolled down the sidewalk, neither one of us in much of a hurry, both lost in thought.

Adam paused just outside the entrance. By the creases between his eyebrows, I could tell that he was still bothered, and it didn't take much guessing on my part to come to a conclusion of what was on his mind. He reached for my other hand and pulled me closer. "Let's leave the shop talk at the door so we can enjoy our dinner tonight."

I snorted. "Just like that, huh? Are you absolutely sure you don't want to talk about anything else? I know something is on your mind."

He kissed my forehead. "I'm okay. I just worry about

what kind of things you could be getting into that others might not have considered."

I knew the "others" he was speaking about was Lydia. I also knew there was something he was keeping from me, but for the time being, I would leave the two topics alone. We were both tired and I could sense the day had worn on him more than usual. "You're better at compartmentalizing than I am, and we both know it. I wish you would have waited until after dinner to tell me about the aconite thing."

"You're probably right about that. I wasn't expecting you to be working on the case with Lydia though. So there's that."

"Fair," I said with a sigh. "I suppose we're even with exchanging information that neither one of us wanted to know. Okay, fine, we won't talk about it during dinner. It's probably for the best anyways."

He released my hand and threw an arm over my shoulders as he ushered me toward the door of the restaurant. "Yeah, especially because that one time we got kind of loud without realizing it and had all those people staring at us."

I snickered at the memory. "Those people probably thought we were some real morbid sickos."

He held the door open. "If they only knew the truth."

I clucked my tongue and he playfully squeezed the side of my waist.

Adam greeted the hostess, and I followed behind him as we were led to our table. I didn't know if I would succeed in avoiding the topic, but I did want time to think about this new bit of information and the implications it had. A poisonous plant might further point the finger at Mr. Zhang, and that didn't sit well with me.

CHAPTER
16

Adam and I had managed to make it through dinner without so much as a word about anything to do with George Wong. But I had to admit—at least to myself—that most of the evening, my mind was drifting somewhere else. Even when the server brought out our crème brûlée, I was contemplating whether or not Adam was on to something with his theory that Felix Hao was connected to the murders in a different way than he was saying. And when I wasn't thinking about that, I was considering the implications of Mr. Zhang and *his* involvement.

All night, even as I attempted to sleep, I wondered about the use of aconite and if that really meant that the sweet old man who was dating my poor, innocent grandmother was even more likely to be involved now that we knew that George's death had been helped along by an herbal poison. I also took a sideways trek into pondering if I would be as compassionate about my thinking if Mr. Zhang weren't older than the proverbial hills.

I woke up the following morning an hour earlier than I normally did so I could make it to my meetup with Lydia in the Asia Village parking lot. Adam didn't question the reason for my adjusted sleep schedule, but seeing as he knew that I was working with Lydia, there wasn't much to keep secret anyhow.

Traffic was much different an hour earlier than my normal departure time, and I'd gotten to Asia Village in record time. It was only 7:15 and I had a little time to waste until Lydia arrived.

There was only one other car in the parking lot, and I wondered if it belonged to any of the employees. Sometimes people left their cars in the lot overnight if they'd been at the Bamboo Lounge the night before and had too much to drink.

While I waited, I kept the radio on low, sipped my coffee, and did a little research on "aconite." The results were pretty interesting, considering mostly all of them talked about how poisonous the plant was and how little it would take to kill someone.

I adjusted my search to include "Chinese medicine" to see what would change.

A lot changed. Turned out that aconite—also known as monkshood or wolfsbane—had been used in the world of traditional Chinese medicine for around two thousand years. And in order to even be considered for use, it would have to be processed by either boiling or steaming the herb.

So had George Wong been using it intentionally and made a misstep? Perhaps he took too much or maybe it hadn't been processed properly? I skimmed for the reasons someone would take it to begin with. It had pain relieving and anti-inflammatory properties, and even appeared to be a fever reducer.

Perhaps two thousand years ago this made more sense, but why would anyone take the chances when there were less risky ways to cure those problems in this day and age? I was for herbal remedies as much as the next modern woman, but not if the risks outweighed the benefits. And sudden death was a heavy price to pay to alleviate some aches and pains.

A car honked, breaking my attention from the article. When I looked up from my phone, I saw a black Mustang pull into the spot next to mine.

Lydia got out of her car, jogged around to the passenger side of mine, and got in. "Morning, chickadee!" She handed me a manila envelope identical to the one she'd given me yesterday. "Try not to lose sight of this one, okay? I'm going to start charging five cents a copy."

I took the envelope from her hands and laid it on my lap. "Don't worry, this is coming into the restaurant with me, and I plan to lock it in the safe while I'm working."

Lydia chuckled. "I'm just razzin' ya. It doesn't really matter, seeing as whoever it is already has their very own copy to enjoy."

"I can't tell you how sorry I am," I said, feeling like a broken record. I once read an article warning assertive and confident women not to apologize too much. It was "unattractive" and "showed a lack of self-esteem." But what else was I supposed to do in a situation like this? That angle was not covered in said article.

Lydia waved the idea away with the flick of wrist. "Nah, don't sweat it. These things happen from time to time."

"If you say so."

"I say so. Don't think another thought about it. I'm just glad I didn't include the crime scene photos like I'd originally intended to."

I blanched. "Actual crime scene photos?"

Lydia nodded. "Yeah, they took photos of everything just in case. I was able to finagle some copies from my contact at the Cleveland PD. I shouldn't have them and they're not currently for public viewing."

"Why did you decide to leave them out?" I shook the envelope.

"Figured I didn't want to scare you right out the gate. They can be pretty difficult to look at if you're not used to that sort of thing. If you decide it'd be helpful for you to look, I have them locked in my filing cabinet at the office."

I sucked in a breath. "I'll hold off for now."

"I don't blame you." She checked her phone screen. "Look, I gotta run."

"Before you go," I said, "I want to tell you about something interesting that Adam told me last night."

Lydia smacked her forehead. "Oh, no, Lana, please tell me you didn't tell him about the case."

I held up my right hand. "I swear, I didn't tell him anything aside from the fact I'm working with you on the case. He's the one who brought up George Wong."

"He did?" Lydia asked. "Why? What exactly did he want to know?"

"Whether or not I knew anything about him. And if he was involved with any type of shady dealings."

"So what's the interesting part?"

"The interesting part is the toxicology screening shows that he had traces of something called aconite alkaloids in his system."

Lydia raised an eyebrow. "What's that?"

"A poisonous plant that is sometimes used for medicinal purposes." I unlocked my phone and showed her the stuff I'd been reading up on while waiting for her.

Lydia took the phone from my hands and scrolled through the article. After a minute of skimming, she asked, "Did you see this part where it talks about paralyzing heart function?"

I nodded.

"This would potentially fit in with Theodore Yeh having an unexplained heart attack. Son of a—"

"It could explain all three murders, actually. *And* if none of them had taken it on purpose and it was slipped to them through food or some type of beverage, was the person who dosed them intending to blur the lines?"

"Entirely possible." Lydia handed my phone back to me. "Look what we're doing right now. We're speculating on whether or not this scenario is plausible. It might have been an insurance policy of sorts to help blur the lines. Maybe they were hoping for no autopsies to be done, but if there *were* any performed that could expose what they did, it could be passed off as an herbal remedy that Asians would be more likely to use."

"So what do we do now?" I asked. "Any developments with Lois Fan?"

Lydia shook her head. "Nada. I've left her a few messages . . . vague ones that I hoped would spark her interest, but she has yet to call me back. Today, I'm reaching out to that financing guy, Douglas Chen."

"They're going to know," I said.

"What do you mean?"

"If they talk to each other, they're going to know that they're being investigated. Which . . . well . . . if it were me, I'd think there was a rat among us."

"Good point." Lydia nodded slowly. "I'll have to mention that to Felix. He may want to come up with a cover story so they think he's also being questioned."

"Yeah, that's not a bad idea."

"In the meantime, forward me the link to that article.

I better get out of here before anyone sees us." Lydia reached for the door handle but paused, swearing under her breath. "Too late. Looks like we have company . . ."

I glanced out the window. It was Mr. Zhang. I slid down in the driver's seat, trying to make myself small as possible "What's he doing here already?"

CHAPTER
17

-- -- -- -- -- -- -- ---

Lydia released the door handle, turning in my direction. "Act natural."

"What do you mean, act natural? We're sitting in an empty parking lot at seventy forty a.m.," I said with a snort, waving the manila envelope. "With this."

"I'm saying don't draw any further attention to us sitting here, and maybe he won't notice. If you crouch down like that and he sees you anyways, you automatically look guilty."

She had a point. I gripped the steering wheel and straightened myself.

In that time, Mr. Zhang had parked his car and begun making his way to the entrance. He hadn't even seemed to notice that we were there, which struck me as odd considering he had just parked one row over. Perhaps Lydia's car was shielding us from view.

Lydia watched him until he disappeared into the plaza. "I thought you said he doesn't normally get here this early."

"He doesn't. At least I didn't think so."

Lydia tapped her index finger on the armrest. "Hmmm.

Okay, I better get out of here before anyone else shows up. Don't forget to find out what you can from Talia Sun. Maybe something she says will help us come up with a way to talk to Lois Fan." She tipped her chin. "I'll be in touch."

I waited until Lydia drove away before I got out of the car. I'd brought a tote bag with me to conceal the files, so I stashed the envelope in there and gathered the rest of my things.

Back inside, I thought I'd find Mr. Zhang waiting to greet me. On the walk from the parking lot, I had already prepared my excuse of needing to rush a meat order request that hadn't gotten done the day before as my reason for being here so early today. But Mr. Zhang wasn't standing at the entrance of his shop, nor had he lifted the metal security gate that protected his storefront.

I scanned the plaza, which was dark except for some light coming out of the windows of Eastern Enchantments. I couldn't see anybody hanging around, but I guessed the car I'd seen in the parking lot must have belonged to Talia. Only, how was she able to get into the plaza before anybody else? Aside from Ian and Donna, Mr. Zhang and I were the only ones with a master key.

Clearly, Mr. Zhang had arrived early to meet with Talia. It couldn't be a coincidence that they were both here well before Asia Village opened for the day. Especially because I knew that the two of them had an association that extended beyond the plaza.

I hurried into the restaurant, making as little noise as possible, not wanting to give away the fact that I had arrived for the day just yet. With a darkened Ho-Lee Noodle House as my cover, maybe I could spy on them and learn something that could shed some light on this case.

Inside the restaurant, I locked the dead bolt and set my

things on the hostess counter. I didn't want to risk missing something by taking the time to stow everything in my office.

I decided to slip into the Matrons' booth and look out that window instead. Propped up on my knees in the booth, I rested my hands on the windowsill to steady myself. I studied the two large windows of Eastern Enchantments, hoping to see shadows at the very least. But so far nothing of interest.

After a few minutes passed without anything happening, I started to grow restless. What were they doing in there? Should I have taken a chance and tried spying from a closer vantage point? Being stealthy was my least favorite part. It always stressed me out and it wasn't exactly one of my strong suits.

Before I could talk myself out of trying, I decided I was going to sneak over to Talia's shop to see if I could spot them more easily that way. I had no idea what I was going to say if I got caught slithering outside her shop, but I didn't see any other options presenting themselves.

I grabbed my purse and slung it over my shoulder. I thought of Lydia's advice to act natural. Maybe if I just walked over there like I belonged, no one would think twice about anything. Plus was it my guilty conscience that was fueling my overactive imagination? Why would I assume that they'd assume my behavior was suspicious?

I went to disengage the dead bolt when a figure appeared just outside the door. I gasped and ducked. It was Ian, Asia Village's property manager, and proverbial thorn in my side. Why was there always someone lingering nearby lately? Couldn't a gal get any privacy to snoop around these days?

"Lana?" Ian's muffled voice came through the door.

"Lana, what are you doing?" He tapped on the glass. "I know you're in there."

"Dammit," I hissed. I closed my eyes, took a deep breath, and rose from my kneeling position. With a forced smile, I opened the door. "Good morning, Ian."

"What is going on with you?" He gave me a once-over. "Is everything okay?"

Movement from behind him caught my attention. I yanked on the sleeve of Ian's suit jacket and pulled him into the restaurant. I shut the door and reached for his wrist. "Get away from the entrance." I urged him to follow me as I scurried back over to the Matron's booth.

"Lana," he said more sternly this time. "What is going on? Talk to me. Are you in some kind of trouble?"

"No, shhhh," I said. "I'll explain in a minute."

Mr. Zhang and Talia were standing outside of Eastern Enchantments. They exchanged some words and seeing as I wasn't any good at reading lips, I had no idea what they were talking about.

They shook hands before Mr. Zhang strolled in the direction of his shop. Talia disappeared back inside her own store. My shoulders dropped. Whatever I had hoped to discover fell flat and I couldn't hide my disappointment.

CHAPTER
18

Ian stood at the edge of the booth right behind me. His arms were crossed over his chest, and his thin lips scrunched into a scowl. "Lana, what are you up to now? Who exactly are you spying on?" He leaned to the side to get a better look out the window.

I shuffled myself out of the booth. Standing up straight, I smoothed the wrinkles from my blouse. "Can you keep this a secret?"

He rolled his eyes. "I've kept a lot of your secrets. What's one more?"

"Do you know anything about the new shop owner, Talia Sun?"

"Not really. She's a bit eccentric for my liking. The other day she told me my Chi is unbalanced, whatever that means."

"Do you know where she came from?"

"Came from?" He scrubbed his chin with the palm of his hand. "I know she lives in Cleveland, if that's what you mean. I think she told me she lives in Lakewood."

"So she just showed up and asked to rent space here? Without anyone else maybe encouraging you to meet with her?"

Ian lifted an eyebrow. "Encouraged? Lana, what are you getting at?"

I huffed. "She seems to have some kind of pre-existing relationship with Mr. Zhang and I was just wondering if you knew anything about that. Maybe she mentioned that he referred her to Asia Village?"

He shook his head. "No, it's never come up. I assumed it made sense to open here if she lives right in Lakewood. Much closer than the east side Asian communities. Do you suspect her of something?"

"I'm not sure yet. I just think it's weird is all."

"I don't believe that for a minute. You know something. And if you do, in fact, know something, then I'd appreciate being clued in. Especially if it's something that could jeopardize the plaza. You know we've already had our fair share of problems and we don't need any more."

"What about Donna?" I asked, ignoring his request. "Did Donna say that she knew Talia from somewhere else?"

"Lana, I'm not telling you another thing until you tell me what this is about."

I groaned. "Fine. Do you remember a while back I worked with a PI?"

"Yes, of course. But I don't know the particulars."

"Well, she called in a favor and asked me to help look into the potential murder of George Wong and two other people."

"George Wong . . . as in the lawyer who was just found dead in his garage?"

"That's the one."

"I didn't realize it was anything nefarious. I had

wondered though. On occasion lawyers can stack up a few enemies."

"It isn't totally conclusive at the moment. Lydia was hired by someone who thinks that George's death was a murder."

"Who's her client?"

"I'm not at liberty to say." That phrase was quickly becoming my go-to statement. "If I say 'Eight Immortals,' does that mean anything to you?"

"You mean the characters from the Chinese folklore stories?" he replied. "Not really my thing. I never got into all that."

I studied his face, checking for telltale signs of lying. I was hoping if Ian had heard of the secret society, his eye might twitch or something. But as far as I could decipher, he was speaking the truth and the only thing that came to mind for him was historical context. "Just curious, is all."

"What does that have to do with George and Talia?"

I didn't want to divulge too much information to Ian because, really, he didn't need to know anything. And if he didn't already know of their existence, there was no reason to involve him. So all I said was, "I'm not sure yet."

"Do you want me to do some inquiring?" he asked. "Gather information, if you will?"

"No, and please don't mention it to anybody. If Talia is involved somehow, I don't want anyone to know that I'm on to something, or even working on anything."

He nodded. "Then I'll keep my mouth shut unless you ask me to do otherwise."

"Thank you," I said. "Do you know if Donna is planning on coming into the plaza any time soon?"

"Not that I know of. Why?"

"I'd like to ask her some questions." I started to edge toward the door to give Ian the hint that it was time for him to move along. I had things I wanted to do before Peter showed up for the day.

He followed behind me. "Good luck with that. I don't imagine she's going to like this line of questioning very much."

"Oh no?" I asked. "Why not?"

Even though it was just the two of us in the restaurant, he lowered his voice. "You didn't hear this from me . . . or at all if you know what's good for you, but Donna was becoming involved with George shortly before his death. Romantically involved."

That made my stomach hurt. "She was? I had no idea she'd started dating again."

"No one knew besides me and her housekeeper. I only found out because of a poorly timed surprise visit I made to her house. Keep it to yourself. Whatever happens with this Lydia detective woman, do not speak a word of it to her."

"I won't say anything. It's probably not relevant anyways."

Ian stopped in front of the doors and looked at me. "Good, because she might come off as some type of black widow."

After Ian left, I gathered all my belongings and headed back to my office. I was more than anxious to review the files from Lydia.

Usually when I worked on cases, I didn't have anything to go off outside of my trusty notebook that remained hidden underneath my mattress at all times. Sometimes, it seemed silly to have it stowed away, but I didn't want anyone who came by my apartment to accidently find it lying about and read the contents.

The notebook contained my ramblings on any case that I was working on, who I considered suspects, and helpful information that might be pertinent.

With the envelope in hand, I unraveled the red string that secured the seal and lifted the flap. There were a decent amount of papers inside and I pulled them out all at once.

The page on top listed the members of the Eight Immortals, and next to their names were their corresponding object and some reference notes that Lydia had made. I noticed the names of the deceased were crossed out, and that Theodore's and Walter's slots had been filled. Lydia had left an additional note by George's name.

1. Wei Zhang—sword
2. Donna Feng—fan
3. ~~Theodore Yeh~~—lotus flower spoon—replaced by Talia Sun
4. Felix Hao—flute
5. Douglas Chen—bottle gourd
6. Lois Fan—flower basket and dibble (*note: dibble—a small hand tool to make holes in the ground)
7. ~~Walter Kang~~—two small boards/castanets—Juliette Chu (*note: castanet—percussion instrument? Aka "clackers.")
8. ~~George Wong~~—bamboo drum—?? Who will fill this?

I'd have to look into Juliette Chu as well. Felix hadn't bothered to mention her during our lunch, but I had to consider that one of the replacements could possibly be the killer.

I thought about the sword hanging above the counter in

Mr. Zhang's shop. That must have been his signifying object.

According to what Felix had said during our meeting, when a member died, the leader of the Eight Immortals was in charge of recovering the artifact that identified their position in the group. In this scenario, that would mean Mr. Zhang was responsible for collecting the item and passing it along to the next member. So had he been the one to say the artifacts were missing, or did Felix come to that conclusion on his own?

But if that were the case, Mr. Zhang wouldn't need to *steal* the object in question because it would go to him regardless and he could pass it along to the next person without anyone batting an eye—further proof that Mr. Zhang being involved in this whole thing was a bunch of phooey.

Felix had said something about the held position being passed down through family, but Theodore Yeh hadn't had any, so it went to a voting system. Lois had been the one to refer Talia to the group to replace Theodore, so it should have meant they were all in agreement for the transition to take place. Yet there had been naysayers, and Talia still made the cut. It made me wonder why *and* who else was up for the position that got passed up.

Perhaps they were the one doling out servings of aconite. Maybe because they didn't get to replace Theodore, they could replace someone else in the group.

And Juliette Chu, who was she in relation to Walter Kang? I'd have to find out if she was a family member. Although, if Juliette wanted in and she'd gotten her way, there would be no reason to kill George.

The next question that came to mind was the "how" of it all. *How* were they poisoning their victims? The little I knew from poisoning came from the very first case I'd worked on—the death of Thomas Feng, Donna's husband.

In my research I learned that women were more often than not the ones to choose poison as their method of destruction. Women were stereotyped as not wanting to be murderous in a hands-on sort of way, which in a large portion of history had proven mostly true. However, that had not held true in the case of Thomas Feng's death. It was quite possible it wouldn't be for this one either. Though, I had Lois Fan to consider.

The person who would have the easiest access to an herbal component and know how the ins and outs worked would be Mr. Zhang. And though I'd concluded that some of the puzzle pieces didn't fit, I had to acknowledge that it was fact.

Then it occurred to me that maybe someone was trying to make it look like Mr. Zhang was at fault. Felix did say this could "cause dissention in the ranks." If someone was trying to frame Mr. Zhang, then it was possible they were trying to get him removed from his position of authority due to what may be viewed as incompetence of protecting the other members.

After all that filtered through my mind, I wondered how this person was choosing their victims. Was it purely random? Or was there a specific reason behind their decision making about who got dosed?

The more I stared at the page, the more questions I had.

Recognizing that time was getting away from me, I decided to quickly flip through the rest of the contents before I had to head back to the dining area. Peter would be arriving soon.

The following pages included photos of each member and a sticky note taped to the ones who were now deceased. After that, Lydia had included a page of contact information for each person: known places of employment, addresses and phone numbers. All neat and tidy . . . more than I'd ever had to work with.

There were also a few pages of screenshots taken from a computer of articles talking about the deceased and the projects they had been involved in that helped the community.

The same glowing article Megan had found on her phone from *Cleveland.com* about how helpful George Wong had been providing free legal advice to Asian Americans was included in the printouts.

With it were articles about the other two victims, Walter Kang and Theodore Yeh, and their contributions to local residents.

The final page was Lydia's suspect list, though she'd titled it slightly different and called it "People to Investigate." All the same, the first name on her list was Mr. Zhang's.

CHAPTER

19

- - - - - - - - - - - - - -

Once Peter had arrived with his typical morning grunts of acknowledgment, I slipped back into my office to give Donna Feng a call. I wanted to meet with her as soon as possible. And in person seemed like the best option. I wanted to gauge if she was telling me the truth or not when I asked her whatever it was that I was going to ask.

As I listened to her phone ring, I knew I had no idea how I was going to approach our pending interview session. And whether being completely forthcoming with her was the best option, but I tended to figure things out on the fly anyways.

I was disappointed to get her voice mail and listened to her message prompting the caller to leave their name, phone number, and the reason for their call.

After the beep, I said, "Hi Donna, it's Lana. I'd really like to talk with you about something important. It's not an emergency but it is time sensitive, so the sooner the better. I'll be at the restaurant until five, so you can call here until then. After five, please call my cell phone. Thank you. Talk to you soon! No time is too late. Okay, bye."

With nothing else to be done at the present moment, I grabbed my travel mug and headed back up front to the hostess station to give everything my final stamp of approval. Since I'd spent most of my time spying, dealing with Ian, and reviewing the file envelope from Lydia, I hadn't handled any of my morning tasks.

I was relieved to find that my teenage, nighttime employee, Vanessa Wen, had dutifully filled the silverware basket with wrapped bundles, restocked the supply of disposable chopsticks, and, from the looks of it, wiped down all the menus.

After I was satisfied with the hostess station and lobby area, I took a lap around the dining room to make sure everything was in place. Finding that all the chairs were tucked in, tablecloths were smooth and centered, and the condiment displays were stocked with soy sauce, sugar, sweeteners, and salt and pepper, my satisfaction was achieved and I returned to the hostess lectern to wait on the Mahjong Matrons.

But just as I was taking a sip of my coffee, something unexpected happened. Talia Sun tapped on the window of the door. When we made eye contact, she waved.

It caught me so off guard that I choked on my coffee, causing me to sputter and cough. I kept the doors locked until the Matrons arrived, and it was five minutes until nine. Aside from Kimmy occasionally dropping by or Ian coming to give me a hard time about whatever he could think of, it wasn't often that anyone else showed up before we opened. What was Talia doing here?

Though her arrival was fortuitous since I had things I wanted to ask her, it wasn't the best time. The Matrons would be here soon and I couldn't interrogate Talia in front of them.

I abandoned my coffee and went to let her in. Had she

noticed me watching her and Mr. Zhang from the window? Was she coming to confront me?

I put on my customer-service smile and unlocked the dead bolt. "Good morning."

Talia's smile was more genuine than my own. "Good morning, Lana." She didn't wait to be invited in and slipped past me into the lobby area. "I thought I would come by and get some rice porridge for breakfast."

"Oh, uh . . ." This was surely the seventh sign of the apocalypse. No one ordered before the Mahjong Matrons, and off-menu on top of that. "Sure . . . we can make that for you."

Her eyes brightened. "Oh thank you. I've heard about the Mahjong Matrons and their special breakfast. I hope you don't mind."

"No, no, not at all," I replied. "I'll let our cook know." Gesturing to a table near the entrance, I said, "Have a seat. I'll be right back."

"Please take your time." She pulled out a chair and sat on the edge of it, her back at a perfect ninety-degree angle. Her posture was impeccable, and I thought about Esther Chin, who was always telling me to straighten my back. She'd love this woman for sure.

I scurried toward the kitchen to put in Talia's order and caught Peter drumming on the grill with two metal spatulas. When he noticed I was there, his hand jerked and he dropped one of the spatulas. It clanked loudly against the side of the grill as it fell to the floor.

"Sorry to interrupt your jam session, but I have an order to place."

He knelt down to pick up the spatula and tossed it into the sink. "The Matrons are a bit early today, huh?" As he stood, his eyes traveled to the clock above the doors.

"No, this order is actually for Talia . . ."

His eyes widened larger than mine had when I'd first seen her at the door. "Wait, you mean the new chick?"

"Yeah, she said she wants rice porridge."

Peter's chin jutted outward. "Come again?"

"You heard me," I said with a smirk. "Believe me, I was as surprised as you."

With a shake of his head, he went over to the fridge and removed a container of chilled rice we always kept on hand specifically to make rice porridge for the Matrons. "In all the years I've worked here, this has never happened."

"Tell me about it," I replied. "I'm going back out there to keep our guest company."

"Right on." He filled a pot with water and set it on the stove. "I'll ding ya when it's ready."

I left the kitchen still lost in my own thoughts. I hadn't realized that the Matrons had arrived while I was gone. They sat in their booth, their heads turning in my direction as I neared the front of the restaurant. I could tell that they'd been chatting with our unexpected guest.

Helen's eyes lit up when I approached their table. "Good morning, Lana. I hope you don't mind that we made ourselves comfortable. Talia let us know that you were placing an order for her."

Talia smiled up at me. "I've been keeping the Matrons company while you've been away."

"Have you all been officially introduced?" I asked. My eyes traveled over each woman and then Talia as I tried to read the room. A slight tension appeared to be present, but I wasn't sure what was causing it.

Pearl nodded and spoke for the group. "Yes, we just finished meeting each other." She then turned to Talia. "We must apologize for not having come to introduce ourselves sooner. We've been a little busy with tending to other matters."

Opal leaned forward in her seat. "Yes, a dear friend of ours recently passed away and we have been busy visiting with his family. We have not been able to spend much time at Asia Village because of it."

Talia seemed to shrink a little in her chair. "Oh? I'm sorry to hear of your friend's passing."

Wendy sighed. "It was a very tragic end. For reasons we do not know, he may have harmed himself."

Talia's jaw stiffened. "That is most troublesome to hear."

My eyes slid back and forth at their exchange. I knew that Talia was perfectly aware of who they were talking about or at the very least had a good idea who they were referencing. She had to, considering they were both part of the same secret society. Even if she was still a newcomer to the group, their time as participants would have had to overlap seeing as Theodore Yeh had been dead for around six months.

I took a step closer in Talia's direction, finally feeling taller than her since I was the only one standing. "Yes, his name was George Wong. Did you know him?" I asked, hoping to get some kind of telling reaction.

Wendy perked up, lifting an eyebrow at my inquiry. She observed me but said nothing.

Talia's eyes flitted in my direction, but she didn't meet my stare. "No," she said, tucking in her chin. "I'm sorry to say that I didn't know him. I'm sure he was a wonderful man."

All four Matrons shook their heads, but it was Helen who spoke for the group this time. Softly, she said, "Yes, he was a wonderful man indeed. We will all miss him greatly."

I could feel my upper lip twitching as I kept my attention focused on Talia. She was clearly lying, and I was the only one who knew it.

The bell in the kitchen dinged rapidly and I knew that was my cue to return to Peter for food pickup. I stifled a sigh. "Excuse me, ladies. I'll be right back."

Helen held up a finger. "Would you please put in our order while you're there? We are all extremely hungry this morning."

"Of course," I replied.

Grumbling below my breath, I retreated into the kitchen. I was going to miss out on whatever was said next and that irritated me. Would the Matrons tell me what they talked about while I was away? Would it seem suspicious if I asked? Because of the nature of this case, I didn't want to involve them, so I didn't want them to know I was nosing around. Though I couldn't see a way not to clue them in at some point. After all, they were the ones who would know the most information out of everyone in the Asian community.

Peter was whisking eggs when I returned. "I'm already prepping the Matrons' breakfast. I know they have to be here by now."

I reached for the paper bag that contained Talia's rice porridge. "They are here. Thanks."

"Good thing I made extra rice yesterday," he said. "I don't think they would have been too happy about being shorted."

"If there's one thing you don't do, it's mess with those ladies' breakfast," I said before turning around to leave.

Back out in the dining area, all focus was on me as I made my way back up to the front. I held up Talia's bag as if it were show-and-tell hour. "You're all set. I can cash you out."

As she rose from her seat, the awareness that I was, in fact, short came back to the surface. "Thank you, Lana." She turned to the Matrons one last time, tipping her head. "Ladies, it was a pleasure meeting you this morning. I hope that you can stop by my shop soon. I have many stones and crystals that can help ease grief."

Helen replied, "Yes, we shall be by soon."

"Nice meeting you too, young lady," Pearl said.

At the register, I handed Talia her bag. "Since rice porridge is an off-menu item, I'll just ring it up as wonton soup. That's how I charge the Matrons."

"That'll be fine. Thank you for accommodating me." Talia pulled a coin purse out of her back pocket. "How are you enjoying the stone that I gave you the other day?" She handed me a ten-dollar bill.

"The stone . . ." I said, as I took the money she offered. "Uh, it's very nice." In truth, I hadn't thought much about it since she'd given it to me, and I'd left it on my vanity, unclear as to what to even do with it. I still didn't understand why she'd really wanted me to have it.

She smirked to herself, but in a good-naturedly sort of way. "Sometimes it takes a little while to become familiar with a stone. Especially if you are new to the idea. You should carry it with you in your pocket."

I pressed a few keys on the register and it sprang open. As I counted out her change, I thought it was interesting that she assumed I didn't already have the stone with me. Instead of saying anything further on the subject, I held out her money. "Here you go."

Gently, she pushed my hand away. "You keep that for a tip."

It was a pretty generous offering considering what she'd purchased. "Oh, um, thank you."

"I feel like there's something you're not saying," Talia

said. "I know we aren't well acquainted, but I can assure you that I'm trustworthy." Her eyes darted in the direction of the Matrons. "And discreet."

It was too early in the day for this level of interaction. I wanted this woman to leave, and I wanted to suck down the rest of my coffee before it got too cold. Now wasn't the right moment to ask Talia anything of importance. "No, not at all," I said, trying to keep my tone light and airy. "I better get going, I have to prep the Matrons' tea still and they don't like to be kept waiting too long."

Talia held my stare for a few moments, though it felt like minutes had passed. "You're right, I should let you return to your duties. But, when you need me, you know where to find me."

CHAPTER
20

- - - - - - - - - - - - - -

Talia's parting words left me with a chill that traveled through my spine, up my arms, and well into my hairline. I couldn't help but wonder if she was, in a matter of speaking, challenging me. She was a difficult person to read and I couldn't make heads or tails of my opinion on her. All I knew was that deep in my gut, I felt like I needed to proceed with caution. Even if she wasn't directly involved, she had to know something about what had happened. Or at the very least, she knew that something wasn't right.

I took a few moments to contemplate why I felt so rattled by a single sentence. I came to the conclusion that it was the calmness and ease with which she presented herself. No skin off her back.

After she left and I'd gathered myself, I hurried back into the kitchen to prepare the Matrons' tea. Peter informed me that their food would be done shortly, so I knew my time was limited as far as questioning them went. I didn't want to be rude and disturb them while they were eating.

As I walked back to the Matrons' table to ask about

their encounter with the new shop owner, I contemplated the possibility that maybe Talia was on the side of good in this scenario and potentially, like me, she was looking for answers. In an effort to remain somewhat neutral, I had to include the notion that maybe she had no idea how she'd gained her position in the exclusive group. Whatever the case may be, the only way I'd find out is if I got to know her better. I decided when Nancy came in for the day, I was going to take a little trip over to Eastern Enchantments and see what I could find out. Hopefully it would be more successful than my last venture.

Not only did I want to move things along for the sake of my own sanity, but I also wanted to be able to tell Lydia something of relevance by the end of the day.

The Matrons were quietly chatting amongst themselves, their faces somber, and I wondered if they were still talking about George.

The four of them looked up as I approached their booth. I set the teapot down in the center of the table. "So that was an interesting change from our usual mornings together," I said. "What did you think about Talia?"

Helen lifted the pot while the other ladies flipped over their cups. She smiled. "Talia seems to be a nice young woman, but we have gathered perhaps that you do not share in this opinion."

I blushed. "Why do you think that?"

Wendy leaned forward, a bemused smirk on her face. "I was not the only one to notice that you questioned Talia about whether or not she knew George Wong. And I was not the only one to find it most curious."

The other ladies nodded in agreement.

Clearing my throat, I replied, "I was just wondering is all. I don't know what to make of her just yet. She seems nice enough but—"

"But she is hiding something," Opal replied. "And you think it has something to do with George?"

"So you agree?" I asked. "You think she is hiding something?"

Pearl answered for her sister. "It is clear that she was pained during our discussion of George's death, but if she claims not to know him, then none of us can figure why this would bother her in such a deep way."

Helen bobbed her head up and down. She'd finished filling all four teacups and placed the pot back at the center of the table. "We also suspected something was odd when she introduced herself to us and began to ask questions about you right away." Her eyes met mine as she ended her sentence.

"Me?" I gawked. "What was she asking about me?"

Wendy responded. "She mentioned that she'd read about you in the local newspapers and wondered if the stories were true and if you had really solved all of those murders."

I felt my veins run cold. "And what did you say?"

Helen sipped her tea. "We told her that they were in fact true and that you have a gift when it comes to such matters."

"She then asked whether you had been tasked to look into these deaths or if the desire had been of your own mind," Pearl added.

Opal continued, "And we told her that whether someone asked you to help them or not, it was your own heart that led you through to find the truth."

Though I was flattered by the Matrons' opinion of my investigative activities, I didn't like where this was going when it came to who was asking the questions. It was clear that Talia was asking about me behind my back instead of face-to-face. And the topic of conversation was even more upsetting. I might have found it less suspicious if she were inquiring about my favorite color. But it was almost as if she'd had an agenda. I began to wonder if her plan this morning had specifically been to be present in the restaurant while the Matrons were here so she could question them. Ordering food so I would be preoccupied and she could spend time with them without me around.

The more I thought about it, the more likely it seemed that was the case. More intriguing still, I had to ask myself why she'd chosen these four women as her informants. Why not go to someone else in the plaza and talk to them without my awareness of her presence? Did she want me to know that she was asking? Could she have guessed that the Matrons would tell me what she said once she left? Just like I had planted information with them in the past, with the hope they told the appropriate parties what I wanted to relay.

Again, I had to consider it as a possibility.

The food bell dinged rapidly. My time was up, but I had a question of my own to ask them before I went to get their food. "Ladies, this might seem out of nowhere, but does Mr. Zhang have any children? I've never heard him talk about any family before."

All four women stared back at me with surprise on their faces. Wendy was the only one to respond. "If this were so, we would know of it, I'm sure. But as far as we know, Mr. Zhang doesn't have any children. He might have been married when he was still a young man, but he has never spoken of that woman and we know nothing of what happened to her."

"I see," I said, wondering if it was something that Lydia would be able to find out.

"Why do you ask about this?" Pearl wanted to know. "And what does this have to do with George?"

"Oh nothing," I replied. "I just heard a rumor and wanted to find out if it was true."

Helen hadn't said a word, which was surprising because that almost never happened. Her chin drooped and she gripped tightly to her teacup with both hands. Finally, she spoke. "Lana, I want you to tell us the truth. Please do not spare our feelings in this situation."

"Okay . . ." I could only guess what she wanted to know.

She tilted her head up at me. "Do you think that Talia Sun had something to do with George's death?"

My heart skipped a beat as I looked at all four weathered faces staring back at me with expectation, sadness spread through their features as they all frowned. Four sets of eyes misting with tears at the mere thought of Helen's suggestion.

I placed a gentle hand on Helen's shoulder, giving her a light squeeze of compassion. "I really don't know, but I promise you, I will find out."

I felt sad for the remainder of the morning. After the Matrons finished breakfast and went on their way, I was left to my own devices in an empty restaurant.

I sat at my lectern, my chin resting in my palm and my sights set on Eastern Enchantments across the way. It felt like eons before Nancy would arrive for her shift, and I didn't know how to occupy my mind.

I'd locked the files I'd gotten from Lydia in my office safe, not wanting Peter or Nancy to meander into my office for something and find it sprawled out on my desk. I couldn't exactly look at the contents of the envelope while sitting at the front of the restaurant waiting for the minutes to tick by. I had to do something else and, seeing as the restaurant was in perfect order, I couldn't distract my-self with mindless silverware wrapping.

I reached under the counter for my cell phone and de-cided that I was going to attempt some internet snooping. I'd been so consumed with what had happened to the men who'd died, but I hadn't schooled myself in what was going on with the surviving members. Maybe I needed a fresh spin from a different angle to spark a good working theory. What was there to gain from these specific men be-ing killed? And at what point could I prove one hundred percent that they were murdered?

Felix had set his sights on Lois Fan as the guilty party. Other than the little bit he'd told us, I knew next to noth-ing about her. I didn't know if I'd even be in agreement with his reasoning. Was Lois really trying to replace all Eight Immortals with female members? Or was Felix's paranoia getting the better of him? And was that her only possible motive?

I opened a web browser and typed her name into the search bar. I didn't have to look long, because apparently she had quite the reputation and dominated the top of the results with a few listings, the first being a website for Golden Flower Modeling, of which Lois Fan was the sole proprietor.

On the home page she touted that she was "a cut above the rest" and would help any young model "blossom and thrive in the world of fashion and photography." There were tabs for portfolios, application submissions, an infor-mational page with history on the company, credentials, and, at the end, one titled "Coming Soon."

I clicked on that and found a mission statement an-nouncement that Golden Flower Modeling would soon be expanding their services to include aspects of talent. In the next few months, Lois planned to add voice actors, along with film and TV prospects. Golden Flower Modeling would be expanding to become the leading agency in Cleveland.

An attached link to a story from *Cleveland.com* about the growing business was provided at the bottom of the page.

Two thoughts were trying to connect themselves in my mind. Felix was a talent agent. So, if Lois upgraded her business dynamic, where would this leave him? Would it affect him at all?

Still, even if it didn't, I couldn't imagine him taking lightly to it. It was likely he'd view it as a threat to his livelihood. I knew that it would ruffle my feathers if someone else came on my turf and claimed they were the number one noodle shop in town.

I opened the Notes app on my phone and typed a quick reminder to find out if they were planning on doing any collaborating. It wasn't likely seeing as Felix viewed her as a threat, but I had to be sure I didn't have any wires crossed. It could also be that they planned to merge businesses and it wasn't going how Felix wanted so he decided to throw her under the bus.

I typed in Douglas Chen's name next. He was both a financier and an investor. I didn't know what a financier was, so I opened a fresh tab to look it up before going any further. I wanted to make sure I understood everything.

The restaurant phone rang, breaking my concentration. "Ho-Lee Noodle House, this is Lana speaking, how can I help you?"

"Hi Lana, it's Donna. Sorry about the delay, I was in a meeting and just heard your message now. Is everything okay?"

"Yeah, nothing to be alarmed about, but something's

come my way and I'd really like to sit down with you and talk it through."

"Can it wait? I have a very packed couple of days coming my way. The kids will be on spring break soon and I'm planning to spoil them a bit and take them to Hawaii for the week. So as you can imagine, I have quite a bit to wrap up before I can leave town."

"It's a very time sensitive situation. It's about . . . well, it's about George Wong."

There was silence on the other end. I wasn't sure if I'd lost the connection.

"Donna?" I asked. "Are you still there?"

"Yes, dear, I'm here. Just tell me where and when you want to meet, and I'll be there."

CHAPTER
21

Donna and I agreed to meet at her house after my shift was over. I'd almost considered asking her to come by the plaza so we could get drinks at the Bamboo Lounge, but I didn't want Talia or anyone else to see us chatting. And I was positive that Penny Cho, the owner of the karaoke bar, would spread word around Asia Village that she'd seen Donna and me together.

Penny was one of the most paranoid business owners we had in the plaza. She always thought Donna and Ian were planning ways to make our lives more difficult, and if she saw me having drinks with Donna, she'd probably assume I was in on their supposed diabolical plans.

When I'd gotten off the phone with Donna, a few customers had ambled in for an early lunch so my internet snooping would have to wait. By the time Nancy arrived for the day, I was seating my fourth table and getting ready to cash out a to-go order.

It was rounding noon once we got down to one table of customers. I caught Nancy at the register after she dropped off a tray of food. "Would you be okay for a little while? I want to run over to Eastern Enchantments."

Nancy tilted her head. "What about your lunch? You should eat something first."

"I'll eat when I get back. I won't be long. I told Talia I'd stop by her shop and visit with her."

"Okay, well take a few almond cookies to give her. It'll be a nice gesture," she replied.

It was a genius idea. Not only would it soften her up, but it might look like the reason I was stopping by versus me just showing up with a barrage of questions in hopes that she would somehow incriminate herself.

I slipped into the kitchen and saw Peter with his back turned to the door, washing dishes. Grabbing a small Styrofoam container, I reached for the cookie box and pulled out six almond cookies, arranging them neatly before securing the lid.

I was just about to slide out of the kitchen undetected when Peter startled me. "What are you up to now?"

One hand ready to push on the swinging door, I turned to acknowledge him. "Why do you assume that I'm up to something? I'm just getting some cookies." I held up the container for him to see.

He pursed his lips. "Because you're sneaking around here like a common criminal."

"I am not," I said, trying to sound convincing. I didn't think it was working because even I didn't believe myself. "I'm getting cookies for the new girl . . . for Talia."

"Don't run the new chick outta here," he replied, wiping his hands on a dish towel. "At least give it a week."

"I'm not going to run anybody out of anywhere. I'm being nice."

"Uh-huh."

Rolling my eyes, I said, "I'll be back." I left before he could say anything else.

I couldn't really get all that mad at people when they assumed I was up to something because nine times out of ten, I was.

Eastern Enchantments was free and clear of customers, which was a relief because I didn't want to stand around like a weirdo waiting for people to leave so I could question the proprietor.

The fragrance of sandalwood was just as strong as the last time I'd come by, and I wondered if she kept a stick of incense burning at all times. Also as before, soft music played in the background, the romantic sounds of the erhu drifting through the shop.

I had to give her credit where credit was due. The environment was welcoming, peaceful, and made you want to linger a little longer—which is what every shop owner wanted.

Without Talia in sight, I took a moment to fully appreciate the artistic design she'd used in creating her showroom. The largest portion of her inventory was comprised of small stones and crystals, like the one she had given me. She carried them tumbled, raw, and even sculpted. I noted a few animal figurines made out of clear pink, purple, and aquamarine stones. I didn't know what any of them were called, but I supposed that's what the placards were for.

I hadn't realized it the previous day, but the entire inventory seemed to be accompanied by handwritten, descriptive cards. I thought about the time it would take to write everything out and was exhausted by the very idea.

Each display sparkled with twinkle lights entwined

with faux strands of ivy that wove in between the bowls on every table.

Against the far wall were shelves lined with pillows, throw blankets, picture frames, and wall ornaments. Next to that were neatly displayed mugs, tumblers, and shot glasses.

I noted that she carried more than just Asian-related items. She also had inventory bearing the symbols of the zodiac, and even things in honor of patron saints. Really, she had a little bit of everything. Which was smart. The variety of offerings would undoubtedly appeal to anybody who walked in.

I was sniffing an incense box when she appeared from the door to the back room. She didn't seem surprised to see me. "I'm sorry to have kept you waiting," she said. "I trust that you were enjoying a few moments of solitude."

Remembering the cookies I brought, I took a few steps to meet her and held out the box. "I thought I'd bring you something to nibble on."

She took the box, popping the lid open. "Oh thank you, I really love almond cookies. They might be my favorite."

"We keep them stocked all the time, so if you ever need a fix, feel free to stop on by."

Closing the box, she set it on the counter. "That's very generous of you. I may take you up on that."

"How's business?" I asked.

Her eyes scanned over the empty store. "I'm still getting settled in. I finally finished setting up my shop pages on Facebook and Instagram to help spread the word that I'm finally open. I'm not very good at posting on social media, but I'm going to have to start now, I suppose."

It felt like the perfect segue, so I jumped on my chance to begin my line of questioning. "What did you do before this? Is this the first store you've ever opened or are you moving from another location?"

She leaned against the counter, appearing thoughtful and as if she were reminiscing about her past. "This is my first store. It's something I've always dreamed of having but never imagined would happen. But life has a funny way of bringing things to you when you believe it's possible."

"Oh?" I kept my tone as light as I could, just two gals having a nice chat.

With a smile, she said, "I'm sure it's much like how you found yourself working for your parents . . . a pleasant surprise but not your intended plan."

She said it with such certainty, it unnerved me. Had I been unaware that she'd been asking questions about me earlier that morning, I would have thought she was a psychic or something. I had to wonder who else in the plaza she had asked about me.

If I had time, I'd have to stop by Asian Accents hair salon and find out if they knew anything about Talia's information gathering.

When I didn't respond, she said, "Anyways. It's been a welcome blessing."

"What did you do before this?"

"Mostly odds-and-ends modeling jobs. I did a fashion show for a local designer and things really began to take off from there, but it wasn't my passion . . . or my calling."

"You're more of an entrepreneurial type then?"

With a soft laugh, she replied, "No, I'm not that either, I'm afraid. But this"—she spread out her arms—"is a way for me to help people, and to hopefully reconnect them with the parts of themselves that they've forgotten." She paused. "Or that they've never known. I've always wanted an official space to do just that . . . and here I am."

It was such a flowery answer, I didn't know what to do with it. It made me wonder if I could ever make selling noodles sound so wondrous and meaningful. "What made you choose Asia Village to open your shop? Do you live in the area?"

"I live in Lakewood actually, above a florist shop. I'd thought about opening a store out there, but with other similar shops so close by, I thought I might stand a better chance on this side of town where crystals are more sparsely found. And I was attracted to the idea of a community. You all seem so close with one another . . . like family."

I noted that she didn't mention Donna or Mr. Zhang as previous contacts and I wondered why that fact remained hidden. It was possible that her original intentions of opening here had nothing to do with either of them, but it felt strange that it was omitted from her explanation completely. "We've all grown on each other, I guess" was my reply.

"I look forward to being a part of that. I cherish the idea of family. I spent most of my life in foster care until an elderly couple adopted me. I spent my late teens living with them in Southern Texas."

"Oh, I didn't know," I said.

She smiled. "That's okay, how would you?"

"So you're not originally from here then?"

"Not originally, no. My foster mother was from New York and had family in Cleveland. So I spent a good amount of time living here, but we moved away for a time because her husband's father was ill and he grew up in Texas. I decided to come back on my own . . ." She paused, tucking in her chin. "It's always felt like home, even with the awful winters."

I felt there was something she wasn't saying. I wanted

to press her further but didn't want to be completely rude. Families could be a sensitive topic, and just in case she wasn't a diabolical genius I wanted to remain somewhat delicate about the topic.

Seeing as I had Anna May and both my parents, plus now my grandmother, I pondered what it might be like if they weren't around and I was left to my own devices. As much as my sister drove me crazy, I was glad she was around. And the same went for my parents. It might be nice to get away for a little while and feel some freedom, but at the end of the day, I'd miss them something awful.

That's not to say I hadn't thought about packing up my grandmother and whisking us away to the Caribbean where we could live on the beach and drink out of coconuts. Supposing she'd even want to do such a thing. Maybe it was because of the language barrier, but my grandmother and I got along the best out of everyone.

Learning the fact that Talia had no one as backup in the city softened me a little bit and I wondered if I was being too hard on her. I thought about Peter's warning not to scare her away. But I still couldn't shake the fact that she wasn't being entirely truthful. I decided to steer my questions in a different direction to see if she'd offer up some telling information. "Have you met Donna Feng yet? Or have you strictly been dealing with Ian? I know he can kind of be a little over the top at times."

She laughed. "Ian is still learning how to handle his fire. He has not settled into himself yet. Still doubting his capabilities."

"So you haven't met Donna then?" While I was intrigued by her assessment of Ian's character, I felt her explanation was another avoidance tactic.

Her eyes traveled toward the store's entrance. "Donna is an old friend of the family. We had not met until I showed interest in opening the shop. She is a lovely woman . . . and very powerful. Strong like a tiger. I'm hoping to learn much from her."

"What about Mr. Zhang, did you meet him?" I asked, knowing that she had.

"Yes, I know Mr. Zhang. He was one of the very first people to greet me when I arrived a few months ago to look at the store location."

I held back the urge to narrow my eyes. Both answers were generalized and provided me with nothing useful. Although, in the end, I didn't know what I expected her to say. It's not like she was going to admit she belonged to a secret society. That kind of went against being in a secret society. I guess I had wanted to poke a hole somewhere in something that she told me.

My phone vibrated in my back pocket. Kimmy was calling. I sent the call to voice mail and returned it to my pocket.

"Well," I said, sighing and wishing I hadn't seemed so exasperated. "I better get back to the restaurant. It was nice getting to know a little bit about you."

"Stop by any time," she said. "I look forward to getting to know you better."

I flashed a quick customer-service smile before heading out. I felt myself trudging along with each step over the footbridge, feeling that I had gotten nowhere and gained nothing.

I watched a black koi fish zip below the bridge and pop out on the other side. They grew more active when people crossed over, knowing that food was most likely on its way.

I had some change in my pocket and stopped on the bridge to put a quarter in the pellet machine to feed my scaly friends and shake the look of disappointment that surely stained my face.

The machine dispensed a small amount of fish food that resembled what SweetTarts would look like if they were all brown. I sprinkled my offering slowly, spreading it out so it didn't all fall in one large clump. Three more fish appeared, sucking up their unexpected lunch, splashing and bumping into each other as they focused on where the pellets had landed.

I brushed my hands off and continued toward the restaurant. What I hadn't noticed while I'd been feeding the fish was Kimmy standing at the end of the bridge, her arms crossed over her chest, blocking my path.

She held up a hand as if she were a crossing guard. "Sorry, Lee, you have to pay the toll before you can cross."

CHAPTER
22

If I had a scowl mean and big enough to deter Kimmy from the interrogation I knew I was about to receive, I would have used it. But at the end of the day, my childhood friend usually got what she wanted, one way or another. Kimmy was persistent and willing to work you until you finally broke down and gave in.

I can't help but admit that very trait had come in handy more than once when I'd needed backup on a case. Although I couldn't say I liked being the recipient.

Balling up both fists, she planted them firmly on her hips. "What gives, Lee? I texted you *yesterday* and you still have not replied. How rude. Clearly I see both of your hands are functional."

I smacked my forehead. "I'm sorry, I genuinely forgot. I've been kind of preoccupied lately."

"Yeah, tell me about it," she replied. Then, pointing in the direction of Eastern Enchantments without caring who saw her, she asked, "What gives with this activity between you and our new fortune teller or whatever she is."

I clucked my tongue. "She's not a fortune teller." I paused. "At least I don't think."

"*Whatever*," Kimmy spat. "You promised you would clue me in if I gave you some time. And I've given you time. What's going on? Don't make me rat you out to Peter."

With a groan, I conceded. "Fine. But not here, okay? I don't want anyone to overhear us and I don't want her to think we're talking about her." My eyes slid in the direction of Talia's shop.

"You better not be stringin' me along, Lee. That's only going to work for so long. I know where you work *and* live."

"I'm not, I swear. I have to meet with someone after work, but I should be done by seven at the latest. Do you want to meet me at the Zodiac? Megan is working until close and it's pizza bar night."

Kimmy chewed on her bottom lip. "Hmm . . . pizza bar night, you say." Dramatically she tapped her chin. "I guess that's acceptable. Okay fine, Lee, it's a date. I'll be there at seven sharp. Don't be late."

"I won't," I replied.

Kimmy strutted back to China Cinema and Song, a little pep in her step after what I'm sure she considered a victory. I made my way back into Ho-Lee Noodle House, squaring my shoulders and taking a deep breath before I opened the door.

I had no idea what I would tell Kimmy when we met later that night, but I had until seven o'clock to figure it out.

When I returned to the restaurant, I'd found three tables with customers, and Nancy with her Mom-like ways shooing me off into the kitchen to eat lunch before I died of hunger.

Peter grilled a handful of shrimp, letting some of it char how I like it, and sauteed some snap peas, baby corn, and straw mushrooms, drizzling all of it with his notorious sweet and tangy teriyaki sauce.

I ladled some white rice from the steamer into a bowl and held it out for him. He maneuvered the shrimp and vegetables onto his spatula in one practiced motion and transferred the contents to my bowl. He then reached for the metal container filled with teriyaki sauce that he kept next to the grill and spooned an extra scoop onto my meal. No matter what ethnicity of food I was partaking in, I was definitely an extra sauce type of gal.

I ate my lunch on the beat-up couch in the back room, my bowl in one hand, my chopsticks in the other. Even though I hadn't turned on the ancient TV that sat across from me, I stared at the screen anyways, watching my reflection.

I began to question myself, wondering if I was looking at things all wrong. Had I spent too much time thinking about Talia simply because Felix had put the thought in my head? Again, I questioned whether that was his intention. If so, his plan worked because my judgment was mildly colored by his opinions of her.

Regardless of the fact that I found something about her mysterious, I didn't know if it had anything to do with the deaths that had occurred or if that was just her personality. And the fact that she had been asking questions about me didn't help anything.

I chomped on a piece of shrimp without worrying about how unladylike I looked at the moment. My thoughts returned to my earlier attempt to research things about

Lois. That was something, wasn't it? I'd found a bit of information, however small, that I hadn't known before. I felt like I should use that as a vote of confidence to keep trying and pushing for answers.

In truth, I didn't know what my problem was and why I felt this case was more difficult than usual. I'd done this sort of thing before, so why did it seem so different this time around? Was it because Lydia was involved and I felt an even greater need to perform? After all, *she* was the professional and I was working on her turf. Or was it because the expectations felt higher than they used to? Because it had become what I do, and if I failed, people would know that I had.

There was a time where I spent most of my energy worrying what other people thought about what I was doing and whether or not I should be doing it. Now I was worried that I wasn't doing it well enough.

It was hardly progress, yet I knew I had to find some compassion for myself. These sorts of things weren't always so cut and dry. And besides, when I thought about how it had only been a few days, I couldn't justify how rigid I was being with myself. Perhaps the rush to an answer came because of Lydia after all, and wanting to prove that I was worth bringing on to the case.

And, if I wanted to get technical, she hadn't asked me to solve the damn thing, she just wanted help with interviewing potential suspects. Surely she wasn't sitting in her office wondering why "that gal Lana" hadn't yet presented the suspect with a neat and tidy bow.

Deciding that all made perfect sense, I gave myself some grace and contemplated that maybe I should delve deeper into Felix and what he was all about. Not to be forgotten was Douglas Chen, who I hadn't finished looking into earlier in the day. He'd barely been on my radar this entire time. I'd been interrupted while searching the function of a financier. Even without being familiar with what they did, from the name I could take a stab at a great guess. Still, I wanted to be sure I understood clearly just in case their positions were of relevance to everything that had happened.

I stared into my now empty bowl, not realizing I'd eaten everything until looking down. This is what people meant when they said they ate their feelings.

Rising from the sunken-in couch, I stretched my legs, cracked my neck, and made my way back into the kitchen, trying to coax myself into a better mood.

Whatever the answers were, they were out there. That I could be sure of. I just had to find them.

CHAPTER

23

I left the restaurant promptly at five o'clock, unwilling to be deterred by anything that might get in the way. Donna Feng was not someone you kept waiting.

Thankfully, Nancy only had two occupied tables, so I didn't feel guilty leaving her. On occasion if we were busy, I'd stay until Vanessa came in at six.

Donna lived in the city of Westlake, about a fifteen-minute drive from Asia Village. I took Center Ridge the whole way there to avoid rush hour traffic on I-480. Instead of heaps of traffic, I was met with practically every stoplight along the way. When I reached Crocker Road, I turned right and headed in the direction of Donna's housing development. She lived in a fancy neighborhood filled with cluster homes far bigger than anything I'd ever lived in. Even though she was now a widow, she had twin teenage daughters and wanted to keep the large house for their benefit because it was where they'd been raised. At least that was the story. Not that anyone questioned Donna's decisions to begin with, but I gathered that the real reason was because she wasn't ready to let go. I'm sure there were many memories with her husband in that house and maybe if she left, she would feel like she was abandoning him somehow.

I only guessed at this, of course, based on the conversations we'd had. It was why I was so surprised to hear from Ian that Donna had started dating again. It seemed out of character.

I pulled into the driveway and took a few minutes to look the house over before getting out of the car. There'd been a fire months ago and the structure had taken quite a bit of damage. But looking at it now, you'd never know that anything happened.

I walked up the drive to the cobblestone path that wove to her front door, and by the time I went up the three steps to reach the landing, the door opened. It was Rosemary, Donna's housekeeper, a stern woman with a conservative bun that would have been approved by the military, a closet full of drab dresses that reminded me of an old-fashioned schoolmarm, and a firm attitude on no-nonsense behavior. On most occasions she didn't take kindly to all of my questions. She never said so, but I could tell by the expression on her face every time she saw me that she thought I was a troublemaker. No matter how polite or syrupy sweet I was, I still felt her judgment leaking from every pore of her body.

"Hello, Lana," Rosemary said with little inflection. "Please come in."

Despite the fact that she didn't smile at me, I smiled at her, just so she couldn't hold it against me that I hadn't. "Hi Rosemary, nice to see you again."

After I stepped inside, she shut the door and spun on her heel to lead me down the hallway toward the living room. "Please have a seat. I'll let Ms. Feng know you're here."

She disappeared up the stairs in search of the lady of the house. I admired Donna's home while I waited. It was decorated in a contemporary style with an Asian flair, which showcased Donna's forward thinking but also her appreciation for culture.

It was similar to how things were designed at Asia Village: heavy use of reds, blacks, and golds that were associated with tradition, but the architectural design and décor leant itself to a more modern time period with clean lines and open floor plans. While it had been her husband's pride and joy to run the themed shopping center, Donna had been the one to handle the interior design of the common areas of the plaza.

I'd been to her house a handful of times, enough to notice and remember specific details. But it was the first time I'd noticed the artwork above her fireplace. The painting was similar to the one Mr. Zhang had hanging in his shop of the travelers sailing an ocean. Had it always been there?

And next to it, instead of a sword, there was a vintage silk fan—black with white and purple flowers.

While I waited for Donna to come down, I pulled out my phone and did a quick search. I hadn't familiarized myself enough with the story of the Eight Immortals since Lydia had brought this whole situation to my door.

I typed a few keywords into my search bar, and someone named Zhongli Quan appeared in my results. A quick skim told me that this person had been the one to possess a fan and that they could bring people back to life with it. This man had also been said to represent men in the military and possess the knowledge to perform alchemy, transforming stones into silver or gold.

Though I knew that not everything should be taken so literally, especially since I didn't know Donna to ever have anything to do with military men, I did think about her ability to create wealth through her charity work, *and* to give people wealth by providing them with business opportunities. Her deceased husband had been the same type of person.

Whatever the case may be, there was growing evidence that this group was real, that Felix wasn't making up their existence. I tried to scour my memory for something significant in Talia's shop, but I couldn't remember seeing a similar painting hanging up anywhere or an identifying object. Then again, I hadn't known what I was looking for.

"Lana?" a feminine voice called from the hallway. "Are you there, dear?"

"I'm here," I said, stuffing my phone back into my purse.

Donna appeared in the threshold of the living room, her makeup fresh as if she'd applied it specifically for our meeting. She was, however, a woman who was always ready for anything. "Sorry to keep you waiting, I had an unexpected phone call from someone who isn't time conscious. I asked Rosemary to bring us some tea. Did you want something different?"

"No, tea will be fine. Thank you."

She held out a hand, gesturing to the couch. "Please have a seat."

I returned to my seat on the sofa while Donna sat in the wingback chair that she normally sat in when I came over. It always made me feel like I was meeting with a mafia boss.

She crossed her legs, leaning backward in the chair enough to rest her back but not enough to mess up the French twist hairstyle she often wore. When her jet-black hair wasn't in a twist, it was in a bun or some other form of updo. Seldom did you see her with her hair down. "It's been a while since we've gotten to chat. To what do I owe this pleasure? You mentioned you had something you needed to talk to me about?"

"What is the significance of this painting?" I asked, pointing to the ocean travelers above her fireplace. It wasn't what I thought I was going to lead with, but I wanted to compare her answer to Mr. Zhang's.

Her eyes turned to the painting and she smiled, taking a moment to appreciate the captured scene. "It is a story of overcoming obstacles, persevering through challenges, and remaining determined. That painting is of the Eight Immortals and their journey across the sea. These eight traveled through the treacherous waters that tested their will—each having to contribute their unique power in order to succeed."

The more I learned, the more I was ashamed to say that I hadn't known a thing about it. At least not in this context. Sure, I knew *of* them, my mother having shown me a Taiwanese soap opera or two that depicted the characters on their various journeys, but I hadn't known how powerful and meaningful it could be.

"And the fan?" I asked.

Donna turned her attention back to me, her eyebrows knitting together. "Lana, this can't be what you came over to talk about . . ."

"It's not, but it might be connected," I admitted.

Rosemary returned with a rectangular tray that held two teacups, a teapot, and a small platter of miniature Danish squares topped with cherries. It wasn't exactly an Asian treat, but again, a mix of cultures.

Without a word, Rosemary placed the tray on the coffee table in front me, filled both cups with tea, tipped her head at Donna, and exited the room as if she'd never been there.

I leaned forward to reach for the cups, carefully handing one to Donna.

Taking it, she said, "Thank you, dear. I hope you'll enjoy a Danish or two. I know that you've got just as much of a sweet tooth as I do."

I took one to be polite, but I knew I would be stuffing myself at the pizza bar in the coming hours.

"Now," she said after sampling her tea. "Tell me, why are you really here? And what this has to do with my fan and a painting."

Popping the miniature Danish into my mouth, I chewed with precision, stalling while I thought about exactly how much I wanted to tell her. I knew she could be trusted, especially because I'd kept her secrets to myself, and I was sure she wouldn't want that to change.

When I was done chewing, I said, "The original reason I wanted to come by is because of George Wong. Did you know him well?" I remembered Ian's warning to stay far away from the subject, but I had to know what Donna was willing to tell me. It was possible something she knew could put the rest of the puzzle pieces into place.

She inspected her fingernails. "I knew him well enough, yes. His death comes at a great loss to me . . . to our community."

"I'm sorry," I replied. "I don't want to be insensitive because I can see that the topic of George is upsetting, but I need to know what kind of person he was and if there was anything out of the ordinary going on before his death."

Her eyes had welled with tears and she blinked rapidly to stop them from spilling out. "He was a good man, a brilliant attorney, and a worthy companion."

So Ian hadn't been exaggerating like I'd thought he might have been. "I didn't know you'd gotten involved with anyone."

"No one knew really. I wasn't ready to announce to any-one that I was attempting to move on. I didn't know if I could go through with it. But one date turned into another, and before I knew what was happening, we were seeing each other on a regular basis."

"The both of you must have really liked each other," I said, feeling a pang of sadness for Donna having to suffer yet another loss.

"It's different, you know," she said, sniffling. "To date at this stage in life, and under the circumstances I find myself in. Having my first husband murdered by an old friend, someone right under our noses. Well, the stories run wild, I'm sure you can imagine."

"I'm sure it's hard" was all I said, but I would never really know what it was like for her.

"George didn't care about all that. He said that this was our second chance at happiness. He was divorced not long ago, a whole ugly matter with a child custody battle and spousal support. Divorcing a lawyer isn't the easiest thing to do, and your only way out is to find a better lawyer than the one you're trying to remove yourself from."

I did know a thing or two about that, seeing as my own sister, Anna May, was in a similar situation of her own. The man she'd been interested in for several months was in a messy predicament with his estranged wife. At times, I didn't know how estranged they actually were and wanted Anna May to tread lightly when it came to pursu-ing her on-again, off-again boyfriend, Henry Andrews. It had become such a sore subject between Anna May and me that we had barely talked in weeks because of it.

I couldn't help but wonder if George's divorce had any-thing to do with his death. Especially if it had been an ugly ordeal.

The whole concept was stirring something in my mind.

The fact that George was a lawyer felt important for some reason. Perhaps I was circling around the idea of lawsuits. A sure recipe for murder that could involve various parties. "I'm guessing since the divorce was final, his ex-wife found herself a decent lawyer?"

Donna chuckled with an air of sarcasm. "It really is as they say . . . a small world. You'll never guess who his ex-wife hired for legal representation."

"Who?" I asked, fearing by her reaction that I already knew the answer.

"Andrews, Filbert, Childs and Associates."

I felt nauseous. That was the firm where Anna May was interning.

CHAPTER
24

"Lana dear, are you all right?" Donna asked, leaning forward.

I sipped my tea, trying to gather my thoughts. "Yeah, I'm okay. I just . . ."

Donna scooted further to the edge of her seat. "It's okay, dear, you can tell me anything. If it's a secret, I promise it won't leave this room."

With a sigh, I decided that I was going to tell Donna more than I originally intended to. I started from the beginning telling her about Lydia showing up at the restaurant on Monday and everything that followed after that. I kept Felix's name out of it for the time being since they had an association, and Felix had made us swear we wouldn't let any of the other members know what he was up to.

After I'd finished relaying most of the story to her, she sat back in her chair and stared at the floor. No doubt her mind was overloaded with information just as mine had been. The only difference is she sat on the other side, being a part of the exclusive group herself.

"So you see," I said in conclusion, "there's a possibility that all three men were murdered."

"That's why you wanted to know about my fan and the painting." Her eyes flitted in my direction momentarily before she went back to staring at the floor. "And . . . George . . . he . . ."

"I don't think it was an accident or"—I lowered my voice—"self-inflicted."

A nervous laugh burst out of Donna. "I never thought so, dear. George was full of life and excited for this next chapter we would explore together. He really had everything going for him. I mean . . . yes, the whole ugly mess of a divorce was lingering in the air and his ex-wife had won full custody over the children, but things were looking up for him otherwise."

"His children," I said. "How old are they?"

"They're seven and nine, two boys," she replied. "Both now with their mother. They had visitation rights in place, but he felt so disappointed that he wasn't able to see them every day anymore."

"So since he was divorced and his sons are both so young, who will take his place as one of the Eight Immortals?"

She shook her head. "I have no idea. It will be put to a vote among the group. Each of us will recommend someone we think is fit to take the place of the former member. However, since everything is so fresh with George's death, we haven't even begun to discuss anything."

"Now that you know what I'm really up to, I hope you don't mind if I ask you a few more questions."

"No, of course not. I'll help any way that I can." She settled back in her seat, cradling her teacup in both hands. "If there is justice to be had for these men, then I'd like to say that I was part of securing it. All three were longtime friends of mine. And well, George . . ."

"If this is too painful for you, I can come back over once you've had time to process everything. I know this is a lot."

Donna gave me a sheepish grin. "I know this is time sensitive though. I'd like to be of some use today."

"Well, two things come to mind that could really get me pointed in the right direction," I said. "Do you know of anybody who would have it out for any of them? Someone in your group . . . or an affiliation? Did anyone get passed over for the position?"

Donna tilted her head upward, staring at the ceiling while her eyes moved back and forth like one of those cat clocks with the swinging tail. "I don't know anybody who'd want to murder them. It seems completely ridiculous. All three men were stand-up citizens who went out of their way to help others in need. As far as anybody getting passed up, nothing out of the ordinary sticks out. Naturally, everyone was upset when their referral was passed over, but no one lost their heads over it."

"Can I ask . . . the person who took over Walter Kang's position . . . Juliette something," I said, blanking on the name.

Donna nodded. "Yes, Juliette Chu, nice girl. She just opened her very first agency and is thriving beyond expectation."

I thought about new beginnings and what Talia had said about her shop being her very first and how life had handed her things at the right time. "How does this work? Your club, I mean."

Donna laughed. "Well, I wouldn't call it a club, Lana. But to answer your question, once a position is filled, that person gets the full support of the rest of the members and we would help get them up and running. Then it is that person's duty to help others, specifically of Asian descent, reach their potential. Consider us benefactors, if you will. Sometimes those we help are aware of our assistance, and sometimes they are not."

"So you all shell out money to help this person open a business or whatever?"

Donna shook her head. "No, the money is handled by one person. Currently, it is Douglas Chen. He fronts the money and then either becomes an investor or puts together some type of loan agreement between himself and that person. He helped our new tenant at Asia Village acquire the financing to open her shop, and he's helped Juliette start her agency."

"I see," I said, readjusting the puzzle pieces forming in my head. "And who exactly selected Juliette? Is she Walter's daughter?"

"Oh, no dear, he only has one daughter, estranged, who went backpacking through Europe, discovered that she enjoyed the French countryside, and decided not to come back. She came home for the funeral services but left immediately after everything was squared away with his estate. She didn't even want to meet with any of us. It was a bit rude, if you ask me, but who I am, dear? No, Juliette came at the recommendation of a woman by the name of Lois Fan. She's one of the Eight Immortals and has an impeccable eye for prospects."

I'd left out the part about Lois Fan, so Donna had no idea that I already knew who she was. I found it interesting—and possibly telling—that both replacements had been referrals of hers. I also couldn't help but notice that all three men who had been murdered weren't able to be replaced by a family member or spouse. I was beginning to form the conclusion that it was the reason they'd been chosen as targets.

I didn't know if Lydia was aware of this commonality between the three victims and it might prove useful when added to the information she'd already collected.

"Mommmmmm!" a young voice yelled from the hallway. A second later one of Donna's daughters came bouncing into the living room, one earbud in and the other dangling from a cord attached to her smartphone. "Oh," she said, when she noticed me sitting across from Donna. "Sorry, I didn't know anybody was here. Hi, Lana." She smiled brightly at me, exposing her braces.

"Hi . . . Jill," I guessed.

"I'm Jessica," she said with a bubbly giggle. Her head of silky, shiny black hair cascaded around her as she moved and I reminisced briefly about what it was like to have pure hair untouched by dye. "Jill doesn't have to have braces—that's the secret to tell us apart now."

I tapped my temple. "Note to self."

She giggled then turned to her mom, her facial expression becoming serious. "Mom, we have dinner reservations at Morton's and we're going to be late if you don't hurry up and get ready."

It amused me to see anyone, even her own children, talk to her in such a commanding way. I don't think I'd ever heard anyone dare to tell Donna Feng, of all people, to "hurry up."

Donna sighed. "I'm sorry, Lana, she's right. I promised a nice dinner and I wouldn't want to disappoint them. Is it okay if we continue this on a different day, after all? Unless you'd like to join us?"

Though it was hard to turn down a dinner at Morton's Steakhouse, I'd promised Kimmy that I would meet her at the Zodiac. Plus, I didn't see having a productive conversation with Donna's kids around. Especially because of the topic that needed to be discussed. "Thanks for offering," I said. "I wouldn't want to intrude on your family time, and I have to meet up with Kimmy Tran anyways."

"Ah, Kimmy. How is the little spitfire?" Donna teased.

"She's doing pretty good," I said, rising from my seat. I placed the teacup back on the tray next to the nearly untouched Danishes.

Donna rose as well. "I'll walk you out." She held out a hand, gesturing to the hallway.

"Thanks again for taking the time to meet with me. I really appreciate it, and the information you've given me will definitely help."

"Like I said, anything I can do," she replied. "I'll keep an ear out for anything useful that I might come across."

We stood at the doorway, and I reached for the knob, but Donna held up a hand, stopping me.

"Lana," she said, "you said there were two things that had come to mind. But you never got to tell me what the other question was before we were interrupted."

"Oh, I wanted to ask if you have anyone in mind to fill George's position."

Donna smiled. "I do actually. I had planned on referring Anna May for the slot."

On my way to the Zodiac, my mind went rampant with speculation. Donna was planning to ask my very own sister to be one of the Eight Immortals. The first thought that came to mind was how this would inflate Anna May's ego to the size of the Goodyear Blimp. She already thought she was the bee's knees, so being asked to be part of an elitist, secret group would surely send her over the top. The next thought that followed was the specific fact that she would have to keep it secret. That brought me a little comfort.

Despite what feelings I had about my sister's potential future involvement, I still had a case to solve and couldn't help but wonder about something Felix had said during our meeting. Not only had he mentioned that Lois wanted to replace the existing male members with females, but he'd also said that Donna had agreed with the sentiment.

For a split second, I considered that Donna might be involved in some way to help Lois achieve her goal, but as quickly as I thought it, I realized two things. One being that I knew Donna better than that, and though she was a determined and powerful woman, she wouldn't resort to violence to get what she wanted.

The other thing being I knew that she wouldn't sacrifice George's life specifically because he had meant so much to her. By the look on her face, I had gathered she'd been filled with hope at the prospect of their new relationship and it had meant the world to her.

Now that was crushed.

The devil on my shoulder insinuated that maybe it was all an act to deter me from figuring out the truth. But I brushed it away, sticking firmly to the fact of reason number one—she just wouldn't do that.

However, I couldn't say the same for Lois Fan. The idea of her being guilty of what Felix accused her of was becoming more and more of a possibility.

CHAPTER
25

- - - - - - - - - - - - - - - -

After I'd parked in the lot at the Zodiac, I checked my phone and found that I had a text from Lydia. *Hey chicka-dee, tomorrow at 6 p.m. we have a meeting with Juliette Chu to look at a house we're going to pretend to be interested in. Forwarding you a link of the listing to review before we go. See you then.*

The next message was a link to a realty website. I decided to look at it when I got home. It was 7:05 p.m. and I felt like Kimmy was waiting to put my head on a platter. Frankly, I'd been surprised she hadn't started calling me like a madwoman at 7:01.

I quickly sent a reply text letting Lydia know that I'd be there at six and that I had some information to pass along that might be useful to the case. I tucked my phone back into my purse and exited the car.

Inside, I spotted Kimmy sitting at the bar next to my usual seat. I couldn't see her face, but by her posture, I could tell she was bored. With her chin rested in one hand, she stirred her drink with the other, swirling her ice cubes round and round.

"Hey!" I said, coming up from behind her.

She jolted as I hopped onto the stool to her right—my honorary seat.

"Geez, Lee, scare a girl, why don't ya?" She checked the time on her cell phone. "Fashionably late, but I'll allow it."

"Sorry, I got caught up longer than I expected. I made good time though . . ."

"Yeah, yeah, it's fine," she said, dropping her straw back into her glass. "I figured I'd wait for you to eat, so before we get into everything, let's go grab a plate of pizza. I'm starving!"

We both made our way toward the back of the room where a buffet-style table was set up. Five pans of pizza were being kept warm under heat lamps, alongside a metal tray filled with breadsticks, another with twisted pepperoni rolls, and the last, boneless fried chicken.

On our brief walk, I managed to get Megan's attention as we passed. She winked at me as she briefly paused from chatting with a customer.

My mouth watered as I inspected my choices of pizza with different toppings. I grabbed a plate and reached for a slice with black olive and onions, and then another with pepperoni and mushrooms. Not being able to help myself, I grabbed a few twists of pepperoni rolls and some fried chicken to go along with my first serving. Depending on how long we were here tonight, I might be able to eat my weight in pizza.

I scoped out Kimmy's plate, which was filled with pineapple pizza—an atrocity in my opinion. But everybody had their favorites.

The idea for a pizza night had been Megan's, and she'd presented it to the owner about a month ago as a way to drum up more business during the week. The Zodiac had no problems keeping the neighborhood regulars, but they were always looking for ways to bring in new business. So, for twenty bucks, you could indulge in the pizza buffet from the hours of six to nine. The hope, of course, was that you spent well more on drinks.

Looking around, it seemed it was going rather well. The place was packed, and pitchers of beer graced almost every table.

With there being so much competition in the bar industry, you really had to keep things fresh if you wanted to survive.

When we returned to our seats, I'd found that Megan had dropped off a glass that looked to be filled with my standard drink of whiskey and Coke. I was relieved she wasn't forcing me to be her guinea pig tonight. I just didn't have it in me to drink one of her latest concoctions.

Kimmy bit into her pizza, a string of cheese tethering her to the slice as she pulled away. Once she'd gotten her mozzarella under control, she asked, "So, what's the what? Fill me in and don't spare any details."

I thought about my promise to Lydia that I wasn't supposed to share details with anyone outside of the case. I'd broken that rule several times already and was trying to avoid doing it again. I'd spent a better part of my day thinking about what I could or *should* say to Kimmy once I'd gotten here, but I'd come up with a whole lot of nothing.

Kimmy, like Megan, was good at telling when I was lying about something, or even just withholding a piece of information. I didn't want to spend time arguing with her because it felt like wasted breath.

I settled on telling her the general story, leaving out names of the involved parties, hoping that would be enough to keep her occupied for at least a little while longer.

When I finished filling her in, she perked up in her seat and set down the pizza slice she'd been holding onto. "I know what this is about . . . This is about that lawyer guy . . . what's his name? George something. It's been all over the news. They're having a charity benefit in his honor."

"George Wong," I said. "They are? I haven't heard about it."

"That's because you avoid the news like it's the plague or something," Kimmy joked. "But yeah, they're starting a foundation that will be named after him, and the money raised will go toward helping people who need legal help but have no income."

"Who is *they*?" I asked.

"Donna and some people I have never heard of."

I held my pizza slice in midair. That's weird, why hadn't Donna told me about it while I was at her house? "When did you hear this?"

Kimmy shrugged. "I think it was first announced yesterday."

I set my pizza down and reached into my purse for my cell phone. I had a feeling I knew who the other people might be. Opening a web browser, I typed "George Wong charity" into the search bar and found a story from WKYC on the topic.

When I clicked on the link, I found a three-minute video that had most likely been what appeared on air. Below it, an article detailed the specifics of the charity event.

Since we were in a noisy bar, I opted to read the post, which mentioned that the event was open to the public and the entry fee was two hundred dollars. Purchasing an entire table would cost a thousand dollars, and an auction would take place during the evening for things like week-long cruises and full-year memberships to local upscale spas.

The event would be hosted at the iconic luxury hotel Metropolitan at The 9 that was located downtown on E. 9th Street—hence the name.

Kimmy leaned in, her arm brushing against mine as I read over the details. She let out a long whistle. "Two hundred dollars a pop is quite the steep admission price, I'd say. But leave it to Donna to pull out all the stops."

I'd hardly paid attention to what Kimmy was saying because my eyes had landed on the four names of the people hosting the event: Donna Feng, Douglas Chen, Felix Hao, and Lois Fan.

Since Douglas was the money man, I wasn't all that surprised that he was listed, but I did find it interesting to see Felix Hao and Lois Fan included. Felix hadn't mentioned anything about the charity event either, although maybe he hadn't felt it was relevant. After all, his main concern was for me and Lydia to find him answers to who'd murdered his three friends.

Kimmy nudged me with her elbow. "I was right, wasn't I? This is about that George guy. He's the person you don't want to name."

"It is," I admitted, closing the browser and putting my phone away.

"But why?" she asked. "What's the big deal? You've always told me stuff before. And I've helped you quite a few times."

I sighed. "Because I had to sign forms this time, promising I wouldn't go around town talking about all this stuff."

"But how are you going to find anything out then?"

"Well, I'm not supposed to share information with

people who wouldn't have direct information. The client wants us to be extremely discreet."

Kimmy picked up her abandoned pizza crust and broke a piece off, popping it into her mouth. Through chews, she said, "Sounds awfully suspicious to me."

I didn't want to explain to Kimmy about the existence of the Eight Immortals. It would only complicate things further, and even though I knew I could trust her, I didn't know if she could promise me that she'd never mention this to anyone for the rest of her life.

The other cases were different. And they'd been publicized—to my dismay—so people had known what went on and how it went down. However, with the secrecy this case involved, I didn't know what details would eventually be relayed through media and I didn't want to be the one who outed this secret society that had existed in Cleveland since Asians first settled in the area.

"A penny for your thoughts," a playful voice quipped.

When I looked up, I found Megan staring back at me with a wide grin on her face. She'd saved me for the moment from explaining anything further to Kimmy. "Hey busy lady, I was wondering when you'd stop by."

Kimmy's shoulders dropped and I knew she was disappointed that our conversation had been interrupted.

Megan leaned forward, resting her elbows on the bar top. "What's shakin', toots? Any new developments?"

My eyes traveled down to the plate of unfinished food in front of me. The pepperoni twists had gone untouched. "I'm not sure," I said, looking back up at her. I was hoping she'd be able to read the expression on my face, knowing that I had something to talk about.

Reaching for my hand, she gave it a squeeze and winked. I knew she'd caught on. She said, "I'm sure you'll figure it out. You always do. Just give yourself a little more time."

Kimmy shook her glass at Megan. "My ice cubes are lonely. Would you mind being a dear and getting me another drink?"

Megan clucked her tongue. "Just when I thought I had a minute to breathe." She took Kimmy's glass and went about getting her a drink.

With Megan gone, Kimmy swiveled in her seat to face me head-on, her determination obvious by the stern look in her eye. "Look, I know there's a ton more you're not telling me, and I'm not going to hold it against you. Not yet anyways. History tells me that you're always reluctant to share because you don't want to burden people. And I know that you say this Lydia chick made you sign papers to keep quiet, but I'm not buying it, Lee. And besides, you know you can trust me with anything. Have I ever let you down?"

I took a moment to try to conjure up an example I could throw back at her, but she hadn't done one thing that I could recall causing me to think she wasn't trustworthy. Butting in when maybe it wasn't the best time and losing her temper on occasion didn't apply toward this argument. Along with Megan, she was truly my most faithful friend.

"Okay, but you have to swear on your life that you won't say anything ever," I said. "Like forever *ever*. If you do, I'll never speak to you again. This is the biggest secret I've ever come across."

Kimmy held up an index finger and drew an imaginary X on her chest. "Cross my heart and hope to die. Now out with it, Lee."

CHAPTER
26

"Not even the Mahjong Matrons know?" Kimmy asked when I'd finished telling her the entire story.

Megan returned with Kimmy's freshened drink and leaned back against the bar.

I shook my head. "Not as far as I know. If they do, they haven't offered it up. I didn't exactly ask them specifically if they knew, only because I didn't want them to take that and run with it all over Asia Village."

"But how could they not know?" Kimmy asked, incredulous. "They know everything."

Megan looked between Kimmy and me. "Who we talkin' about? The Matrons?"

"Yeah," I said, taking a sip of my drink. I felt like I'd been talking for hours and my throat was becoming scratchy.

"Well, don't forget, they also don't know about Kimmy's moonlighting gig at the Black Garter," Megan replied.

Kimmy nodded thoughtfully. "This is true. How we've

managed to keep my secret serving job from them is beyond me. But it's saved me a trip to the mountains of China."

Asian parents still wielded the power to scare their children well into adulthood when it came to life choices. And with Kimmy's parents being slightly conservative and old-fashioned, they would not approve of her working at a gentleman's club, especially if they saw what she wore to work.

"So," Megan said, "it's very possible this has slipped their radar as well."

Kimmy exhaled. "I still can't believe this is real. I mean, I'd totally not think it was real if I wasn't dating Peter." She turned to me. "You know how he's super into conspiracy theories and whatever. I mean, granted this isn't really a conspiracy, but you know what I mean . . . it sure feels like one. Like, how . . . I just can't."

I nodded. "I know. It threw me for a loop too. It made me wonder how many things have been affected by the actions of eight people. They're intervening in people's lives without everyone involved really being aware of their presence. And if one of them were a bad seed, well . . . imagine what they could do. They could help someone get into a position of potential power they either didn't deserve to be in or had ill intentions of their own."

Megan said, "What's really got me thinking is the fact that this type of thing had to exist at all. I did a little bit of reading on Asian history in Cleveland during my break. I happened to stumble across a story about a guy named Wan Lee Yew. Have either of you ever heard of him?"

Kimmy and I both shook our heads.

Megan continued, "It was like the 1880s or whatever and he was marrying an Irish woman."

Kimmy interrupted. "So? What's the big deal about that?"

"It's what happened next that will shock you," Megan replied.

We both looked at her expectantly.

Megan let out a deep sigh as her shoulders drooped. "Interracial marriages were extremely looked down upon and the townspeople weren't exactly having it—"

Kimmy covered her mouth. "Oh gawd, don't tell me they did something to them."

With a frown, Megan said, "They threw stones and tried hitting them with clubs . . . It was an awful story. After that, I didn't want to read any more."

"Ohmigod!" Kimmy blurted out.

Megan pursed her lips. "Yeah, right in the middle of Ontario. It's outrageous to think about."

The thought of it left me feeling saddened and uneasy that things like that happened in the past, not just to Chinese immigrants but to other cultures as well. "So a secret society that's been in existence since those times doesn't seem so out of this world if you take into account how they were treated. The people who started the group had to protect themselves or they'd feel like they could never win."

"Or maybe someone would have tried to disband them and ruin their chance at a better life." Kimmy groaned. "A different way of living for sure. I'm thankful it wasn't us living back then—I wouldn't have lasted a day. I'd be throwing stones right back at those jerks."

"And you with two marks against you," Megan added. "A woman *and* an Asian."

Kimmy balled up a fist and shook it with passion. "I would've given 'em hell. You can be sure of that."

After keeping quiet for a few beats, not wanting to take away from Megan's moment of sharing knowledge, I decided to interject. "Well, my meeting with Donna pretty much solidified the history of this group. She didn't get into the specifics of their timeline or any ordeals the original founders had to go through though. Not that I'd really asked either."

Megan was the one to speak next. "When were you going to tell me you met with Donna?"

I blushed. "I was getting around to that. It's been a lot."

Kimmy patted me on the back, a little forcefully. "Well don't worry, Lee, you have your bestest pals to help you figure out who this slippery slimebag happens to be, and we'll make quick work of this. Who even needs Lydia Shepard?"

"It's her case," I reminded her.

Kimmy blew a raspberry. "Oh, right. Well, still, we'll get it straightened out. Now who are your suspects? My money is on that Douglas Chen guy. He's the one doling out cash, maybe he doesn't like who it's being given to or something. Or . . . maybe the guys he took out of the picture all owed him money and weren't willing to pay up."

"Or couldn't," Megan added.

I was just about to tell them the angle I'd come up with involving the lack of replacements when something else dawned on me. I slapped my forehead. "Oh my god, the files!"

"The files?" Kimmy asked.

"Lydia gave me a file folder with the information she's collected since first meeting with Felix. I left it at the restaurant in the safe. I was so preoccupied with meeting Donna that I forgot to bring it with me." Panic overtook me as I came to the realization that Nancy and Vanessa had access to the safe and would put the till in there right before closing. "I have to go."

Quickly I gathered my things, stuffing my phone into my purse and pulling out my wallet to leave money for my tab. Megan brushed my hand away. "Don't worry about it, it's on the house. You go."

Kimmy sucked down her drink and slapped the glass down on the counter so hard I thought it might break. "Hold up, Lee, I'm coming with you. I wanna take a look at this file for myself." She hopped off the stool and slung her purse over her shoulder. "You better drive us there," she said, pointing at her glass. "We can come back after we get the files."

I could tell that Megan felt left out because she was stuck at work, but there wasn't anything I could do about that. "Okay, let's go," I said to Kimmy. "If we leave now, we'll catch them before closing."

I said goodbye to Megan and promised we'd return soon. As Kimmy and I walked into the parking lot, I found myself relieved that I had barely drank anything and thankful that I hadn't forgotten about the files until the following day.

Just imagine what sort of trouble I would have been in had I completely forgotten that the folder was at work and Nancy or Vanessa happened to take a peek. Now I only hoped that I'd make it there in time.

We arrived at Asia Village at 8:50 p.m. The plaza, except for the Bamboo Lounge, would be closing in ten minutes. At 8:45, the main doors locked so customers could only get out, not in, but thankfully I had a master key, so we didn't have to walk through the karaoke bar.

I parked right up front near the doors, not worried about dealing with the employee lot, and I hurried to the entrance with Kimmy trailing behind me.

"Slow down, Lee," Kimmy shouted. "I can't move that fast after all the pizza I ate."

With my keys already in hand, I unlocked the doors and waited for Kimmy while she caught up. "We have to get there before Vanessa puts the cash in the safe. I don't trust a teenager not to go snooping through something that isn't normally there."

Kimmy snorted. "But you trust her with money? Lighten up, Lee."

As we sped through the plaza, Kimmy used me as cover when we passed China Cinema and Song. I spotted her mother behind the cash register of their shop, but she was preoccupied with something below the counter and didn't notice us walking by.

With more force than necessary, I whipped open the door to Ho-Lee Noodle House and found Vanessa at the register getting ready to remove the cash drawer. Her long ebony tresses appeared to be freshly curled and I noticed she had on more eye makeup than usual. "Sorry, we're closing early," she said, her words faltering as she realized it was me. "Oh, hey boss, we weren't closing like super early, but our last table left about five minutes ago and—"

I held up a hand signaling for her to stop explaining. "I'm not worried about that. You know I don't care if you guys cut out a few minutes early if the place is empty." I looked behind her to inspect the state of the dining area. It appeared immaculate from my brief assessment. "You can actually go." I held out my hands. "I'll handle the register tonight."

She raised her perfectly plucked eyebrows. "Really? Oh thanks, boss. I have a chemistry test tomorrow that I'm dreading and if I could bail just a few minutes early I can get in some extra study time."

Kimmy sidled up to the counter, a devious grin forming. "Kid, I don't know who you think you're talking to, but neither one of us believes that leaving work five minutes early is going to help with a chemistry test or any other subject, if you wanna get technical. Also, I feel like studying chemistry doesn't involve hot pink lip gloss."

Vanessa blushed. "I swear."

Kimmy folded her arms across her chest. "Uh-huh. You're speaking to a master of deception right here."

Vanessa handed the register drawer over to me, her face reddening even deeper. "Okay, fine, my boyfriend's been out in the parking lot waiting for me to get out of work. But don't tell my mom," she pleaded. "I'm not supposed to see him on school nights unless I have good grades in all my classes. I really am bombing in chemistry, so I've only been seeing him on the weekends. It really sucks."

I chuckled. "Don't worry, your secret is safe with us." I thought about all the secrets I had to keep lately, and of them, this one seemed the most innocent. "But also, don't fail chemistry. Your mom isn't going to let you work anymore if you do, and then you won't be able to save up for that car you want."

She sighed. "I know. I won't fail it. He's actually helping me with my homework."

I knew her well enough now to know that she understood the importance of doing well in school, but I also knew the pull of teen romance and how it seemed so dire in that phase of your life to be with the person you considered your sweetheart. "Well, go on," I said, shooing her with my free hand.

"Thanks boss," she said before zipping through the restaurant to get her things from the back room.

Kimmy and I ambled our way toward the kitchen. She snickered and said, "Ah, to be a teen again . . . the excitement of it all."

"Pft," I snorted. "No thank you. The hormones, the awkward growing phases, gym class. Ugh."

"You'd rather do what you're doing now just so you wouldn't have to go to P.E. class?"

I laughed. "I wouldn't trade it for the world. Nothing is getting me back into those awkward shorts they made us wear."

Vanessa flew through the kitchen doors again, almost barreling over Kimmy and me. She managed to sidestep just before colliding right into us, her hair whipping back and forth. "Sorry. See you later, Boss."

When Kimmy and I reached the kitchen, we found Lou, our nighttime cook, scrubbing down the grill. He looked up, surprised to see us. "Oh hey there, boss lady. Kimmy. How are you ladies doing on this fine evening?"

"We're okay," I answered for the both of us. "Just have some business to take care of in the office and Kimmy came to keep me company."

"Do you want me to stick around?" he asked. "I can escort you ladies out when you're done."

"No, that's okay," I said. "We'll be fine. You can go whenever you're finished. Have a good night."

"You too. Always nice to see you!"

Once we were tucked away in my office, Kimmy snorted. "That guy is like the Asian version of Mr. Rogers. He's so peppy and positive."

"It used to bug the crap out of me," I admitted. "But his attitude has been kind of refreshing lately. Things can't be that bad if people like him are still chipper." I typed in the safe combination on the keypad, it beeped as the lock disengaged, and I pulled the handle open. I exhaled a breath of relief as I found the envelope undisturbed and in the same position as I'd left it. "Phew."

Kimmy grabbed the manila envelope out of my hands. "Dibs!"

I clucked my tongue. "Would a 'please' kill you?"

"No, but it might damage my soul," she said with a wink. She plopped down in my guest chair and went about opening the envelope.

I shimmied behind my desk with the register still in hand. We always left fifty dollars and some change in the drawer to use for the next morning. The rest went into a bank deposit bag with a calculated receipt, which I'd then take to the bank the following day.

I worked on tallying the money while Kimmy flipped through the pages. Occasionally when I looked up to see what she was doing, I'd notice a perturbed expression on her face. Her eyebrows scrunched together as she got further into the documented information.

Once I'd finished my tallies, I organized the money in the drawer to all face the same way before I placed everything into the safe and secured the lock. My parents had been big sticklers on keeping the appearance of the drawer organized, and the habit had grown on me.

Kimmy shook her head as she reached the last page. "This stuff is . . . like, how do you even deal with it all?" she said, looking up at me. "It's a lot."

I shrugged. "I've hardly looked at it. It's much more detailed than anything I jot down in my notebook at home."

"Imagine the resources she has at her fingertips." Kimmy straightened the papers before stuffing them back in the envelope and securing the clasp. "Also, I can't help but notice there was a page with notes from your meeting with that Felix guy. He really said that he thinks Mr. Zhang has a daughter? Who is this Lois Fan woman anyways?"

"I don't know yet, to be honest," I said. "Lydia is trying to get us a meeting with her, but last I heard, Lois hadn't returned any of her calls."

Kimmy rose from her seat and handed me the envelope. "Well, the answer is obvious."

"What do you mean?"

"You have to go undercover to get to her."

"I'll let Lydia call the shots on that, it's her case."

"Suit yourself, Lee, but if you need someone to suit up and pretend to be a model or whatever, you know where to find me."

I rolled my eyes. "I can just see it now." I tucked the envelope under my arm, grabbed my purse, and opened the door. "Come on, let's go."

The kitchen was empty when we passed back through, but Lou had left all the lights on for us. I went to the switch panel and darkened the kitchen, then waited for Kimmy to reach the front of the restaurant before I turned off all the lights in the dining area.

She held the door open and I reached into my pocket for my keys to lock up, but just as Kimmy stepped out into the plaza, I noticed lights on across the way at Eastern Enchantments, and two figures standing in close proximity to each other right near the entrance.

With a gasp, I pulled Kimmy by the arm, dragging her back into the restaurant.

"Hey!" Kimmy shouted. "What's the big—"

"Shhh," I hissed. "Get back in here and be quiet." I locked the doors and urged her to come with me to the Matrons booth so we could get a better view.

"What are we lookin' at?" she asked as she shimmied into the booth next to me.

I took a few moments to make sure I was in fact seeing what I thought I was seeing. I'd only seen her picture twice. Once in the file, and once again on her website. When I was sure, I said to Kimmy, "Remember how you were asking me about Lois Fan?"

"Yeah?"

"Well that's her in Talia's shop."

CHAPTER
27

"That's her right there?" Kimmy asked, as she leaned forward, her nose almost touching the window. She then twisted her body to edge herself out of the booth. "Well, let's go say hi then."

"What?" I tried reaching for her arm, but she escaped my grasp. "No, we can't go over there; we don't want to give ourselves away."

Kimmy kept heading for the door. Without turning around, she said, "Nah, it'll be fine. How would they even think to know anything."

My friend had made it out of the restaurant before I could stop her, and I left the doors unlocked to try to catch up with her. She marched over the footbridge with all the confidence of a tightrope walker.

"Kimmy, wait," I pleaded.

She looked at me over her shoulder. "The time for waiting has passed, Ms. Lee. Kimmy Tran is on the case and around here we take action."

I groaned with frustration. "I knew I shouldn't have brought you with me. This isn't going to go well."

"Nonsense," Kimmy chuckled. "It's going to go swimmingly. Now you just let me do all the talking."

We'd reached the double glass doors that made up the entrance to Eastern Enchantments. Talia and Lois were so preoccupied with their own conversation they hadn't even noticed us walking up. But that was about to change because Kimmy walked right up and knocked on the tempered glass with enough force to cause the doors to vibrate.

Talia and Lois both jolted with a start, and Lois gasped, her hand flying up to her chest. I heard a muffled "Oh my!" as Talia came to unlock the doors.

Besides the jolt, Talia seemed otherwise undisturbed by our presence. The pleasant smile on her face appeared genuine as it always had the few times we spoke. If I was looking for her to show signs of guilt at being caught in the act of a secret meeting, I was thoroughly let down.

"Good evening, ladies," she said in a soft, wispy tone. "I'm afraid we haven't officially been introduced . . ." she said to Kimmy.

"Kimmy Tran." She stuck out her hand. "I help run my parents' entertainment shop." She bobbed her head in the direction of China Cinema and Song. "You're Talia."

Talia laughed, taking Kimmy's hand into her own. "Yes, that I am. So nice to meet you."

"And who's this?" Kimmy asked, turning her attention to Lois, who hadn't said a word.

Talia released Kimmy's hand. "This is . . . an old friend . . . of mine, Lois Fan."

Lois raised an eyebrow at Talia but said nothing. She didn't offer a hand either, but instead tipped her head at Kimmy and me. "Hello."

I nodded a hello while wishing for probably the eight hundredth time in my life that a vortex would open below

my feet and swallow me whole. While Talia seemed un-
encumbered by our impromptu visit, Lois didn't appear to
feel the same way. She tried to cover the scowl that was
forming by fidgeting with a ring on her finger, but even
as she tried to occupy her attention it was clear she didn't
want us there.

Aside from stifling the discomfort she felt, she looked
exactly like she had in the photos I'd seen of her. Her
black hair was all one length and cut with blunt edges
that stopped at her shoulders. The tips were curled in-
ward so that the style framed her face ever so slightly.
Her makeup was minimal and to the point. Soft blush,
tattooed eyeliner and brows, but no lipstick like she'd had
on in her pictures.

The black, pinstripe suit jacket she wore had padded
shoulders, and the matching pants were pleated down the
front. A white tie-neck blouse added a little playfulness
to her otherwise conservative look. Sensible black heels
completed the outfit.

Talia looked among the three of us. "Is there anything
I can help you ladies with?"

Kimmy skirted the question. "How do the two of you
know each other? Aren't you new in town?"

Lois cleared her throat.

I went to reach for Kimmy's arm. "We should probably
be going and leave these two—"

Talia cut me off and replied, "She's actually my modeling agent . . . well, former modeling agent. I haven't
modeled in about six months now. She came by to see the
new shop."

"A modeling agent?" Kimmy feigned surprise. She
clasped her hands together and took a step closer to Lois
who, in turn, took a step back. "I've always wanted to
model, but I've always been told I'm too short."

Lois narrowed her eyes, sizing Kimmy up with a discerning glare. "You are too short—"

Kimmy tsked.

"For runway," Lois continued. "But I might have a modeling opportunity for something else for print ads that could use your figure." She slipped a hand into her Chanel bag and pulled out a card, handing it over to Kimmy. "If you're serious about modeling, and I mean serious, contact me and we can talk further. Now, I'm afraid, isn't the time to discuss business. I have to be going soon and I still have things to discuss with *Ms. Sun.*"

Kimmy looked the card over. "Great, I'll give you a call tomorrow and we can set up an appointment."

"Sorry to have bothered you," I said sheepishly. "We'll get out of your hair."

Lois regarded me with the same look of critique that she'd used to evaluate Kimmy. "You're not bad looking either. You've got a look about you. Is that your real hair dyed or do you have extensions?"

Self-consciously, a hand flew up to the side of my head. I smoothed my hair down, sensing I had tons of flyaways after chasing after Kimmy. "It's my hair," I said.

"If you're interested, I know a dye company that needs someone to sample their product. Why don't you take my card too."

"Uh, okay, thanks," I replied, taking the card and shoving it in my pocket. "Nice meeting you. Talia, we'll see you tomorrow."

Kimmy cheerfully waved goodbye and began to prance away with an air of accomplishment.

I pulled her arm for the third time that night and led her back over the footbridge. "Come on, I still have to lock up."

"Oh, right." She sidled up next to me and playfully nudged me with her shoulders. "Also, no need to thank me."

"Thank you?" I snorted. "That was embarrassing as hell."

"Oh whatever, Lee. You just don't want to admit it, that's all."

"Admit what?"

She held up Lois's business card. "Day one on the case, and I've already made headway. Now you have your chance at meeting with Lois Fan in private."

After I locked up the restaurant, Kimmy and I left Asia Village and headed back to the Zodiac, where business had simmered down. With the pizza bar now closed, the place had cleared out except for some of the nightly regulars who milled around until closing time at two a.m.

I was too tired to remain social, so I only stayed long enough to fill in Megan on the story of what happened when we got to Asia Village. She didn't want to admit she was impressed by the progress we'd made by introducing ourselves to Lois Fan because I knew she could tell that I was annoyed with Kimmy's forwardness, but she complimented her anyways.

The two of them had been getting along a lot better since I'd gotten back from my trip to Irvine, and I wondered if my time away had forced them to make amends somehow. I found it strange that they were getting along so well, but I didn't dare question it. I wasn't going to look a gift horse in the mouth. After all, I'd spent less time breaking up their arguments in the past couple of months.

I left shortly after, wanting to have time to myself so I could review the files, jot down some notes in my own notebook, and look over the house listing that Lydia had sent me earlier that evening.

On my way home, Adam texted that he'd managed to wrap up early at the station and asked if I wanted some company for the night. *Of course I do*, I replied. He needed some time to shower and shave before coming over, so I'd still get at least a little bit of alone time to do the things I needed.

I walked Kikko before jumping into the shower. Twenty minutes later, I was in my pajamas and at the dining room table with the contents of the envelope and my trusty notebook sprawled out in front of me. Kikko sat at my feet with her favorite stuffed duck, snorting as she chomped on its head. It was a wonder the thing wasn't totally decimated by now. I'd tried replacing it with a newer one, but it sat untouched in her toy bin.

I pulled out my phone, opening the text thread from Lydia and clicking on the link that took me to the house listing she'd provided. She'd chosen a four-bedroom colonial in Fairview Park. I sped through the listing photos and found a renovated home decorated completely in neutral tones, a lavish patio with a built-in stone grill, and a healthy-sized yard with immaculate grass that almost didn't look real.

I noted the listing included the name Juliette Chu as the agent and Chu Realty as the broker. A small headshot of Juliette appeared next to her name, and I'd realized then that Lydia hadn't included a photo of her or Talia in her file. I wondered why, considering she'd felt that Talia was a potential suspect. Obviously, Juliette would have to fall into the same category.

Juliette was a pretty girl with long hair that was loosely curled and accented with caramel highlights. She wore a full face of makeup, which was done tactfully and with precision. It was apparent that she was good at contouring; it almost looked as if a professional makeup artist had styled her for the photo. I began to wonder if she had also been a model, seeing as she was a referral from Lois Fan.

I'd taken a few sparse notes about the slivers of information that I'd gathered before the doorbell rang.

Kikko sprouted up from her relaxed position below my chair and furiously waddled to investigate, barking and snorting along the way. Her wiggly tail swept back and forth as she reached the crack below the door, bending her head down and sniffing to identify if the person on the other side was friend or foe.

She always seemed to know when it was Adam. She'd perk up her ears after catching his scent, and then whimper and whine until I let him in.

When I opened the door, Adam held up a brown paper bag spotted with grease in one hand, and in the other, a bouquet of flowers.

"Oh!" I said, greeting him with a kiss. "What's the occasion?"

He handed over the flowers as he stepped in and shut the door behind him. "No occasion, just saw these and thought of you. It's been a while since I've done something semi-romantic."

I stuck my nose into the bouquet, crinkling the cellophane wrapper. "You didn't have to do this." It was a beautiful spring mix filled with pink tulips, blue hydrangeas, orange lilies, and peach snapdragons, accented with a touch of baby's breath.

"Work has been keeping me busy lately, and I'm slacking on my other job." He held onto the paper bag he was carrying while he investigated the papers I had spread out on the table. "What's all this?"

"Wait, what's your other *job*?" I asked.

He turned his head, blew me a kiss, and winked. "Why keeping tabs on you, of course. Making sure you don't land yourself in an orange jumpsuit."

"Har har," I said, sticking my tongue out at him.

"I'm filled with jokes. Now, back to this . . . What exactly is all of this?"

Moving around him, I slid some of the papers off to the side so he could set the paper bag down. By the tangy smell that was emanating from it, I suspected barbeque wings, one of his favorite after-work indulgences. "It's a case file from Lydia. Wanna have a look?"

"Babe, I just got off of work . . . doing this very exact thing." He set the bag down and wandered into the kitchen to grab a beer from the fridge. "This isn't really the kind of thing I want to look at while I spend quality time with my girlfriend."

I'd followed after him in search of a vase to display my flowers. "Well, I thought maybe you'd want to see what she had that you didn't . . ." It hadn't been my original plan, but once I'd started sorting through the papers, I didn't think it would hurt to have Adam take a gander. Sure, I was failing at this not sharing information thing, but he was a police detective. He knew how to be discreet.

He popped the twist cap off his beer bottle and returned to the table to casually skim through the papers I'd laid out. "We have nothing to connect these murders. I'm trying to find out from Westlake P.D. if there was an autopsy done on Walter Kang. The detective in charge of the case hasn't gotten back to me yet."

I pulled out the vase I had in mind, filled it with water, and added the attached packet of flower food. "Aren't autopsies always done?" I didn't really know how that worked, and in a lot of the cases I'd handled in the past, the cause of death had more times than not been pretty obvious.

He shook his head. "Not always, dollface. In the instances where death appears natural or the cause evident; and if a family member requests one not be done, then they skip it. And seeing as Walter Kang was found at the bottom of a staircase with a twisted neck, there's a big possibility there wasn't one performed."

As I arranged the flowers, I thought back to what Donna had told me about Walter's estranged daughter and her rush to be done with the particulars and return to her life in France. It was likely she'd opted to pass on an autopsy so she could wrap things up quickly and get the services under way.

"Would Theodore Yeh have had one?" I asked.

"Maybe. In instances of a heart attack, they can do the autopsy to find out if a cardiac event took place and if that was the cause of death. Now whether a toxicology report was included with that autopsy is another matter."

"How will we find that out?" I joined him at the table, shoving aside some of the papers to make a spot for the flowers at the center.

He pulled out a chair and sat in front of the paper bag he'd yet to open. For a split second I thought I caught a glimpse of longing in his eye. Looking up, he said, "I'm inquiring into that as well. The chief wants to know what I'm up to and so far isn't backing my play, so I've been trying to acquire all this information on the side. He's working me to the bone trying to figure out if we can catch a lead on George Wong's death. It's pretty high profile, considering the legal work he was into . . . and I'm sure you're well aware, lawyers can make a lot of enemies."

"I am, and you're not the first person to say that. But I

don't think it was a client or anyone that had anything to do with his profession. I don't think so, anyways. Do you know if he was involved in any lawsuits of his own?"

"Like was someone suing him?"

"Yeah . . . maybe a group lawsuit?"

"Nope, nothing has turned up of that nature."

"Then I really think it has to do with this secret group," I concluded.

Adam pursed his lips. "Something that I can't mention to anyone . . . at your request, remember? I can't exactly tell the chief that's the potential connection between these deaths if you don't want me to expose the truth."

I sighed. "I know. It throws a giant wrench into the whole thing. But at this stage I find it hard to believe it's a coincidence."

Adam was preoccupied by something he'd just read on a page of Lydia's handwritten notes. "What's this about Mr. Zhang?" He held up the paper up for me to see. "Like Mr. Zhang, your grandmother's boyfriend?"

"Yes, ridiculous isn't it?" I replied, rolling my eyes. "I feel awful that it's even written down anywhere. My guilt has caused me to totally avoid the man. He's got to be wondering why I'm dodging him recently. Normally I stop by at some point during the day to chat with him."

"Where did this absurd notion even get started?"

I sighed. "Lydia's client, Felix Hao, said he saw each of the men arguing with Mr. Zhang shortly before their deaths. Then after you told me George Wong had aconite in his system, well that only makes it look worse. If there was anyone who would know how to use or misuse something like that, it would be him."

"What exactly were these arguments about?" Adam asked. "I find it hard to believe that Mr. Zhang could even manage to get himself remotely riled up over anything."

"I'm not sure. Felix said the topics of conversation were confidential."

"Convenient," Adam commented. "Confidential arguments that Felix witnessed and won't divulge. And forget asking the parties involved when they're all deceased. *And* you can't exactly ask Mr. Zhang, because that would imply you knew about the group. Which I'm guessing you don't want to do?"

"I don't," I said, finally sitting in the seat diagonal Adam. "He's wrong about Mr. Zhang, but I'm telling you, their ties to the group have to be part of the motive. At least a little bit. Felix did say that the objects were missing from each person's possession after their death. Which means that, at the very least, whoever did it has an awareness that those objects are of value. And so while Felix is trying to implicate Mr. Zhang, he's also got another finger pointed in Lois Fan's direction. Which is a whole other story."

"How does he know?"

"About what?" I asked. "That the objects were stolen? Or about Lois?"

"The objects, how would he know they were stolen to begin with?"

I paused. "Well, I don't know, I just assumed that he found out when Mr. Zhang couldn't find them."

"No, you're missing my point," Adam said. "I'm saying, how did he specifically know that they were *stolen* and not just misplaced or potentially lost in the shuffle somehow."

"Oh," I replied, feeling dumbfounded. "I hadn't thought about it like that." After thinking about it for a few more seconds, I said, "Maybe Lydia knows. She didn't seem intrigued by his word choice or anything. Maybe he told her in more detail how he knew and just didn't mention it to me."

"I'd find out if I were you," he said. "Especially about what these supposed arguments were pertaining to. The content of those conversations could implicate someone else who perhaps Felix is trying to protect."

"You think so?" I hadn't even considered the idea that Felix was protecting someone he knew or assumed to be guilty. Times like these I was extra thankful to be dating a police detective.

"What I think, is that I'm hungry." Adam rose from his seat and walked into the kitchen, opening the cupboard where we kept our dishes. "But I do also think there's something this guy isn't telling you. The key to this whole thing could be finding out what he's omitting and why."

I peeked into the paper bag while he went about gathering utensils and napkins. It was as I'd guessed, a large container filled with wings drenched in barbeque sauce. I pulled it out of the bag and placed it on the cleared side of the table. Before anything got ruined, I collected all the loose papers scattered on the other side and put them back into the folder where they'd be safe from the mess we were surely getting ready to make.

He handed me a plate. "You'll have to tell me about this Lois Fan person and what the deal is with her, but with everything else you've told me so far and the fact that this guy happens to know more than he should about everybody else's business, I wouldn't assume he's telling you everything."

CHAPTER
28

Adam and I munched on the barbeque wings while we chatted about the particulars of the case and I felt a sense of appreciation at all the progress we'd made in our relationship. There'd been a time when I had to hide these things from him or ask questions in a hypothetical manner that usually led to him figuring out what I was really up to. There wasn't much I'd gotten past him undetected. He was very good at his job.

He didn't form a judgment on Lois because he said that everything had been Felix's opinion and he'd want someone to corroborate the stories that Lydia's client had been so willing to share about Ms. Fan's character.

After taking the time to talk through things with Adam at length, I wondered about everything I'd learned and what information had been twisted to meet the needs of Felix's story. Sure, the replacements so far *had* been women, and based on Lois's website, I could confirm that she seemed very interested in women's empowerment. But most women were, so that didn't mean she wasn't up to anything scandalous like picking people off until she had everything just as she thought it should be.

So, if Felix *was* protecting someone, who could it be? It obviously wasn't Lois he was trying to shield. And that theory meant that Mr. Zhang and Talia were also not on his favorites list. That left one person: Douglas Chen. Was it possible Felix was protecting him from being exposed?

I knew very little about Douglas Chen, and I recalled that at the meeting Lydia and I'd had with Felix, he'd written off Douglas's involvement with barely a passing remark. Was that a clue?

When I asked Adam what he thought about that, he agreed that it could be very likely. Especially if Douglas was the man with deep pockets. Maybe Felix needed something from him, and Douglas had baited him into helping cover up his dirty deeds in exchange for a favor.

We went to bed shortly after I'd cleaned up the kitchen. Adam took Kikko for her nightly tinkle while I filled the dishwasher and wiped down the table of stray barbeque sauce.

In bed, I laid awake while Adam and Kikko both snored away happily into dreamland. I was always the last to fall asleep on nights like these when my mind refused to shut off, organizing and re-organizing information as I processed it from different angles.

I couldn't even fathom how I'd get through the following workday before I finally met up with Lydia for our undercover mission with Juliette Chu. Sometimes I wished there was a fast-forward button to get through the not so fun parts of life. But then again, maybe you needed those dull parts. It sounded like something Mr. Zhang would say.

That's when my thought roller coaster returned to the idea of Mr. Zhang and his alleged involvement. I wondered how I could find out if what Felix was saying about the arguments he'd witnessed was true. It dawned on me that I could ask Donna. Seeing as I'd told her more than I'd intended and I knew I could trust her to tell me the truth, she seemed like my best option.

I also made a mental note to ask her if she knew anything about Mr. Zhang's history and whether or not it was possible he'd had a child. I hadn't thought of the obvious connection that she might know something because her husband, Thomas, had been so close to Mr. Zhang. Close like a son. Surely, he would have known some of the elderly man's secrets and potentially have told Donna along the way.

It was worth a shot and I would leave no stone unturned until I found something that would make sense of all this mess. And maybe if I could figure out why Felix pointed Lydia and me toward a specific set of people, I'd be one step closer to discovering who the guilty party actually was.

In my heart, I knew it wasn't Mr. Zhang. It couldn't be. I didn't know what I thought about Lois yet, and like Adam, I agreed I should withhold further judgment until I had my chance to talk with her myself.

I fell asleep thinking about how the first thing I'd do in the morning was call Lois Fan and request to meet with her as soon as possible. I didn't know how Lydia was going to feel about it, but that sounded like a problem for tomorrow.

I struggled to wake up, having slept soundly for only a few hours. I hit the snooze button four times before finally giving in and forcing myself to plant both feet on the ground. I sat on the edge of my bed rubbing sleep out of my eyes while Kikko found her way out of the burrow of blanket she'd created.

Since Adam's day started earlier than mine, he'd woken up and left an hour prior to me getting up. Even though I hated for him to leave while I was still sleeping, it helped keep my morning routine on schedule. The less distractions I had, the better.

Dog walk, coffee, makeup application, and I was ready to go. Traffic moved along steadily as I headed to Asia Village.

I slunk in through the main doors, scouting for Mr. Zhang and hoping to avoid him once again. The guilt was too clearly written on my face and I didn't want him to question me with his perceptive abilities. Thankfully, he was not at his usual post outside of his shop, so I skittered over to Ho-Lee Noodle House undeterred and locked myself safely inside.

My day went as it always did: Peter arrived half an hour before opening, the Matrons came at their usual time, a smattering of customers popped in and out at various intervals, Nancy showed up for her split shift, and the clock ticked on as I waited for my shift to end.

On my lunch, I'd called both Donna and Lois, but neither one picked up so I left messages for them to call me back at their earliest convenience.

I'd hoped that somewhere during my day something would happen to help speed things along, but nothing out of the ordinary occurred. I didn't know if that was good or bad.

Part of me had expected at the very least a visit from Talia to inquire about the real reason we'd come by her shop last night. But that was my paranoia getting the better of me again. I'd also anticipated Kimmy dropping by, but when Peter arrived he'd told me that Kimmy's mom had come in early so that both of them could work on an inventory project. She usually found a way to slip out and do things she wasn't supposed to do, but to my surprise it didn't happen.

At five o'clock, I left without incident, which I was thankful for because Megan had to do a double shift at the bar and someone needed to go home and let out Kikko. Since the house Lydia and I were checking out was in Fairview, I'd have plenty of time to run home, let out the dog, change out of my work clothes, and make it back by six.

At 5:58 I pulled up behind Lydia in the single-car driveway that sat to the left of the house. There was a black SUV in front of Lydia's Mustang, which I assumed belonged to Juliette. Lydia got out of her car when I turned off my engine.

She walked over to meet me halfway. "Hey there, chickadee. Are you ready for this?"

"I am. What exactly is our plan?" I said, looking up at the two-story house. It was just as attractive as it had been in the listing photos with its sage green shingles, black shudders, and white trim. "I mean, we're pretending to look at this house, but how are we going to get any information out of her?"

"Well"—she tapped her temple with her index finger—"I got to thinking a good idea might be to pretend like we knew Walter and that he used to be our real estate agent before he passed. She has no way of knowing if that's true. Once we're all like, *oh hey, what a small world*, we can ask some questions about his death. See if she has any reactions to what we say or maybe she'll confess that she doesn't believe his death was an accident."

"Okay," I said with a nod. "That sounds like it'll work." Behind my back I crossed my fingers, hoping it really would. It could be tricky to get people talking, especially when a line of questioning didn't seem altogether natural under the given circumstances, like say for example, showing a home. The hook was to get that other person to feel comfortable, as if they had your total confidence to speak freely.

"I've done this hundreds of times," Lydia reassured me. "Just let me kick off the conversation and then you can jump in. If you think you can make it convincing, you can even say you knew him from Ho-Lee Noodle House or something. I'm sure Walter must have come by Asia Village at least once in his lifetime, so you're not totally lying."

I hadn't thought about it like that prior to her mentioning it, but now that she did, I wondered if we had ever crossed paths. "Okay, I'm ready. Let's go."

She shimmied between our two cars and we made our way up to the covered front landing. There was an ornate brass knocker Lydia used to rap against the door. We waited a few beats, but no one came to greet us.

She tried the doorbell. We could hear it ringing through the house, a repetitive *bing-bong* signaling our arrival. A half minute later and still nothing.

"That's odd," Lydia said. She cupped her hands around her eyes and stood on her tiptoes, trying to peer through the tiny, rectangular window that was a smidge taller than she was. "We know she's here."

"Maybe she's on a phone call or something," I said.

Lydia pounded on the door, adding force with each knock. "Still, she could answer the door at least."

Adam sprung to mind, and I ventured back over to the driveway to where the black SUV was parked and did something he'd mentioned to me in the past. One way to get a grasp on someone's recent activity was to feel the hood of their vehicle for heat. Lydia didn't pay me any attention as I walked away. Now at the front of Juliette's SUV, I held out my palm and pressed it against the hood. It was cool to the touch, which meant that the realtor had been here for at least long enough that her engine was no longer warm.

A sense of uneasiness was beginning to form, and I felt a slight tightness in my chest. When I returned to the covered landing, I found Lydia trying to force open the door, twisting the knob repeatedly and pushing with her shoulder. "It's locked," she said with a groan. "Okay, let's go around back."

It felt like we were trespassing as I quickly scanned the surrounding houses to see if anyone was watching us through their living room window. I followed behind Lydia back to the driveway as we went around the side of the house to the backyard. We were met with the image I'd seen online: an immaculate lawn, unnaturally green, and the patio with its stone grill ready for a summer barbeque.

There were sliding glass doors leading into the house and as we approached them, I realized that my palms had started sweating. "Maybe we should call her cell phone first. You have the number, right?"

Lydia didn't respond, but instead pulled on the handle. To my surprise, the glass door slid open without a hitch. She turned to face me. "You ready?"

The way she said it made me think she'd understood something long before I had. Perhaps I'd been naïve, or maybe I wanted to be more positive than I normally was in these situations. Whatever the case may be, I felt sick to my stomach, and despite my better judgment, I followed Lydia into the house.

There had been venetian blinds obstructing our view and they clattered noisily as we pushed past them into an enclosed dining room area. There were two doorways on opposite sides of the room. One leading down a hallway, and the other presumably to the kitchen.

"Hello?" Lydia called out. "Juliette Chu? Are you in here?"

I stood next to Lydia. "Something doesn't feel right."

"You're not the only one thinking that," she mumbled. "You check the kitchen, I'll go this way." She pointed down the doorway that led to the hall.

With trepidation coursing through my veins, I took small steps toward the kitchen. When I made it to the threshold, I found the all-white kitchen with its granite-top island and stainless-steel appliances. On top of the island sat a cell phone, a box of pastries that I couldn't make out, a red handbag, and a bottled water. Someone was definitely here.

But it wasn't until I took a step farther into the kitchen that I noticed a pair of feet sticking out from behind the island, one black high heel on, one off.

My heart raced and beat so loudly as I took another step forward. "Lydia!" I yelled. "Come in here!"

"What?" she yelled back from somewhere in the house, sounding a world away.

Another step forward. I held onto the island as I rounded the corner. That's when I screamed.

Lydia came storming into the room. "What? What's going on in here?"

I clenched my eyes shut and pointed to the floor. "I found Juliette."

CHAPTER
29

I'd frozen in place, keeping my eyes shut for as long as possible, but Lydia was quick to act. She pulled me out of the way forcing me to open my eyes and steady myself. I watched her as she stepped in front of me and knelt down to where Juliette's body lay. She placed her index and middle fingers on Lydia's throat, checking for a pulse. I wanted to smack myself for not having done the same, but I'd panicked and assumed the worst.

Lydia rose from her knelt position. "Well, she's dead. There's no pulse." She ran a hand through her hair. "Dammit, we have to call this in."

I stood there staring and feeling useless. Despite everything I'd been through, death was a hard thing for me to deal with. I didn't accept it in all its grim finality.

"What do you think happened?" I stammered. "It doesn't look like there's any blood or anything."

Lydia surveyed the spotless kitchen. "No clue. It doesn't look like she hit her head either. At least not at this angle. I'm going to run out to my car for something, do you mind calling this in? I figure you have the Fairview Police Department on speed dial."

Without waiting for me to respond, Lydia disappeared into the other room. She didn't use the front door and instead went back the way we'd come in. My guess was that she didn't want to touch anything she didn't need to.

I pulled my cell phone out of my purse with a shaky hand and found the saved contact I had for the police station. Lydia was right, I did have it on speed dial. The number I called was their emergency line and when the dispatcher picked up, I told her what I'd found. I couldn't remember the location's address off the top of my head, but there was a printout-listing page laying on the counter next to Juliette's purse with informational tidbits about the house. I recited the address to the dispatcher, letting her know that it wasn't my house and that it was up for sale. When she asked my name and I gave it to her, she paused, and I wondered if in her head she was saying, *Oh, you again?*

She promised that someone would be there within ten minutes, and I dreaded to think that Adam would be the one to show up for this. But, he and his partner, Higgins, were the only two detectives the station currently had, so the chances were just about one hundred percent.

While I waited for Lydia to return, I reminded myself that we hadn't done anything wrong. Juliette Chu had been dead prior to us even arriving, and aside from Lydia checking her pulse our fingerprints weren't on anything aside from the slider door we'd used to come in.

It was going to be fine. I was fine. We were fine. It was all fine. Well, except it wasn't fine for Juliette.

Thankfully, Lydia returned to save me from my thoughts and I noticed right away she had on a pair of latex gloves.

"What are you doing?"

"I'm snooping through her stuff before the cops get here," she said. "There might be a clue in her things."

"Why did you have me call the cops then?" I asked. "They're going to be here in the next ten minutes."

Lydia went about opening Juliette's handbag, shuffling through whatever items it held. "Because if any of the neighbors are watching us, I don't want there to be a gap in time. If the cops know we were here for longer than a few minutes, they're going to wonder what we were up to . . . no matter whose girlfriend you might be." She pulled a wallet out of the purse and rifled through it.

"What can I do to help?"

"I need you to be lookout. Watch for the cops and then we'll go out the back way and circle round to meet them. Don't use the front door. Leave everything as it is as much as you can. The last thing we need is to implicate ourselves any further."

"Should I even be walking through the house?"

Finding nothing of consequence in Juliette's wallet, she stuffed it back into the purse and kept digging around, checking side pockets and the zippered pouch that was standard in almost every purse ever made. "From what I can see, most everything is hardwood, so you won't leave any prints on the carpet. Now go, so I can concentrate," she said.

I left her to finish snooping through Juliette's things and went to stand watch in the living room. I stood in front of the large bay window, trying to get a good angle through the mini blinds that were opened at an awkward slant. It felt like a godsend because I didn't think any of the neighbors could spot me here if they happened to be spying on us.

Though I felt uncomfortable and rigid, it was a relief

to not have to stay in the same room as Juliette's body. I gave Lydia a lot of credit for being able to keep herself together mentally while she did what needed to be done.

Eight minutes later, I spotted a police cruiser coming down the road and an unmarked black sedan trailing behind it. "Lydia!" I yelled as I sprinted back to the kitchen. "They're here."

I found her taking snapshots with her phone camera of all the items on the island when I returned. I dreaded wondering if she'd also taken photos of Juliette to review at a later time. I didn't ask because I thought it would be better if I didn't know the specifics. Edward Price's job offer to join his team of investigators popped into my mind and I concluded that even if there'd been any interest, I didn't think I'd have the stomach for the job.

"Let's go," she said. She stuffed her cell phone into her back pocket, removed the latex gloves, and stuck them in the pockets of her denim jacket.

I followed as we moved quickly through the house to the back door and into the back yard. We reached the driveway just as two uniformed officers whom I recognized got out of the patrol car. No one had exited the unmarked vehicle just yet. They'd parked in the street in front of the house because my car and Lydia's car, plus Juliette's SUV, took up all available space.

My stomach flip flopped as I thought about my first initial eye contact with Adam. I had failed to mention to him last night that I was going to attempt a meeting with Juliette Chu. It hadn't been my intention to leave it out of everything else that I told him, and I hoped he wouldn't perceive it as if I'd been holding out on him on purpose.

I recognized the two cops, officers McNeeley and Gonzalez. More times than not, they were the beat cops who showed up to secure a scene when I called.

They greeted Lydia and I with head nods, their hands resting on their duty belts.

Lydia stepped in front of me, extending her hand to Gonzalez. "Lydia Shepard, I'm a licensed PI and I am carrying a concealed weapon."

My eyes bulged and I tried to cover my shock. I hadn't known that Lydia was hiding a gun under her jacket. It made sense to me now that she'd had it on this whole time. Despite it being spring, it was a little warmer than usual and I'd been running around all day with short sleeves.

She produced a business card from her back pocket and handed it over to them. Gonzalez took it and read it over. He then looked up and asked, "So what exactly were you doing here?"

As she started to answer, the front doors of the unmarked car sprung open at the same time. I watched Adam get out with a look of exasperation on his face. I could tell from all the way over here that his jaw muscles were tense. His tie flew over his shoulder as the breeze caught it, and he hurried to adjust it.

Higgins ambled out of the car with little expression, his demeanor always on the side of good-natured observer. They joined at the head of their vehicle, exchanged a few words, and then split as they neared the driveway. Higgins went in the opposite direction of where we stood; Adam came directly toward us.

I'd missed half of what Lydia had said and caught the tail end of her answer as Adam was walking up. ". . . and so we headed round back when no one answered. The slider to the patio was unlocked and fearing that something was wrong we decided to enter the property. I'm glad we did," she said, her eyes sliding in my direction. "No telling how long she'd been there like that."

"And you're sure that the victim was deceased upon arrival?" McNeeley asked.

Adam winked at me from behind McNeeley. Though the gesture was affectionate, his face remained stoic, in what I have come to refer to as "detective mode."

Lydia answered, "Yes, I checked for a pulse when we arrived on the scene and unfortunately she didn't have one."

Gonzalez noticed that Adam had arrived and nudged McNeeley. They both turned around to acknowledge him. McNeeley said, "Hey, Detective Trudeau, EMT and someone from the coroner's office are both on their way. ETA around twenty-five minutes."

Adam nodded. "Good, McNeeley, secure the scene. Gonzalez, you're with me. Grab some statement forms from the cruiser first so we can have these ladies fill out an initial report."

"You got it, boss," Gonzalez said with a two-finger salute.

When the two officers went about their duties, I held back the natural instinct I had to hug Adam. He squeezed my hand, and then greeted Lydia. "Shepard, good to see you again."

"Trudeau." Lydia reached for his hand. "Always nice to see you, but of course, not under these circumstances."

He grimaced. "Yeah, you should try calling on my better half when the situation doesn't involve a growing list of dead bodies. What the hell is going on?"

With an awkward laugh, Lydia said, "I wouldn't get her mixed up in anything I didn't think she could handle. She's quite capable." She nudged me with her elbow. "But as far as what the hell is going on . . . well, that I have no idea about. It's what I've been trying to figure out."

"Can you tell me anything about the vic?" he asked.

Lydia shook her head. "I'm afraid not. I didn't even get to question her. The most interaction we had is when I set up the appointment to meet her here."

"Cause of death?" Adam's eyes flitted in my direction.

"Unknown," Lydia replied. "If my suspicions are right though, I'm guessing she was poisoned. There's a box of some type of cake things on the counter and a bottle of water that she'd clearly drank from . . . Potentially one of those items is laced?"

Adam pursed his lips. "I better go inside and see for myself." He squeezed my shoulder, truly looking at me for the first time since he'd shown up. For the briefest of moments, his eyes betrayed the concern of a significant other before he returned to detective mode. "You okay?"

I nodded, smiling to ease his mind. "I'm okay. Don't worry. Lydia is here with me, go do what you gotta do."

Gonzalez returned with two sets of clipboards, which both came with matching statement forms and Bic pens. "Fill these out," he said, handing one to each of us. "Maybe sit in the car." He jerked his head to the side. "People are starting to watch."

I saw a few people standing in their doorways and noticed that Higgins was talking to someone next door. I couldn't see his face, but he had his mini steno pad out and was scribbling furiously as the neighbor spoke. I was horrible at reading lips, so I had no idea what was being said.

Lydia pulled her car keys out of her pocket. "Come on, we can sit in my car together."

We got into her car as Adam and Gonzalez disappeared into the backyard. McNeeley was busy putting up crime scene tape across the front door.

When we were inside Lydia's car where no one could hear us, she pulled out her phone and turned to me. "Look at this," she said, handing her phone over.

"Am I going to see anything that will scar me for life?" I asked.

She smirked. "Never fear, I wouldn't do that to ya. It's just a picture of the stuff Juliette had with her. Take a look." She encouraged me by offering her phone again.

I took it gingerly into my hands and studied the picture she wanted me to see. It was the box of pastry I wasn't able to identify upon first glance. The lid had been removed and placed off to the side. It touted that the contents were a dozen gourmet pineapple cakes. The bite-sized, short-bread-covered treats filled with jam were not individually wrapped as they often came. Instead the twelve cakes sat unwrapped and nestled in slotted, plastic dividers. Two of the slots were empty.

"My money says that right there"—Lydia paused, pointing at the picture—"is the murder weapon."

CHAPTER
30

When we were finished filling out our statements, we tracked down McNeeley, who'd completed his task of securing the perimeter. In the meantime, an EMT had shown up followed by a car emblazoned with the seal for Cuyahoga County and below it a decal that read Medical Examiner.

McNeeley directed the newcomers to where they needed to go before turning his attention to the two of us.

Lydia handed over her clipboard first. "Do you think they need us to stick around? I have someplace I need to be."

McNeeley took my form. "I think you're all set to go. If we need anything else or have questions, we'll give you a call. Thanks, ladies." He turned to me. "Lana, nice to see you again."

I blushed. "Be safe out there."

He tipped his head at us, then made his way back up the drive, disappearing into the backyard.

"You want a drink?" Lydia asked. "I sure could use about sixteen of them right about now."

"I thought you had to be somewhere?"

"Nah, I just said that so we could get out of here. I had a not too pleasant chat with the coroner a few weeks ago and I'd rather not stick around."

I could only imagine what that had been about. Since it had to do with the coroner's office, I didn't ask her to elaborate. "Sure, wanna go to the Zodiac? Megan's working tonight and I'm sure there's a free drink in it for us."

She shrugged. "Yeah, why not."

We hopped in our cars, and I took one last look up at the house before pulling out of the driveway. I wondered who would end up buying it now that it had a giant stain on its reputation.

The Zodiac had enough people that it felt lively, but it wasn't packed and I was okay with that. The last thing I needed right now after what we'd just been through was overstimulation.

Megan knew immediately that something was wrong, and probably having Lydia with me was somewhat of a giveaway. She rushed over as we took our seats. "What's going on?" she asked, her eyes shifting back and forth between me and Lydia. "Something happened didn't it? What happened?"

"You know how we were supposed to meet with Juliette Chu?"

"Yeah . . ." She covered her mouth. "Oh god, what."

Lydia beat me to the punch. "She's dead."

Megan's eyes widened. "You've got to be kidding."

"Nope, I'm afraid not," Lydia replied. "We both need something with whiskey in it."

Megan reached across the bar and squeezed my hand. "Are you okay?"

I nodded. "I'm fine. I mean, as fine as I can be. You know this kind of thing is never easy for me. And she was . . . young," I said, looking down at my feet. "Too young."

"She was thirty-two," Lydia added.

Megan sighed. "Ugh, that's terrible. Do you know what happened?"

Lydia shook her head. "Not for sure, but I'm betting she was poisoned. Just like the others."

"Well, like George," I corrected her. "We still don't know for sure that's what happened to everybody else."

"Oh come on," Lydia said. "You know as much as I do that these murders are connected. There is no other explanation."

Megan held up a finger. "I'll be back with strong drinks."

When Megan was gone, I shifted to face Lydia. "I agree with you and I don't think they're separate happenstance deaths within the same group of people. But officially we don't know for sure. It's probably Adam's influence causing me to say that."

Lydia pulled out her phone, opened her photo album, and chose the same picture she'd shown me earlier in the car. "I'm telling you, this is how whoever it is, is doing it. Hopefully they get fingerprints off the packaging or something lucky."

"I think at the very least Adam will have the pineapple cakes tested for aconite. That'll connect the two deaths and hopefully prove that George Wong was murdered. It might be enough for them to open up the cases for Walter and Theodore again."

"I should probably meet with Felix and ask him if he'd know anything about who could have given these to Juliette."

"I wouldn't tell him anything," I replied.

She raised a brow. "Why not?"

Megan returned with our drinks, just in the nick of time. I took a long sip of my whiskey and Coke before going into story-time mode and updating Lydia on everything that had transpired since last we spoke. I held off on telling her about the parts that involved Kimmy inserting herself into Talia and Lois's after-hours conversation until the very end.

By the time I was finished, she had her elbows propped up on the bar with her hands in her hair. Her face was covered and I couldn't read her facial expressions.

Megan had to leave to tend to some customers, so it was just Lydia and me hashing it out.

We sat for a full minute in silence, which felt like eternity, while I waited for some type of reaction to anything I'd said. Finally, she let out a groan. "Lana, you suck at this confidentiality thing. No offense, but you do."

"I know," I said. "I'm sorry, but you have to admit, it got us some headway with Lois Fan."

Lydia lifted her head. "If she'd called me back by now, I may not be so willing to agree with that statement. I even went so far as to stop by her office unannounced hoping to catch her off guard, but I couldn't get past the damn receptionist."

"I put in a call to her this morning, and she hasn't called me back yet, but I'm hoping to get some face time with her in the next couple of days."

"Hopefully it's soon," she said, sipping her drink. "These two murders are closer together, which means whoever is doing this is becoming impatient."

"What do you think changed?" I asked.

Lydia dropped her chin, shaking her head. "I don't know. And it's really pissing me off. The other murders were all men and longstanding members of the group. Juliette was a female and a new addition. She didn't have time to even get her feet wet. The only other options are that she saw something she wasn't supposed to and became a liability, or she wasn't stepping in line and someone wasn't having it."

I nodded. "And it also throws Felix's theory right out the window. If Lois was the one who recommended her for the position, I doubt she'd be the one to get rid of her."

"Well, his theory about Lois, maybe. It might still be possible that Lois recruited her but then, like I said, Juliette wasn't falling in line with her plans. Either way, it doesn't remove Talia or exonerate Mr. Zhang." When she caught the pained expression on my face she added, "Unfortunately. I wish that it did."

"What do you think about Adam's theory that Felix is misdirecting us?" I wanted to get away from making Mr. Zhang a part of the discussion. And when I'd told her about the misdirection idea a few minutes earlier she hadn't made any comments or shown interest in it.

She shrugged. "Trudeau has some good theories, but I don't know if I'm sold. I think it would be pretty risky for Felix to try misguiding us. One slip-up and he could incriminate himself or whoever he's protecting. But the idea of someone doing that isn't totally unheard of. I need time to re-evaluate the situation with that in mind."

I decided to leave it alone for the moment versus trying to convince her of anything. I had begun to form some ideas of my own, but I wasn't ready to share them with her just yet. I needed to find out some more information from Donna before I felt comfortable even mentioning what I had in mind. What I did end up saying was, "I think it's a possibility that the lack of a direct replacement has something to do with who's being killed, and looking at it that way might serve us better than trying to figure out what Felix knows and isn't saying."

Lydia slid her drink back and forth between her hands, letting it move a few inches through the condensation the chilled glass had created. She was deep in thought and I assumed she hadn't heard me, but then she said, "Actually, you bring up a good point. Juliette had no kids, was an only child, and wasn't married."

It felt like a punch in the gut thinking that Juliette's parents would now have lost their only child. Just as painful to think about was that Juliette had been robbed of a future that held so much promise. It also infuriated me to think that whoever was doing this thought they were getting away with it. "So maybe we have to look at who's going to be next . . . or at least potentially. We can't assume this person is done . . . can we?"

"No, we can't." Lydia removed the cocktail straw from her drink and emptied the contents of her glass in one big gulp. "There are five members left. If memory serves me correctly, the two women—Talia and Lois—don't have kids and are both single."

"Talia is a foster child, so I know she doesn't have any other direct family," I added.

Lydia massaged her forehead. "And I remember seeing that both Douglas and Felix have sons in their twenties. I haven't confirmed anything about your good friend Mr. Zhang yet, or about whether or not what Felix said about Lois being his daughter is factual. I wrangled up her birth certificate, but under the father's name it's blank."

"So, I think—and maybe I'm being bold in saying this." I paused. "But I think instead of being the guilty parties, maybe Lois and Talia are actually the ones in danger."

Lydia inspected her empty glass and then signaled

Megan from across the bar for another drink. "Lana, I think you might just be on to something."

That night after I'd gotten home, walked the dog, and showered, I took a full five minutes to just breathe and stare into nothingness. Afterward, I got out my notebook along with the files from Lydia and made myself comfy at the dining room table.

With Kikko at my feet, I mumbled to myself while jotting down the significant events that had happened since the previous day. I spent considerable time notating the details of Juliette's death while the whole thing was fresh in my mind.

Normally I would have spent time trying to find out who her enemies were or riffled through her social media in hopes of finding a telling post. But, in this instance, I didn't deem it immediately necessary, seeing as I suspected a few specific people and I doubted they would be mentioned anywhere on Juliette's social accounts.

Even though I didn't include Mr. Zhang in my list of suspects, I knew that Lydia was still holding space for the possibility. I began to wonder if clearing his name should take precedence ahead of anything else I did. In some ways, it felt self-serving, and I didn't know if I was being objective or not.

Mr. Zhang did have the means. And I supposed he did have the opportunity as well. But still, no clear motive. I could not see him hurting people just so he could confiscate power from the others. Also, how would that even serve him? There was a slim chance that perhaps he wanted to doctor the group in his favor. If the victims in question were noncompliant, he may have wanted others who were more malleable.

But it still wouldn't explain withholding the original objects, which he could just rightfully pass to the next candidate. He also wasn't a demanding man, and I couldn't see him acting in this way under any circumstance. No, it wouldn't work for me. Objective or not.

I twirled my pen like a baton, my mind roaming this way and that. Nothing made sense anymore. Looking at the pile of papers, the files that Lydia provided, I childishly blamed them. I normally didn't have this much information, and maybe it wasn't jiving with me. This wasn't how I worked.

My phone rang, causing me to jump and drop my pen. It fell to the ground missing Kikko's head by an inch. She jerked her body back and grunted.

It was already ten p.m., who would be calling me? When I checked the readout, I didn't recognize the number. I almost let it go to voice mail, but with everything going on, I decided to answer. "Hello?"

"Hello, is this Lana Lee?" a woman asked.

"Yes . . ."

"Hi Lana, sorry to contact you so late. This is Lois Fan returning your call."

"Oh, hi," I said, sitting up straight. "Thanks for calling me back, no worries about the time. I was up anyways."

"Yes, well regardless, I do apologize. I was caught up in some business for most of the day that required all of my attention."

I considered for a minute that her business might have something to do with Juliette Chu.

There was a brief silence while I contemplated this theory. I didn't know what Lois wanted me to say in return and I was having a hard time thinking of words to string together as a sentence.

Finally, with some exasperation in her tone, she said,

"Do you have time to meet with me tomorrow? Say nine a.m.? I'd like to meet and go over the specifics for this dye manufacturer that needs a hair model. You'd be perfect for their new fashion colors poster."

"I have to work tomorrow morning. I'm the manager and I doubt I can get anyone to cover for me at this time of night. Could I meet with you at eleven thirty?"

She made it a point to huff. "I suppose I could move some things around."

"Great, thank you. I really appreciate it."

"My office address is on the card. If you have any existing headshots, bring them. We'll take new photos of you anyhow."

"Photos?" I asked. "Tomorrow?"

"Well yes, I need to give something to my client."

I cringed. "Uh, okay."

She paused, and I worried whether she was rethinking her decision to meet with me. But she said, "Okay, I'll see you tomorrow then."

We hung up and I wondered what I'd just gotten myself into.

With my head in my hands, I let out a groan that could have very well been heard in the neighboring apartment. When I'd put in the call to Lois, I hadn't imagined that I'd actually have to go through with any of the modeling parts.

Whether I wanted to go through with it or not, it was the only current way to speak to Lois.

Kikko, sensing my upset, began pawing at my leg, whimpering until I pet her. I looked down at her, scratching her wrinkled, fuzzy head. "I tell ya, Kikko, the things I do for justice."

CHAPTER
31

The following morning, the hours of nine to eleven dragged on like the slow drip of a leaky faucet, even with the Mahjong Matrons filling in part of the time. If they'd wanted to ask me any questions about what I was up to, they kept it to themselves, and I didn't offer up any new information. I was still feeling raw from the previous day, and being social wasn't at the top of my to-do list.

The news of Juliette Chu's death had been on the eleven o'clock news the night before, and by morning, it was all over the internet. But the Matrons said not one word about it. At first, I thought it was strange, but then I realized they probably had no idea who she was. And if they didn't know anything about the Eight Immortals, they wouldn't put together the association.

I sludged through the first two hours of work with a pit in my stomach. I kept thinking about how I'd have to take photos and wondered if I could manage not to look self-conscious during the process. Truth was, I had no intention of going through with the whole thing. I just needed to buy enough time to have my meeting with Lois Fan.

Then another thought occurred to me. What if I *didn't* get picked for the modeling job? Would I be offended? Would I take it personally? I hadn't considered what effect this whole thing might inadvertently have on my ego.

Juliette Chu's headshot flashed in my mind, and I put all the superficial worries I had aside. This wasn't about me.

Finally, when Nancy arrived at eleven I felt that my day could truly begin and I quickly spouted off an excuse that there'd been a mistake with the bank deposit from the previous day and I had to go to the bank in person and correct it right away.

Neither Nancy nor Peter questioned me, though I could tell that Peter had wanted to make a comment before I left. He refrained, and I left with a bank deposit bag just as I normally did.

Because I was really going to need to stop at the bank, I had no time to waste. I flew through the plaza, hoping that Kimmy, or Mr. Zhang for that matter, wouldn't notice me passing by. Thankfully I didn't see either of them and neither of them saw me, as far as I knew.

The bank wasn't far from Asia Village but it was in the opposite direction I needed to go in order to get to Golden Flower Modeling.

With patience, I made it down Center Ridge Road, getting stopped repeatedly through the cluster of traffic lights that littered the business section of the busy street.

After I used the night deposit box, I backtracked down Center Ridge and made my way toward I-90. Golden Flower Modeling was on Superior Avenue in the heart of the city's true Chinatown.

My eyes flitted back and forth between the clock on my dashboard and the road as I made sure to obey the speed limits. It wasn't going to do me any good to get stopped by a cop, or to get a ticket.

I did manage to make it with a few minutes to spare, and thankfully the old brick commercial building had its own lot so I wouldn't have to worry about street parking. Finding a spot easily enough, I parked the car and scurried into the back entrance of the building.

Lois's business card said that Golden Flower Modeling was on the second floor. There was an elevator that showed it was sitting on the seventh floor. There was a wrought iron staircase to the right of the elevators. I opted for taking the stairs since I only had about three minutes before being late. Who knew how long the elevator car would take to come back down?

I took the steps two at a time, losing my breath quickly and realizing just how out of shape I was. The hopes I'd had since the beginning of the year about getting into a solid workout routine had yet to be actualized and I berated myself as I made my way to the second floor. I was too young to be this worn out by two flights of steps. *When this case is over*, I promised myself.

I whipped the door open to the second-floor landing and was met by a young Asian receptionist sitting behind a semicircular desk.

She gawked at me while I gasped for air. "Can I help you with something?" She said it with such disdain, you'd think I'd soiled her precious waiting area with my sheer existence.

"Yes, hi," I said, catching my breath. "I have an appointment for eleven thirty with Lois Fan." I walked up to the counter, leaning on it for support.

Without so much as a smile, she turned her attention to the computer monitor in front of her, clacking on a few keys with her acrylic nails, her charm bracelet jingling with the motion. Then she clicked her mouse a few times before looking up at me. "Lana Lee?"

"That's me."

"Have a seat," she replied with all the personality of a flat tire. "Lois will be out in a moment to get you."

The waiting room was empty except for the two of us, and I was relieved that there wasn't another model prospect to contend with. My self-consciousness had already elevated beyond the level of "through the roof."

The walls were covered with framed magazine ads and covers featuring predominantly Asian models. I assumed they were Lois's clients, and I took a moment to scan through the images instead of sitting down.

One photo caught my eye. The woman in the picture was definitely younger, but there was no mistaking that it was a younger Talia Sun. She was standing at an angle, her hair tossed into a high ponytail secured by a gold coil. The hot pink dress she wore was skimpy—something Kimmy might wear to her job at the Black Garter—and had a taffeta bottom that was just long enough to cover her butt. Matching sparkling stiletto heels covered in hot pink rhinestones accentuated the height she already had and made her legs look a mile long.

Though the photo was impressive, the Talia that I knew . . . yeah, this wasn't her at all. I wondered what the rest of her portfolio looked like and if she'd done anything that was more her style. I didn't have time to think about it for too long because my mind registered that a door was opening somewhere and then I heard Lois calling my name.

When I turned to greet her, I noted her look of dissatisfaction. If I'd had any doubts, they were quickly squashed by the bluntness she met me with. "You didn't style your hair?"

I walked toward her, smoothing down any stray fly-aways I'd acquired going up the two flights of stairs. "I ironed it . . . but I didn't know if I should do anything else. I've never done this before," I said.

She'd been holding the door open to a long hallway and ushered me to walk through. "We'll make do, I suppose." Stepping in front of me, she led the way to her office, and I tried peeking in the rooms we passed, but they were windowless and all the doors were shut.

We got to the end of the hallway and she opened the door, motioning for me to follow. "Have a seat." She pointed to the leather chairs across from her desk.

I did as I was told without adding any further comments about my hair. *Remember why you're really here, Lana.*

Behind her desk, she busied herself on her laptop without so much as a word to me. If I was in a different position, I might have called her out on her rudeness, or at the very least, made some type of passive aggressive remark. But I didn't think I could afford to lose this chance to meet with her and finally get some answers.

She finished typing something and then her eyes darted back and forth as she read through whatever she'd been looking at. Clasping her hands together, she nodded. "Okay, great. My stylist, Hope, can fit you in. She's working with someone else but is available in about twenty minutes. That gives me enough time to get some information from you before we go any further."

Lois searched through a tiered filing organizer, plucking pages from each tray.

I had to somehow take control of the conversation before I got sucked further into this mess. "How long have you known Talia?" I asked.

"A long time," she said, focusing on the forms she was gathering.

"Was she discovered or did she seek you out?" I had no idea how else to get her talking. We had nothing to talk about and I wasn't ready to show my hand.

She inhaled deeply. "You could say in a manner of speaking that she sought me out."

What the heck did that mean? I wanted to ask, but she didn't give me the chance.

"If you want to know more about Ms. Sun, you should ask her yourself. I'm sure she'd be willing to discuss all of this with you at a more appropriate time. Right now, let's try and stay on task."

Lois didn't know it, but I was staying on task. With Talia as our only common link, I didn't know what other line of questioning I could go forward with. It suddenly felt like I didn't know what I was doing, yet I'd done this sort of thing several times in the past.

I concluded again that it was because I was working under different circumstances and maybe it just wasn't me. That had to be the explanation.

Lois straightened the papers she'd collected by tapping them firmly against her desk. Outstretching her hand, she offered them to me. "I need you to fill these out. They're all very standard."

I sat there, unwilling to take them. *It's now or never, Lana. Don't get sucked into this.*

Lois waved the stack at me. "Well, go on."

I didn't know if I was going to regret this later or not, but I'd run out of time. And I had to do things my way. Especially after what had happened to Juliette. "Did you know George Wong?"

It was clear that I'd caught her off guard because she sputtered her reply. "Wh-what . . . why would you ask about him?"

She hadn't denied knowing him, so that was a start. "How about Juliette Chu?"

The assertive façade that she'd held on to was deteriorating and I could sense that I'd struck a nerve by bringing up Juliette. "What exactly are you doing here, Ms. Lee? I'm gathering you're not actually interested in a modeling job. Who are you and what is it that you want?" The question came out with a sound of defeat. Her shoulders sagged and her eyes appeared to glass over with tears.

Gently, I said, "I'm someone who can help."

CHAPTER
32

- - - - - - - - - - - - - -

Her eyes widened with disbelief. "You? How exactly do you qualify as someone who can help? And what exactly is it that you're helping with? I still don't understand what's going on."

I was making a snap judgment call on believing in her innocence, but I had to take the chance that she was free of any guilt because there was a large possibility based on what had been discovered so far that she was actually in danger. "I'll get to all that, I promise," I said. "But I need you to be honest with me about some things because I think . . . based on your reaction . . . that you're not guilty of any wrongdoing. However, I think that there's someone out there who's trying to make it look that way."

She gasped, dropping the papers on her desk. She'd been holding onto them as if they were her lifeline. "Me? Why would anybody want me to look guilty? I haven't done anything. Who sent you here?"

"No one sent me," I reassured her. "I came here because I'm looking into the deaths of George Wong, Walter Kang, and Theodore Yeh. And . . . unfortunately Juliette Chu as well. I don't think any of their deaths were accidents and whoever did do it is trying to make it appear as if you were involved one way or another."

She didn't respond immediately, flopping backward in her leather executive chair. I gave her a minute to process what I'd said. Finally, she replied, "If you're mentioning these people, then you must know about . . . us."

"I do."

Lois clutched the arm rests with both hands and thrust herself forward. "Who told you? Have you told anyone else?"

"I'm not at liberty to say," I said, taking a page out of Lydia's book. "And no, I haven't told anybody." It was a fib, but I didn't want to waste time explaining about Megan, Kimmy, and Trudeau. "There is a PI that knows, though. She was the one originally hired to look into the deaths."

"And how exactly are you involved in all this?"

"Lydia Shepard, the PI, she was the one to bring me on as a consultant."

"Lydia Shepard? So not the girl who I saw you with the other day?"

I laughed. "No, she's not a PI. She and her family have a shop at Asia Village. She's a childhood friend of mine."

"If someone has asked you to look into this and has connected the deaths, then that means this person must belong to our group."

I chose not to respond and hoped that my face didn't betray me by exposing the truth. It wouldn't be hard for her to narrow down who'd hired Lydia considering there were only four people it could have been. And I'm sure she'd have eliminated Talia as a possibility since they were so close.

"Miss Lee . . ." She paused. A moment later, she held

up a finger. "Just one minute." She reached for her desk phone, typed in a few numbers, and waited. When the other person picked up, Lois said, "Justine? Be a doll and do me a favor. Can you get in touch with Hope and tell her that the thing I needed her for is no longer necessary?" Another pause. "Yes, thank you."

Hanging up the phone, she regarded me once again. "Miss Lee, you have to tell me who hired you and who is trying to pin their deaths on me. I won't stand for it."

"I'm sorry," I replied. "But I can't do that."

She groaned, slamming a fist down on her desk. "It can only be a handful of people, Miss Lee. I demand you tell me who it is."

"Right now, who hired Lydia isn't my biggest concern." *At least not yet*, I thought. "But what I do need to know is who would go after these specific people? And why would they work so quickly to get rid of Juliette? Did something happen with her to put a target on her back?"

Lois inhaled deeply through her nose. "Juliette has done nothing. Absolutely nothing but excel at her job. She was in the process of working with a developer to create affordable modern homes in Parma. One of those cluster developments that are now all the rage. With her impressive list of clients to offer as buyers, she felt confident it would go through. It was the last thing we talked about. We planned to celebrate once they finalized their deal."

"Do you think that could have anything to do with it?"

She shook her head. "I wouldn't think so. And she hadn't said anything that would raise any red flags in my opinion."

"What about the others? Were they involved with anything that would put them in danger?"

"If they were, I didn't know anything about it." She gritted her teeth. "I knew they didn't all just up and die. I knew it. Theodore never had heart trouble. And Walter wasn't a klutz, he had impeccable grace and practiced tai chi every morning. He'd never go flying down a set of stairs." She glanced up at me. "But you can never be too sure of these things. Who am I to say who has heart trouble and who doesn't? And anyone can be involved in an accident no matter how balanced they are. But deep down I knew that something wasn't right."

"Did you share that opinion with anyone else?"

"Only with one person," she said. "If you know of the Eight Immortals, then you surely know Wei Zhang."

"Yes, I've known Mr. Zhang my entire life."

She cocked her head at me. "How?"

"My family owns Ho-Lee Noodle House and we've been friends with Mr. Zhang since the plaza first opened."

Lois sat up in her seat as recognition set in.

"He's also dating my grandmother," I added.

Her eyes widened at this. "You're the Lee daughter that he is always speaking of . . . Betty's girl. With Lee being such a common surname I hadn't realized you were the same person. You are Jing Hua's grandchild."

"Jing Hua" translated to something along the lines of "Peaceful Flower," and I remember thinking how beautiful that was when I'd first heard it spoken and translated. But much like Mr. Zhang, few people reference my grandmother by her first name. "How do you know about my grandmother?"

She looked down at her hands and then back up at me. "Not many people know this, but Mr. Zhang, as you call him . . . he's my father."

I tried my best to keep my jaw from dropping but failed. So it *was* true. I collected myself and then asked, "Why have we never heard of you? Why is it such a secret?"

Again, she sat back in her chair, this time leaning her

head against the cushioned headrest. "My parents were briefly married . . . and when I say briefly, I mean less than a year. My mother, for all her high points, had some very low ones as well. When my father failed to give up his business to become part of the corporate world like she desperately wanted him to, she left him without so much as a note. A few weeks later, she sent divorce papers to him. She didn't tell him she was pregnant or anything, wanting to have no ties to him. She moved to Chicago, where her father's business was headquartered."

"What kind of company did your grandfather own?"

"An extremely large chain of laundering service companies across the United States. He had a shop in every Chinatown across America and wanted my father to manage the Eastern territory. It was quite a big deal for an Asian who'd immigrated here to have such a successful business back then. It was nearly unheard of when my grandfather first started. He was smart to operate within the ethnic parts of the cities, because he had so much support."

Knowing Mr. Zhang, I knew he liked the simple life, and I couldn't imagine him wanting to be a businessman that traveled back and forth between every major city east of the Mississippi. "So if your parents split, and Mr. Zhang didn't know who you were or that you even existed . . . how did you end up here with him?" My mind was spinning, but I had to stave off my shock until after our meeting was over. And here I'd thought Kimmy's secret employ at the Black Garter was the best-kept secret in town.

"Shortly before my mother died, she came clean with me. When I was still a baby, she'd remarried the man I'd come to think was my father. They divorced when I was still young, and she remarried two more times after that.

Always finding something wrong with everyone around her . . . including me." She looked away. "I also didn't want to be a part of the family business. I wanted to be a model. I didn't want to manage laundry companies or spend my life jumping from one city to the next. So I stopped speaking with her when I turned eighteen and moved out on my own, living in New York for a little while."

"That must have been hard," I said, imagining what it would have been like if I had moved away at such an early age, especially to a city like New York.

"It was indeed, but it's where all the best fashion and modeling opportunities were, and I knew that if I could make it there . . ." She snorted. "Well, you know the song, I'm sure."

I chuckled with ease, forgetting for a couple of seconds why I was really here. "You'd make it anywhere," I finished.

Lois smiled, genuinely, for the first time. "Exactly. And I did well, being one of the few Asian models out there. I was different . . . exotic"—she rolled her eyes—"but I was thriving. It hadn't been easy and that's when I knew that I wanted to help other girls like me achieve the same thing."

"I have to say, that's a commendable goal."

"Yes, well, before I could go forward with any of my plans, I needed more money than I had. And perhaps an investor of sorts. I didn't know what to do, really. I hadn't gone to college or had any official training with running a business. So I went home to ask my family for help."

I leaned forward. "And did they help you?"

With a sigh, she replied, "No. And on top of it, I found out that my mother was severely ill. I couldn't bring myself to leave her like that, so I stayed to help take care of her until she passed away. Shortly before her death is when she told me about my real father. She said she couldn't let the information die with her. She regretted keeping me from him for her own selfish purposes."

"I'm so sorry," I said.

"Don't be," she replied. "I've made peace with it. I'm only glad that I was able to find my father still alive and well. I worried that he might have died before I'd have a chance to meet him."

"So that's why you came here and stayed . . . but . . . how . . . ?" I couldn't find the words to the questions I wanted to ask. There were so many.

Lois continued, seeming to understand what it was I wanted to know. "I found my father and introduced myself. It took him a long while to accept the truth and come to terms that he'd had an adult daughter. I was in my thirties by the time we first met."

"But why all the secrecy?" I wanted to know. "I don't get it."

"While getting to know my father, he'd asked me questions about what I wanted from life. I think he was a bit worried that I was coming to him for money. As you know, he isn't a rich man. He has enough to live comfortably and has never wanted anything more. I did admit to him that I needed financial help, but I hadn't come here to empty out his wallet. With my mother gone, I'd soon have access to an inheritance, but I was waiting for the legalities to be completed."

"So that's how you eventually started Golden Flower Modeling?"

"Not quite," she said. "Once the lawyer reached out, he alerted me to the fact that my mother had dipped into my inheritance with the approval of my grandfather.

There was less than half of what had originally been there and not nearly enough to get a modeling agency up and running."

"So what did you do?" I felt myself scooting to the edge of my seat.

"That's when my father came up with the idea to recommend that I take the place of an Eight Immortal who'd recently withdrew his position."

"Someone withdrew?"

"The elderly man was beginning to lose his memory, and his family had put him in an assisted living facility because he could no longer be unattended. His intention was to pass the torch to his eldest son, but when my father and the others approached him, he declined anything to do with our secret organization. He said it was archaic and no longer needed in today's modern world. My father, being the leader, had no idea what to do because this was unprecedented. No one in the history of the group had ever declined a position."

Walter Kang's daughter had also declined, and it made me wonder what I would do if I were in their shoes. "So you ended up taking that man's spot."

She nodded. "Yes, and it breaks the rules to have me in a position of authority with my father also as leader. It appears as though we're trying to stack the odds in our favor. In an effort to keep things balanced, there's a strict rule that only one member of a family may participate at a time. So, my father made me swear that I would keep our secret between the two of us. I thought you might know because you seemed to know so much already. That maybe there was a slim chance that he confided in you."

"No . . ." I replied, holding back that Felix had been the one to mention the possibility. And it made me wonder how he knew. If he'd managed to get his hands on Lois's birth certificate like Lydia had, he would have also found the father's name missing from the document.

"At first, as we began chatting, I thought it might be that my father hired you," she said. "Although, he'd never try to turn me into a villain. It's not in his character."

"No, Mr. Zhang doesn't even know what I'm up to." I looked down at my feet. "I've kinda been avoiding him the past couple of days."

"He's not involved in what's happening," she said firmly. "I can promise you that. I wish you would tell me who it was that hired the private investigator."

I started to toy with the idea of telling Lois everything because I was inching closer to what I thought was the truth. And it was quite possible that Lois might be able to give me all the information I needed to take my theory back to Lydia.

"I'd like to ask you something first," I said, remembering there was one piece of business I needed to clear up before I told her anything else.

She held up a hand. "Wait. There's something I want to say first. It's only fair that you know because, after everything I've just told you, I wouldn't want you to find out from anyone else."

"Okay, what?" I felt a swarm of butterflies fluttering in my belly.

"There's another connection in our group that you should know about." Lois rested both elbows on her desk, steepling her fingers in front of her face. With a renewed sense of calm, perhaps relief, from divulging one of her most guarded secrets, she said, "Talia Sun is my daughter."

CHAPTER
33

It was one of those earth-shattering moments where if I had been drinking coffee, I would have sprayed it out of my mouth every which way. It was something I hadn't seen coming nor could have guessed at by a long shot.

As I took some time to process this new, and rather large, detail, it all came together. A daughter perhaps following in the footsteps of her own father, a generational cycle that some families found themselves destined to repeat.

I sucked in a deep breath, remembering what Talia had told me about her upbringing. "So . . . Talia . . . she told me she was in foster care . . . was that true?"

Lois cringed. "It's true. When I first arrived in New York, I found myself wanting to tether myself to someone for protection. The city intimidated me more than I care to admit, and like most women were taught back then, the way to safety and security was through a man. Only I found myself attached to the wrong person. When he found out that I was pregnant, he left me. Completely disappeared without a trace. I never tried looking for him," she said with a sneer. "If he was that rotten as to leave me, I didn't want him in my life anyways. But at nineteen, and without having any success to speak of, I didn't see a way to keep the baby. So I did what I thought was best."

"Why didn't you go back to your family for help?" I asked.

"I hope you're not judging me for my past choices, Miss Lee," she said. "You're beginning to grow on me and I wouldn't want to ruin that with your criticisms."

I shook my head. "Please, you can call me Lana. And no judgment at all. I get it. You were still a kid yourself. I was just wondering because your family had a lot of money and could have helped you raise a child."

She scoffed. "Not my family. You didn't do things like have children out of wedlock. It was looked down upon, and my mother already disliked me for not being what she wanted me to be. She didn't exactly try to convince me to come back when I left."

"Okay, so how did Talia find you? Or did you find her?"

"She found me," Lois replied. "There were no upsetting circumstances in her situation. She wasn't looking for money . . . just curious to find her birth parents."

"Did she ever find her father?" I asked, wondering what had ever happened to the man.

"If she's found him, she hasn't shared the information with me. I did give her his name when she asked, but I also told her that I was not interested in ever speaking to him again. And I didn't feel she should either. But I didn't want to repeat history and hold onto the information until I was on my deathbed. If there was one thing I could do differently than my mother, it was that."

"So like Mr. Zhang, you helped Talia secure a future by placing her within the Eight Immortals." *And breaking the rules for a second time*, I thought.

Lois nodded. "She'd taken up modeling as a way to get close to me, and she excelled at it. Perhaps it's favoritism that she's my child, but she is quite stunning." She smiled to herself. "However, she wasn't happy doing it. Then when Theodore died and had no one to replace him, we found ourselves in a similar predicament. That's when I thought, well, if this isn't fortuitous then I didn't know what would be. I recommended Talia right away."

"Does Mr. Zhang know she's his granddaughter?"

"Yes," she said. "I wanted him to know as soon as I found out who she was. He warned me that we might be dabbling in something that could get us all in trouble, but we've managed to keep everything under wraps. We're not doing anything with ill intent, Miss Lee. But these positions within the Eight Immortals can help both Talia and me to thrive and help many more people. More people than if we had acted alone."

"I need to ask you something."

She held out both hands, palm up. "I have nothing else to hide."

That was a relief to know. I half expected her to tell me that Juliette Chu had been related to them as well. "Have you noticed that all of the people who were murdered have no one to replace them?"

She sucked in her cheeks. "I had considered the possibility, but thought it had to be a coincidence. There has never been this much trouble in our group before. But with these modern times comes a shift in the dynamic of families. It's something I don't think the original members accounted for, though I suppose they couldn't have guessed how the world would be over a hundred years later."

"Lucky for you," I said. "I don't believe in coincidence. And I have a feeling that a lot of the original facts that were given to me were only laced with the truth."

"Yes, you mentioned you wanted to ask me something. What was your question?"

"Is it true that your father argued with each member before their deaths?"

Lois snorted. "My father? Argue? Come now, Lana. The man doesn't have an argumentative bone in his body. I think him letting my mother go without a word demonstrates that very fact."

"I know," I replied. "I had a hard time believing it too, but I needed to be able to confirm it."

Lois let out a heavy sigh. She lifted a hand to her cheek, and I noticed she'd begun to shake. "This whole ordeal has me completely rattled. Not only have I just given you the keys to my skeleton closet, but there is also someone out there trying to use this against me. Or frame me . . . or whatever it is that's going on." She pushed her seat back and pulled out a drawer, digging through the contents. A moment later, she produced a slender red and gold box. "I snack when I'm nervous." She laughed. "Well, I drink when I'm nervous, if you want me to be truthful, but seeing as it's the middle of the day . . ."

She opened the box, plucked out a miniature, rectangular shortbread cake and displayed the box for me to see. "Would you like one?"

I nearly choked on my gasp as the box and its contents registered in my mind. Struggling to speak, I watched as she raised the pineapple cake she had in her hand toward her mouth. Reacting on instinct, I jumped out of my seat and knocked it out of her hand. "Don't eat that!" The tiny pastry went flying, smacked against the side wall and plunked to the floor where the edges of the cake crumbled.

"What the hell is the matter with you?" she shouted.

I let out a breath. "Juliette Chu had the same box in her possession before she was found dead. My partner—"

I paused, correcting myself. "The private investigator thinks that the pineapple cakes might have been poisoned."

Lois became rigid. "What do you mean?"

"Lydia has the idea that all of these people were poisoned with aconite. They found a huge dose in George Wong's system."

With a gaping mouth, she looked down at the pastry box still in her hand and dropped it onto her desk with a thud.

"Lois," I said, my cheeks warming with panic. "Where did you get those pineapple cakes?"

She closed her mouth, her eyes narrowing in on the box of disowned pastries that sat in the middle of her desk. "They were a gift . . . from Felix Hao."

CHAPTER
34

There are moments in life where you almost feel guided
by something greater. Especially when you think of the in-
finite number of possibilities that exist in the universe.
The reason for you to be at a specific place at a specific
time might not always reveal itself, but today, it sure felt
like I had been exactly where I was meant to be. If I hadn't
been there, Lois would have eaten the pineapple cake
without a care in the world.

When I'd asked Lois when she'd received the box of
pineapple cakes from Felix, she'd told me that he'd delivered them on Monday. The same day that Lydia had
first come knocking on my door. Which meant that he'd
planned on taking further action before our investigation
had ever truly begun.

But for whom? Was he doing this on his own be-
half? And why? Naturally what sprang to mind was to
overthrow the group and gain power, Lydia's original theory. But he hadn't tried to eliminate Donna, Douglas, or
Mr. Zhang . . . at least, not to my knowledge. He'd had his

sights set on Lois, but he'd circled around to Juliette, the newest member.

There must have been a different reason. And I wondered again if there was another party involved. Maybe it was possible that Felix was only a middleman. Someone to deliver the goods and take the fall if things went awry. A patsy.

My mind was operating at a hundred miles a minute, and Lois observed me with anticipation. Her lips curved in a frown, her eyebrows scrunched together as she tried searching my face for an answer.

"Should I call the police?" she asked. "What do we do now? That rat!" she yelled suddenly. "I'll kill him for trying to kill me. I knew his congratulatory visit was a bunch of BS. He said he'd stopped by to wish me well on the expansion of my business." Her words came out rapidly and strung together as if the whole sentence were one long word. "I tried to deal him in, thinking we could collaborate on something. Of course, I didn't really *want* to because he's always rubbed me the wrong way—he's got some kind of superiority complex—but my father saw the best in him and I wanted to give him a chance. That'll teach me to go with first impressions of someone from now on."

Her continuous ramble was making me more nervous than I already was. I needed to breathe, and I needed a moment to think. I interrupted her. "You need to take these to the Fairview Park Police Department and ask for Adam Trudeau. He's my boyfriend and the person working on both George's and Juliette's cases. Let him know that I sent you and you want these pineapple cakes submitted into evidence and tested for aconite."

Lois glanced back down at the pineapple cakes. The twelve-inch box felt larger than life now that there was an awareness they could be poisonous. It may have ruined my love of pineapple cakes, but my emotions were running hot so I didn't want to think about never eating another one for all of eternity.

She gingerly reached for the lid and slapped it on to the base of the box. "I'm so grateful that you were here. You quite possibly saved my life. I've been stalling on eating one because I've put myself on a strict diet to shed some of my winter weight. I almost broke down when the news of Juliette came through, but I managed to squelch it. I would have given in eventually. They're my favorite and hard to resist."

I smiled sheepishly. "I'm just glad everything worked out the way that it did and you didn't eat one of those cookies after all. I don't know how many it takes to cause problems, but Juliette had only eaten two."

"Yes, well, she was *model* thin," Lois commented. "So I'm not really surprised if that's all it took."

My brain was still trying to catch up with everything that had transpired. Then I remembered that I was on my lunch break. "Ohmigod! I have to get back to work. They're going to be wondering where I've been." My panic heightened as I dug my cell phone out of my purse. "It's already past one." I sprang up from my seat. "I'm late." When I unlocked my phone, I saw I had three missed calls. Two from Nancy, and one from Peter. I'd have to call Nancy on my way back to let her know I was okay.

Lois rose, her chair bumping against the wall behind her. "You go on back to work. I'll get these delivered to the police station. What did you say your boyfriend's name is again?"

"Adam Trudeau," I replied. "Detective. If he's not there, ask for Detective Higgins, that's his partner."

"I'll do that," Lois said. "Oh, and Lana . . . I hope I can

trust you won't breathe a word about my relation to my father or to Talia. At least not until this whole ugly affair is sorted out. I wouldn't want to add more problems to what's already going on."

"Don't worry," I said. "I wouldn't want to put your family in any danger."

I hustled all the way to the parking lot, unconcerned about what the receptionist or anyone else I passed thought about my odd behavior. Back in my car with the doors locked and the engine running, I called Nancy on the restaurant line, hoping that Peter wouldn't answer for some reason.

Luckily, Nancy answered and I blurted out a string of apologies saying that I'd gotten held up—but not literally—at the bank and was making my way back to the plaza shortly. She assured me that she wasn't mad that I was late, only worried, and wanted to make sure that wherever I was that I was safe.

I confirmed that I was and she told me to drive carefully before hanging up.

I switched over to my car's speaker phone, calling Lydia next. She didn't answer so I left a message telling her I needed to speak with her right away. Then I went about calling Donna, who had yet to call me back. She didn't answer either, so I left her a similar message but also added that if she'd received any gifts of pineapple cakes or something that she shouldn't eat whatever it may be.

Then I called Megan and got her voice mail too. "Doesn't anyone answer their phone anymore?" I said in my message. "Call me back. It's super urgent. I have so much to tell you and you're not even going to believe the half of it. Okay, call me . . . bye."

After I disconnected the call, I was getting ready to head back on the freeway, so any other calls I wanted to make would have to wait. I needed to concentrate on the road, and the portion of I-90 that I was approaching could be a little bit tricky with its added twists and on-ramps right on top of each other.

As I maneuvered and dodged vehicles that were merging into traffic, I released a string of expletives that would have surely gotten my mouth rinsed out with soap if my mother had been within earshot. Even at this age, it wasn't appropriate in her mind for a lady to say some of the words that were coming out. But I was beyond frustrated with the fact that I had to go back to work. I didn't see how I was going to function as "Lana, the restaurant manager" when "Lana, the unofficial detective" needed to be out and about getting things done.

What were we going to do about Felix? Clearly he had been lying to both Lydia and me, but to what extent? And if he got wind of what we'd discovered about the pineapple cakes, there was no telling what his next steps might be. Would he come after us? Or would he try to flee?

I considered the probability of us being wrong. There wasn't any official evidence to say that the pineapple cakes were even poisoned to begin with. I had assumed it because what were the chances of both ladies having the same exact box and Juliette having them in her possession at the time of her death. Lois had received her box from Felix himself, which increased the likelihood that Juliette had gotten them from him as a gift as well. Again, what were the chances?

But I realized now as I headed west on I-90 that there was a sliver of possibility that the pieces of the puzzle that had looked like they fit, didn't.

I scolded myself for having acted so rashly as an image flashed through my mind of me knocking the pastry right out of Lois's hand. Was I letting my emotions get the best of me? Had yesterday and finding Juliette's body caused me to jump the gun? No one enjoyed the thought of there being a killer on the loose . . . a maniac hell-bent on harming others. So maybe, my reactions had been somewhat justified. Yet, I knew I couldn't go around accusing people if I had nothing to truly base it on. There was too much at stake. These people's lives depended on it.

I followed my exit to Hilliard Boulevard and turned down a side street to make my way back to Center Ridge.

Once I'd arrived at Asia Village and parked my car in the employee lot, I took a few moments to breathe like a normal human being before heading back to work. If the restaurant was slow, I could hibernate in my office and come up with a plan of action to propose to Lydia. I'd only need to come out to cover Nancy's lunch. I could manage a lunch break, couldn't I?

I thought about calling Adam before I went back inside, but I knew what he'd say. He'd tell me that we'd have to wait for the results to come back on the pineapple cakes before we could take any further steps. Then he'd most likely remind me how I was partial to working off of speculation and that legally, he couldn't.

I might have been getting ahead of myself and ultimately I would wait for Lydia's say-so, but I thought the best route to take next would be to apply pressure directly to Felix Hao. If we told him we had new information that advanced the case and wanted to sit down with him, there was a chance we could get him to screw up his story, potentially giving himself away in the process.

No doubt Lydia would want to meet with him and con-front him in some capacity. If my theory was correct, I didn't think she would be too happy when she found out she'd been duped by her own client, and maybe the two of us together could get the ugly rat to squeal.

CHAPTER
35

When I reached the entrance to Asia Village, Kimmy was standing on the other side of the doors with pursed lips and a hand on one hip. She pushed the door open when I reached for the handle.

"Peter called me, asking me if I knew where you were," Kimmy spat. "And where exactly were you, Lee?"

"Are you my keeper?" I shot back. With everything going on, I was in no mood for Kimmy's attitude.

She clucked her tongue. "Don't get lippy with me, missy. I'm on your side, remember?"

I huffed. "Look, I got held up meeting with Lois Fan . . . Things are developing fast and I'm really frustrated." My eyes shifted over to Wild Sage. "I have to talk to Mr. Zhang."

"I'm coming with you," she said, trailing behind me.

I whipped around, stopping her from going any further. "No. I have to talk with him *alone*. Not because I don't want you there, but because I don't want to make him feel like we're ganging up on him."

Kimmy groaned. "Fine. Whatever you're up to, I don't want to make Mr. Zhang feel bad either."

"Nancy should be taking her lunch in about a half hour. Meet me at the restaurant, I'll be waiting for you at the hostess station. I'll tell you everything."

She seemed to perk up. "Okay. Yeah, okay, I'll meet you there."

We separated in front of Wild Sage.

I found Mr. Zhang adjusting some glass containers of dried herbs on the shelf. When he realized I was there, he turned to greet me. "Oh, hello there, Lana." He shuffled a few steps closer to me, inspecting my face. "I haven't seen you in a few days. Is everything alright? You look worried about something."

"Mr. Zhang, has anyone delivered any pineapple cakes to you?"

He scratched his chin. "Not that I know of. Should I be expecting something?"

"No," I said, "but if anyone drops off anything edible, don't eat it, okay? And maybe give me a call."

Mr. Zhang remained expressionless. His eyes moved back and forth as he studied me. "What is this about, Lana? I am concerned for you."

I chewed on my lip. I really didn't have time to tell him the whole story because I had to get back to the restaurant. On top of that, I still needed to warn Talia to take the same precautions. "Listen, I promise I'll tell you everything later, but I'm kind of in a hurry. There's a possibility that you're in danger."

I'd expected him to become alarmed by this ominous statement that held no explanation, but he remained calm, only nodding before outstretching a hand and squeezing my arm with encouragement. "Then I shall not eat anything that is brought to me and wish you luck in what needs to be done."

"Thank you," I replied. "I also need to ask you a favor."

"Anything."

"Can you tell your granddaughter . . . I mean, Talia. Can you tell her to do the same thing? She may also be in danger and I really have to get back to the restaurant."

We shared a silent moment of understanding. It was clear that he understood I knew everything there was to know.

"Yes," he said. "I will go right now and tell her."

"Thanks, I'll be in touch." I started to walk away, but he reached for my arm again.

"Lana?" he called softly.

I turned back around to face him.

He gave me a reluctant smile. "I've only held on to secrets to protect the ones I love . . . not just for my family, but for those outside of my family. I hope you can understand this."

I did something that I normally never do. I hugged him. His frail body felt small and fragile in my arms, so I didn't squeeze him too hard. Just enough to let him know that I cared. "Don't worry, Mr. Zhang. This isn't your fault and all your secrets are safe with me."

Back at the restaurant, Nancy greeted me with kindness and made no comment about my extended lunch period. Her pleasant nature radiated throughout her demeanor as she went about serving a table of four. They were the only customers in the restaurant and I was glad that the place wasn't packed, which would have added to my guilt.

I told her I was going to drop my things off in the back.

As I entered the kitchen, I ran into Peter, who was sweeping the floor on the other side of the door. He held the broom out in mid-stroke. "Do I even want to know?" he asked.

"No" was all I said, continuing to the back room and finally my office. Despite my Hallmark moment with Mr. Zhang, I still wasn't in the mood to be lectured by anyone. I was tired, overwhelmed, and ready to take the longest nap of my life. This whole ordeal had been too much and I didn't want to deal with someone giving me a hard time.

I set my things down on my desk and pondered what my next steps would be. I had a few minutes before it would be time for Nancy to go on break, so I checked my phone to see if I'd missed any calls or messages. But there was nothing from anybody.

I shuffled some papers around on my desk, thinking that moving things around would help settle my mind, but it was only making me more frustrated. There were so many things I'd left unattended while I worked on this case, and no doubt when it was over, I'd have a lot of things to catch up on.

Yet, I wouldn't want it any other way. I thought about how this was Lydia's life . . . it was her work. And she was paid decently for what she did. No doubt she felt a certain amount of gratification at the end of the day when she helped someone get whatever closure it was that they needed. It was meaningful work.

It made me think of what Talia had said about her own situation and how she'd been called—or felt she'd been called—to help people discover themselves.

In this whole process, had I become worried that I wasn't living my life's purpose? Had that thought been there the entire time and I hadn't noticed until others spoke of their own lives? Or was I making something out of nothing?

I didn't know the answer to either question, but what I *did* know was that I needed to get back to work.

Nancy had decided she was going to the Bamboo Lounge for lunch, and I was glad she hadn't decided to stick around, because it was one less person I had to worry about over-hearing anything Kimmy and I had to say.

I sat up front with my cellphone in my hand, watching it and the absence of its chimes accentuating the fact that not one person had called me back. Where the heck was everyone?

Kimmy sashayed into Ho-Lee Noodle House a few minutes after Nancy had left. "So, what happened with Lois? I'm jealous you got to see her without me."

I set my phone down on the lectern, face up, so I could see if someone called. Because I was technically working, I had my ringer silenced. "It was a snap decision to meet with her. There was a situation with Juliette Chu," I told her.

"I saw it on my phone," she replied. "What the hell happened?"

I told her everything that had transpired the day before, including the pineapple cakes being a potential murder weapon. I then explained why I'd gone to see Mr. Zhang and why I'd wanted it to be private.

Kimmy let out an exaggerated whistle. "So the old man has a deep, seedy past." She smirked. "Looks like I'm not the only one keeping secrets around here."

"I don't know if I'd call it 'seedy,'" I said. "But his history is definitely more complex than I could have imagined. The number of secrets in all of Asia Village is enough to set the world on fire," I said.

"So what's our next step?" she asked, rubbing her hands together. "We goin' undercover? I think we go pay Mr. Hao a visit and play a little good cop, bad cop. Maybe he'll fess up to whatever it is he's trying to pull."

"I don't want to do anything without Lydia," I reminded her. "At the end of the day, this is *still* her case. I'm just—"

"A consultant." Kimmy wobbled her head back and forth. "Yeah, yeah, I know. But, come on. When has Lana Lee ever taken a back seat when it comes to this sort of thing?"

My phone screen lit up with a number I recognized but it was not saved to my phone. I answered before it could go to voice mail. "Hello?"

"Lana?"

"Yeah?"

"It's Lois."

"Oh hi," I said. "Is everything okay?"

Kimmy mouthed, *Who is it?*

I waved my hand, signaling for her to be quiet.

Lois replied, "Everything is fine. Well, as fine as it can be. I met your boyfriend, good-looking fellow. Strong jawline. If these were different circumstances I'd have offered him a job. But anyways, that's neither here nor there. The reason I'm calling is because when I gave him the box of pineapple cakes, he told me it could take a few weeks before we'd know anything for sure. He said since it's the weekend, they wouldn't even get submitted to a lab until Monday and then who knows how long it will take."

"A few weeks?" I asked. "That can't be right."

"He said based on past scenarios that he's seen it happen. Lana, that's too much time. Action must be taken now. I can't sit around and wait while Felix is out there running around trying to scheme against the rest of us. No, I won't stand for it."

"Lois," I said for Kimmy's benefit, "let's hold off until I hear back from Lydia. She's the professional and she knows better what to do in a situation like this."

Kimmy's eyes lit up when she realized who I was talking to. She shuffled around the lectern, standing next to me with her ear close to my phone so she could hear our conversation.

"Is she paying you?" Lois asked.

"Excuse me?"

"Is she paying you?" Lois repeated. "Because I will pay you double. This can't go unchecked a moment longer, and if you don't do something about it, I will take care of him myself."

Kimmy elbowed me in the ribs.

Ignoring her, I replied, "I don't think that would be wise." My stomach was beginning to hurt again.

"Let me ask you this, young lady." Her voice became stern, more like the woman I'd originally met at Talia's shop. "Would you sit around and wait while you knew someone was out there trying to hurt you or someone in your family?"

I didn't want to answer the question because I knew what the answer would be. And that answer was no, I wouldn't sit idly by and wait for someone else to rescue me. That's how I'd gotten myself down this whole path to begin with. I sighed into the phone but kept my feelings to myself.

"Lana," Lois said, clearing her throat. "You have until tomorrow to do something or I'm going to confront Felix myself. I'm going to let him know that his stupid plan didn't work and that I gave his wretched cakes to the police department. I'll take pleasure in watching him squirm."

CHAPTER
36

Lois hung up on me without so much as a goodbye. I sat holding the phone to my ear even though I knew no one was on the other end. The room felt like it was closing in and I couldn't breathe.

Kimmy gave me a gentle shake. "Lee, snap out of la-la land. You heard the woman, she's going to pay you double." She took the phone out of my hand and placed it back on the lectern. "And seeing as I'm such a generous young lady, I'll only ask for fifteen percent of whatever it is that she pays you."

I gawked at her. "Fifteen percent? What are you even talking about?"

"For my services," she said, batting her eyelashes.

I gave her the largest eye roll I could muster and picked my phone back up, searching my recent calls for Lydia's number. I tapped the listing, initiating a call, and waited—not so patiently—for her to pick up. When I got her voice mail again, I grunted. "Call me back ASAP!" I said before hanging up.

Kimmy looked too satisfied by the scenario for my liking. She placed a hand on her hip. "Call Felix and set something up. You heard what Lois said, she's going to go confront him herself."

I didn't know if it was Kimmy's influence or my own anxiety, but I thought the best thing to do would be to call Felix and set up a meeting for later this evening. Assuming he'd even be willing to meet with me. He might not accept a request from me seeing as Lydia had been the person he hired. But maybe he wouldn't have to know that I was the one setting up the meeting, and then the appointment would be set by the time Lydia called me back. What were the chances she wouldn't call me back by five o'clock?

I did a quick search online for Felix's office number and selected the option to call once I found it. While the phone rang, I glared at Kimmy. Somewhere in my mind, I knew I was hoping that Felix wouldn't pick up just like everybody else I'd tried to call that day.

But, to my dismay, he picked up on the fifth ring. "Felix Hao," he said into the phone.

"Hi Felix, this is Lana Lee. Lydia Shepard's consultant."

"Yes, Lana, so nice to hear from you. To what do I owe this pleasure? Have you ladies made some headway on my request?"

"There was something that came up," I said, trying to dodge saying anything of consequence. "A few questions about . . . Mr. Zhang that Lydia wanted to ask you about. Could you meet with the two of us later today? Maybe five thirty or so?"

He was quiet for a few moments, then asked, "Why didn't she call me herself?"

"Uh, well, she's tied up with something and asked if I would do it for her. I guess that's the beauty of having a helper." I let out an uneasy chuckle, hoping I was the only one who noticed I sounded anxious.

Felix sighed. "I had dinner plans this evening, but I suppose I could bump my reservation to a later time. Where would you like to meet?"

Formulating my plan on a whim, I said, "We could meet at your office if that makes things easier for you."

He took a couple seconds to think it over. "Yes, that will actually work out nicely. See you at five thirty and please don't be late. I won't have much time to wait on you."

"No problem, we'll be there," I said.

We hung up and I rested my phone back on the lectern, feeling queasy.

Kimmy's shoulders drooped. "Ugh, no fair. It was my idea and I can't even come with you. It's no fun when Lydia's around."

I cradled my stomach at the thought of what lay ahead of me. "Trust me, in this instance, I'd trade places with you if I could."

The rest of the afternoon went by surprisingly fast. Most likely because I was dreading what would come next. In the time since my call with Felix I'd become a ball of nerves; my hands shook as I lifted plates on and off tables.

Nobody else I'd tried calling earlier in the day had bothered to reach back out. I'd even called Lydia once more hoping she'd answer. I had no idea what Donna was up to, and I concluded that Megan must have been sound asleep seeing as she'd worked a double yesterday.

When five o'clock came, I had made no progress and wondered if I should cancel the meeting I'd made with Felix. But then Lois's threat came back into mind. If I didn't do something before tomorrow, she'd take action into her own hands. And there was no telling what kind of trouble that would cause. Not just for me, but for her. I didn't think Felix would take kindly to her accusations. I couldn't risk that something would happen to her in the process. Especially now that I knew she was Mr. Zhang's daughter. If she were harmed, it would devastate him, and Talia, their family finally together after all this time.

Before any more time passed, I zipped out of the restaurant and headed over to China Cinema and Song hoping that Kimmy hadn't left for the day.

As luck would have it, I bumped into her on her way out. She gasped as we nearly collided into each other. "Lee! Watch where you're going! Geez."

"Kimmy, I need your help after all," I said. "Do you have time to go with me to meet Felix Hao?"

Her mouth dropped open. "Um, yes! I'm supposed to work a shift at you know where, but I can have Autumn cover for me." She grabbed my wrist. "Come on, let's go before Peter sees us."

I allowed her to drag me along as we exited Asia Village and made our way through the parking lot. For all her faults and quirks, I knew that Kimmy Tran always came through for me in a pinch.

CHAPTER
37

"I don't understand why I have to wait in the car," Kimmy said with a pout. "I could be very useful. I've been honing my interrogation skills."

We were sitting in the parking lot of Felix Hao's office building, which was located just a few blocks away from Lois Fan's agency. Though the buildings were built of the same old brick that was common in the neighborhood, Felix's was much smaller, only containing two floors, but the entire property was his.

"We've gone over this," I said. "It would be weird to him if you were there since he knows I'm working with Lydia. I need you to stay here and wait for Lydia to show up." *Hopefully*, I thought. "When she does, fill her in on what's happening so it looks like we're on the same page."

Kimmy tsked. "This is ridiculous."

"Kimmy, please, this is the help I need. And you said you wanted to help no matter what that meant."

She groaned. "Ugh, I know. Okay fine, I'll stand watch for Lydia."

"If I don't come out for some reason . . ." My stomach flip flopped at the thought. "You need to call Lydia again. And if she doesn't answer, call Adam . . . he'll know what to do." I found a pen in my center console along with a piece of scrap paper. I scribbled down their numbers. "Whatever you do, don't come in . . . I don't want to put you in any danger." I began to regret bringing her along because if something did happen to us, it would be my fault. However, she would work as my fail-safe. I had no idea what I was walking into.

"Okay, go," she said, shooing me out of the car. "Your anxiety is leaking onto me."

I inhaled, steadied myself, then reached for the door handle.

"Be careful, Lee," Kimmy said before I got out. "You got this."

I gave her a curt nod as I shut the door behind me. I really hoped that was true.

The parking lot was empty except for one car. It was a black sedan with tinted windows and struck me as familiar. I must have noticed it at the meeting with Felix the first day we met.

The door to the building was covered with a washed-out blue fabric awning held together by metal beams. Considering the nature of Felix's work, you'd think he'd take the time to make his building as beautiful as the people he intended to fill it with.

I found the door unlocked and stepped into a plain-looking lobby area that had a few oversized potted plants in front of the window and black leather furniture that surrounded a dark wooden coffee table. The magazines that lay fanned out on the table appeared to be industry related and well worn. I wondered how old the issues actually were.

Most of the office was dimmed and the receptionist desk was empty. "Hello?" I called out. "Felix?"

A few moments later, I heard the tapping of dress shoes against tile. The sound was coming from the second floor and reminded me of a teacher walking down a quiet hallway in search of someone playing hooky. "Hello?" a masculine voice returned. No doubt it was Felix.

"Hi, it's Lana," I said.

He appeared on the staircase to the right of where I stood dressed in a black suit and glossy bloodred tie. Whatever dinner he was heading to must be on the formal side. "Where is Ms. Shepard?"

"Uh, she's running late. We agreed to meet here."

Felix pursed his lips. "I told you on the phone, I don't have time to sit around and wait tonight. Is this something that you and I can discuss or did she not fill you in on what it is that she needed from me?"

"It might be better if we wait a few minutes. I'm sure she'll be here soon," I lied. "You know how traffic can be coming from the west side."

"Very well," he said, turning to head back up the stairs. "Come to my office. We can wait there for a little bit. She has five minutes to get here before I'm going to suggest we reschedule this for another time."

I followed him up the steps, quiet as a mouse. I didn't want to be here. I felt like I'd done an injustice to Lydia by doing all of this behind her back. But I hadn't known what else to do and Kimmy had been right about one thing: I usually didn't take the back seat on anything.

He disappeared into a doorway without signaling me to follow him, but I went through the same door he did. I found his office to be just as plain as the lobby area. Black leather furniture, a solid oak desk with a two-monitor setup. Behind his desk was a matching oak cabinet with several drawers and stacks of magazines on top of it. Above the cabinet was a bronzed flute next to a painting that was similar to the ones I'd seen in Mr. Zhang's shop and at Donna's home.

"Do you play?" I asked.

Felix tsked. "No, of course not. That is the symbol of my position in the Eight Immortals . . . my object." He lifted his chin. "It doesn't make much sense, does it? Though that's the way the *order* has become, I suppose. Nonsensical and . . . unequal."

He appeared agitated as he paced between his desk and the door. I wondered if the dinner he had planned for later that evening had something to do with what had been going on. Was it possible he was meeting with Douglas Chen? Part of me was still circling around the idea that he was working with or *for* someone else.

"I'm sorry to keep you," I said with genuine apology. I didn't want to be here either. I didn't know how to stall for time because I'd assumed that Lydia would have contacted me by now. Checking his wall clock, I noted that three minutes had passed. I decided to sit in one of the chairs in front of his desk to make my visit less temporary feeling. Maybe if I made myself comfortable he wouldn't be so quick to rush me out in the two minutes I had left.

He regarded me with indifference. "It's not your fault really. Do you know what this was about?"

Thinking quickly, I decided to ask a question I'd been wondering myself. "I think it had something to do with what you said about Mr. Zhang having a daughter."

His eyebrows raised and he stopped pacing. "Oh? Did you find the evidence you need to prove that I'm right?"

"Well, that's just it . . ." I said, taking my time to reply. "Lydia did find Lois's birth certificate . . . but the only thing is . . . well, the name of the father is blank."

Felix didn't try hiding his disappointment. "Dammit! There must be a way to find this information out."

"Can I ask how you stumbled across the information to begin with?"

He flared his nostrils. "That's irrelevant. What's important is that you find solid proof. I'm not shelling out all this money for the two of you to come up empty-handed. And now, Juliette Chu is dead."

That's when it struck me that Felix's prediction hadn't come true. He hadn't been next after all. And of course he hadn't been because it was most likely him passing out tainted pineapple cakes. Since he'd brought up Juliette Chu, I decided to see if I could push any buttons about the inconsistencies in his predictions. "About that . . ." I started. "You said that you were sure that you were next, but clearly that didn't happen."

He turned away from me, his hands clasped behind his back. He was clenching both fists. "It was a miscalculation on my part. I assumed it would be me that was in harm's way. Partially because of what I know about Mr. Zhang's secret."

Felix glanced at me over his shoulder. Probably to see if I was falling for his adjustment to the story, throwing in Mr. Zhang's name for good measure. I played along. "That does make sense, I guess."

"Juliette must have known something," he said. "See? This is how these people operate. None of us are safe." He turned around, taking a few steps closer to me.

My mouth went dry. "You have a good point," I said, continuing my charade. "Juliette must have posed a threat to whoever is responsible."

"I think we both know who that is," he said, towering over me.

I cleared my throat, feigning a coughing spell. "Ooh,"

I said in between my exaggerated fits. "I have a tickle in my throat. Do you think I could have some water?"

His eyes darted to his office door and then back at me. "Sure. Not a problem." With stiff movements, I watched him as he left his office and disappeared to find me water.

It didn't afford me much time, but I needed a moment to think of what to do next. I checked my phone and there were no missed calls from Lydia. Noting the time, I realized that I'd stalled long enough to buy myself more than the five minutes that Felix had originally proposed.

I listened for sounds in the hallway and heard nothing. His door was wide open, and I rose, peeking out into the hallway. There was no sign of him so I shut the door, leaving it open just a crack. I crossed my fingers that he wouldn't notice.

I went behind his desk, scanning the items that sat in front of his two monitors. Contracts, information packets, a to-do list. Nothing that interested me. I turned around to face the cabinet unit, and my eyes flitted upward toward the bronzed flute. It was definitely old and needed a good polishing. I resisted the urge to touch it, acknowledging that the instrument was older than most anything I'd ever come into contact with outside of a museum. It held weight, and I wondered why it wasn't locked into a case or something more secure.

Taking a quick look over my shoulder to make sure Felix hadn't crept up behind me, I started riffling through the drawers of the cabinet. Maybe he'd have a spare box of pineapple cakes tucked away. Something to implicate him further.

However, when I got to the third drawer, I found something I hadn't anticipated finding. Sitting all by themselves, wrapped in a red velvet cloth, were the following items: a silver spoon shaped like a lotus flower, a bamboo drum, and two circular wooden objects that had hollowed-out centers. Based on the Google search I'd done after getting the file from Lydia, I gathered these were castanets.

I gasped at the realization that I had found the missing artifacts.

I'd just picked up the spoon to inspect it when I thought I heard the door creak open behind me. I froze.

"You shouldn't have done that," Felix barked. He stormed through his office, grabbing my wrist before I understood what was happening. He applied pressure, forcing me to let go of the spoon, which clattered back into the drawer. In one quick motion, he reached above his head and lifted the bronzed flute off its display stand. The last thing I saw was a metal cylinder coming at my face.

CHAPTER
38

I woke up to find myself tied to one of Felix's guest chairs. He'd tied my left arm with an extension cord around my wrist; my right arm with some type of cell phone charging cord. That one he'd tied tighter, and I could see circulation leaving my hand as it turned a lighter shade than the rest of my skin.

I yanked on my left wrist, but it only caused me pain. My head was throbbing on top of it. I winced as I turned my neck. Felix had been sitting calmly on his guest couch, a leather love seat that was just large enough to fit two people. "I had to improvise." He motioned to my wrists. "It's not like I have rope laying around the office."

"Are you out of your mind?" I spat. "Let me go."

"I should think not." He was still holding onto his flute, hitting it against his palm like a baseball bat. He shook it in my direction. "This little flute, though not my cup of tea, comes in handy."

I realized that he'd left my legs free and I was hoping to use that against him at some point, but he'd tucked in the chair so close to his desk that I couldn't move very well. My eyes searched for the clock on the wall, and I realized twenty minutes had passed. Any minute now, Kimmy would call for help. I just hoped they'd make it in time. I had no idea what Felix's end game was going to be. The best I could do was try to stall him, praying that he didn't do anything rash.

"Why are you doing this?" I asked, trying to sound like I wasn't pleading. I didn't see someone like Felix taking pity on me. He hadn't seemed to care about anybody else's life.

"Because you wouldn't leave well enough alone. I knew I shouldn't have trusted you. I've looked into your history, *Miss* Lee, and I know exactly what kind of nuisance you can be. But I had hoped to play it to my advantage."

"What is that supposed to mean?" I investigated my left wrist again. With the cord being thicker than the other, it would be easier to get out of and I might be able to wiggle my hand free. I started casually twisting my wrist in circular motions to try to loosen its hold. I didn't know if it would work, but I had to try something.

"Do you think it was luck that I would hire Ms. Shepard?" he asked, one corner of his lip curving up in a sinister smile. "Come now, Miss Lee, I'd expected just a tad more from you. I was wondering if you'd ever figure that out. I sought her out because I knew she'd go looking to you for help. Especially when I played the part of mistrusting client. That someone *like her* wouldn't understand someone *like me*."

That caused me to stop what I was doing. "Wait a minute . . . that was all an act?"

"I'm not an actor's agent for nothing, Miss Lee. I do have some firsthand experience." He lifted his chin. "Impressive, I know. I think that little performance was good enough to win me an Oscar."

"But how did you know that she'd ask me for help?"

"Why do you think I made sure to throw in Wei Zhang's name as much as possible? It was only a matter of time before Ms. Shepard went down the path I set her on. Your ties to him were perfect." He exhaled through his nose. "I wasn't planning for you to go the route you did though. I set up everything nice and neat for you to come to the conclusion I wanted you to. The herbal poison that would signify Wei Zhang's involvement, his daughter . . . and his *granddaughter*." He said the word with venom. "The Zhang family overtaking a group of well-meaning Samaritans to fulfill their own selfish purposes. It was all right there."

I began circulating my wrist again, gently so as not to attract his attention. One of his computer monitors was right in front of me. Though my left hand wasn't my dominant, I was still going to try and smash that monitor in his face. Payback for bopping me on the head. The place where he'd hit me was still stinging and I knew a welt would be forming there if it hadn't already. "Well, you ruined your own plan all on your own, *Mr. Hao*. You should have left Juliette Chu alone. It gave us exactly what we needed."

Felix sneered. "All that's not going to matter very soon. *And* I would have left her alone if it hadn't been for that meddling Donna Feng. The woman can't keep her two cents out of anything."

"Donna?" I gawked. "What does Donna have to do with this?"

He rose from his seat on the leather couch. "Imagine my surprise when Donna suggests to the group that someone by the name of Anna May Lee should take George's position. Another Lee?" he asked sarcastically. He tapped the flute to his chin. "Now, what are the chances that you two are related? I'd say one hundred percent, wouldn't you?"

"I don't see what that has to do with me." I was making progress with loosening the cord.

He stormed over to my chair, hovering over me with a menacing glare. "Because that spot was intended for my son! How many people do I have to kill around here to get what I want?" He leaned down so his face was only a few inches from mine.

I stopped trying to free my wrist while he stood over me. He was too close and I didn't want him to realize what I was doing lest he try to tighten the cord back up. "So is that what you've been doing? Trying to secure your son a spot in your little club?"

He held out the flute, pushing it into my neck. "It's not a *club*. Don't belittle it with your casual, uneducated vocabulary. This is an elite society of members that holds power and can change the outcome of someone's future."

I tried leaning back as far as I could, the edge of the flute pushing on my windpipe.

"My son deserves to be one of the Eight Immortals, and why should he have to wait until my death before he can take the reins? After all, Wei Zhang managed to weasel his daughter in without so much as anyone batting an eyelash."

"You killed Theodore so your son could take his place?" I asked. It was insanity what this man was saying.

"Theodore was a mild-mannered man . . . him and his Qigong, or his tai chi, and whatever other Eastern custom he found necessary to impart onto whoever would listen. What did he contribute to the order . . . I ask you. Tell me now, what do you think learning these practices could accomplish to heighten our success?"

He softened his grip on forcing the flute into the side

of my neck. I tried catching the breath I'd been holding while he continued to stand over me. "I don't know what you want me to say."

"Exactly," he said through gritted teeth. "He offered nothing. But my son, following in my footsteps, could make something of our family name. And the two of us together." He outstretched his arms. "We'd be able to do so much good."

I forgot myself momentarily and snorted with indignance. "So much good? Look at all the bad you've done."

He glared at me, tightening his grip on the flute. "The other men were more of an asset. I didn't want to betray them, but they were the only ones that would be difficult to replace. I knew that Walter Kang's daughter wanted nothing to do with any of us, including him. He'd confided in me about the problems he'd had with her . . . *the brat* . . . It was supposed to be an easy fix. I hadn't wanted to go after George, but circumstances left me no choice."

"So were you planning to kill my sister then too?" The idea made me sick, but I couldn't hold back the question.

"I'll take care of her if the time comes. But I'm hoping this situation with Juliette will put a pause to just including any old person into the fold. Maybe now they will see that my son is exactly who they need to choose. The rightful replacement."

"Do you think your son would really want to earn his spot this way?" I asked. "Think about what you're doing."

Felix's lip curled up. "Are you going to be my conscience now?"

"Someone has to be," I retorted.

"Hmm," he said, turning his back on me. "I have other plans for you besides worrying about what I'm doing."

While he was turned away, my eyes darted up toward the clock; fifteen more minutes had passed. It had felt like

I'd been trapped in this room with him for days. I had also used the time while he wasn't paying attention to me to finally free my wrist.

But because I wasn't watching what he was doing, I wasn't prepared for what he did next.

Felix had been digging around in one of his drawers and though I'd heard the commotion of it all, I hadn't noticed that he'd pulled out a red and gold box, exactly like the one that both Juliette and Lois had.

Before I could finish freeing my hand, he was standing over top of me. He'd pulled a pineapple cake out of the box, discarding the rest on his desk. He noticed that I'd loosened the knot of the extension cord on my left wrist. "Before you go," he said, his free hand grabbing my wrist and using it to pull the chair back, "why don't you have something to nibble on?"

I cringed at the pressure he'd applied to my already sore wrist. And as he inched the pineapple cake closer to my face, I clenched my teeth, sucked in my lips, and turned my head away as far as possible.

He dragged the chair to an angle where I was now facing him directly, and he straddled my legs, the cake crumbling in his hands as he tried to force it into my mouth. He lifted his free hand to squeeze my cheeks, but before he could, I jerked up my right knee and forced it right between his legs.

He yowled in pain and doubled over, dropping the cake. I took my chance, pulled my leg back, and with all the force I could manage, I flung my foot forward, kicking him in the stomach. He tumbled backward with a yelp.

I pulled my left arm back forcing my hand to fit through the loosened knot, nearly dislocating my thumb in the process. With my left hand free, I hoisted myself out of the chair and, dragging it with me, ran for the door.

As I reached for the knob, a loud thud came from the other side. The door was closed and locked, probably to deter a quick escape on my part. Another bang came against the door, startling me.

"Lana?!" a female's voice yelled. I knew it was Lydia. "Lana?! Are you in there?"

"Yes!" I tried to yell. It came out as a croak, and then I felt Felix pulling me back by my shoulders. He had a difficult time getting a good grip on me because the chair was still attached to my right arm. I fumbled to unlock the door.

Once I managed, the door came flying open and knocked me back, causing Felix to fall once again.

Lydia stormed into the room with her gun aimed at Felix. A young man with sandy blond hair and a badge around his neck came in right after her.

Lydia took a few steps forward, her eyes locked on Felix. "Stay right where you are, creep."

The sandy blond removed a pair of cuffs from his back pocket and moved around Lydia to get to Felix. With a firm tone, he said, "Cleveland P.D. Felix Hao, you're under arrest."

While the sandy blond went about putting the handcuffs on Felix and forcing him to his feet, Lydia helped me up and removed the power cord from my right wrist, finally freeing me from the chair.

I massaged my wrist, my hand tingling from the lack of circulation.

"Looks like I got here in the nick of time."

"My hero," I quipped, trying to make light of the situation for the sake of my own sanity.

"My hero nothing," she replied. "You have a lot of explaining to do. But let's get the hell out of here first. I think you've been in here long enough."

CHAPTER
39

Outside we were met by Kimmy, who was trying to break through the barricade the Cleveland police had set up near the entrance of Felix's office building. Alongside her stood Adam and Higgins, Higgins trying to calm Kimmy down.

The sandy blond who had escorted Felix out ushered him to a police cruiser that was waiting to take him away.

Kimmy's face brightened when she saw me. She jumped up and down. "Lana! You're okay."

The cop standing in her way let her through, and she wrapped her arms around me, nearly knocking us both over with the motion.

"I was so worried about you," she said when she let go. "I didn't know what to do, so I called everyone." Her head tilted toward where Adam and Higgins were standing. They were now talking to the cop who had been guarding the entrance.

Lydia huffed, placing her hands on her hips. "When your friend blew up my phone with a barrage of calls, I knew something must have been up."

"Yeah," I said. "Where have you been all day?"

The sandy blond walked up to us just then, standing next to Lydia. "She was with me digging up dirt on this case," he answered for her.

Lydia looked between the two of us. "Lana, I'd like you to meet a friend of mine, Jason Fox. Jason, this is the woman I was telling you about, Lana Lee."

I noted again that Lydia said the word "friend" with an air that would imply that something more was going on between the two, but I knew this definitely wasn't the time to ask. Instead, I extended my hand. "Nice to meet you, Jason," I said.

He returned the gesture with a hearty shake. "Likewise. I've heard some stories about you. Nice to meet you in person finally."

"Fox?" Adam said, coming up to us with Higgins trailing behind. "Foxy Jason, is that you?"

Jason grimaced. "Trudeau, well I'll be damned. No one's called me that horrible nickname since the academy."

Adam extended his hand, giving Jason a hearty shake. "The prettiest boy in all the land," he teased.

With a chuckle, Jason replied, "Yeah well, if there's someone up for the job, you know it's me."

Adam's eyes darted between him and Lydia. He pointed from one to the other. "Wait a minute here . . . are you two . . . ?"

Jason blushed, massaging his neck. "That . . . uh . . ."

Lydia cleared her throat. "I think it's time we got going. Don't all of you? Those police reports aren't going to fill themselves out."

Adam burst into laughter, wrapping an arm around my shoulders and kissing me on the cheek. "Universes collide. Looks like I'm not the only who has my hands full."

EPILOGUE

Late Sunday morning, my family, along with Mr. Zhang, Adam, *and* Lydia as our special guest of honor sat around a large table at Li Wah's for our customary weekly dim sum get-together. When my parents had learned about everything that had transpired two days ago, they insisted on treating the private detective to a special meal as thanks for saving their daughter from impending doom. I informed Lydia it was in her best interest to accept the invitation.

Adam was seated to my right and Lydia sat on the other side of me with Anna May on the other side of her. The two women got on surprisingly well as they talked about their chosen professions and how meaningful their work was to them.

After they'd exhausted the conversation, Lydia took the opportunity to fill me in on the things I hadn't known once I'd left the police station the day of Felix Hao's arrest.

She'd been able to find out from Jason that Felix was

lawyering up, though he was having a hard time finding someone to represent him. Certainly, no one in the Asian community was willing to do it once news had broken out all over the local stations that Felix had been caught red-handed with items that connected him to the deaths of three prominent figures in the community. There was also mention of a fourth potential murder victim that would be attributed to him as well: Juliette Chu.

On top of that, while the police had been searching through the rest of Felix's personal effects, they'd found the copy of Lydia's files that had been stolen out of my trunk stashed away in the drawer below where the artifacts had been.

When Lydia told me that piece of information, it clicked as to why I'd recognized his car in the parking lot. It had been the same one tailing Lydia at Asia Village the first time she'd dropped off the files.

Lydia also warned me that I would most likely have to testify in front of a jury because Felix had clammed up and was holding onto the fact that he wasn't guilty, despite all the evidence against him. He wanted a fair trial, he'd proclaimed to his public defender, causing quite a scene at the station in the process.

In the police report I filled out, I'd gone into detail about the things that Felix had admitted to me while he'd held me captive. So whether he wanted to say he was innocent or not, there was much working against him, and I was happy to help in any way I could.

My mother ushered over the server walking around with the cart of dim sum offerings, and because it was a special event, my parents decided that we would have one of each.

The table quickly filled with small plates and metal

baskets containing steamed dumplings, shrimp rolls (my favorite), barbeque spareribs, spring rolls, sticky rice, and, of course, one of my mother's own favorites, chicken feet.

My mom held up her chopsticks, waving them at me and Lydia. "That is enough police talk for today," she commanded. "Now you eat and enjoy. Both of you."

Lydia's eyes roamed the table. "There's so much to choose from, I don't even know where to start."

I picked up the platter with the shrimp rolls and showed it to her. "Do you like shrimp? These are my favorite."

She unwrapped her chopsticks and grabbed the noodle roll on top, almost dropping it before it plunked down onto her plate. "Hey, I'll try anything once. Well, maybe not the chicken feet."

That warranted a laugh from everyone at our table.

I had my eyes on the spring rolls next. "So, tell me about Jason. Are you guys together?"

Lydia smirked. "No . . . well, sorta. I don't know. It's complicated."

I could sense Adam eavesdropping on our conversation so I nudged him under the table with my knee, hoping he'd take the hint not to add his two cents on the subject.

"What's so complicated?" I asked. "I see the way he looks at you. And I know the way you talk about him."

Her chopsticks froze in midair. She turned to me. "So you noticed that, huh?"

"I know I'm not a professional detective, but I'm kinda good at figuring these things out."

Lydia laughed. "You caught me. But in all seriousness, our jobs get in the way. With both of us always on the go, it's hard to cultivate anything meaningful." She reached for a spring roll after seeing me take one. I sensed her mood faltering. "Plus . . . I don't know . . . it's hard for me. I'm not above admitting that I have some trust issues."

"Who doesn't? Am I right?" I said, trying to lighten the topic.

I heard Adam snort beside me.

I nudged him more forcefully with my knee. "I think you should go for it," I said to her. "Life is too short not to take chances."

Lydia inspected the chicken feet and, officially deciding against them, grabbed a sparerib and set it on her plate. She put her chopsticks down while she sipped her tea, probably stalling to reply. A few moments went by before she said, "What, are you a matchmaker now too?"

I chuckled. "Hey, if you need me to be. I also know a great place for a first date."

She looked down at her plate, then back up at me with a bright smile. "You know, Lana Lee, I might just take you up on that."

"Eat!" my mother reminded us.

While everyone dug into their food, I took a minute to appreciate the scene in front of me. Surrounded by family and friends, I thought about what lengths we go to protect them, or to see them succeed.

I thought about Mr. Zhang and all he'd had to endure in his long life, and I was happy that toward the end he'd been able to find someone like my grandmother to spend time with. Not only that but he'd been reconnected with a daughter he hadn't known he'd had, and by extension, a granddaughter.

When no one had been paying attention earlier as we were waiting to be seated, Mr. Zhang had pulled me to the side to thank me for putting myself in harm's way to ensure his family's safety. He admitted to me that he'd worried Felix was up to something because he'd thought he'd caught him eavesdropping on a private conversation that he'd been having with Lois about their family dynamic.

Without a way to prove it, Mr. Zhang had hoped that his secret hadn't been revealed. But now with everything that had transpired, he wanted to come clean to the other Immortals *and* to my grandmother. Once he'd told the necessary parties the truth from his own mouth, he'd share the information with the rest of Asia Village. He begged me to keep quiet for the time being. I promised that I would, giving him my support and telling him I'd help ease blows if there was any way I could help.

He still swore me to secrecy when it came to the Eight Immortals, reminding me how important it was for the legacy of their families to keep the tradition going, but he assured me that they'd be making changes in the way they recruited their members.

He also hinted to me that they were planning to ask Anna May if she'd like to take the position that Donna had recommended her for, and that I mustn't tell my sister that I was all the wiser.

There was a small tinge of jealousy that had poked through at the mention of Anna May filling the coveted position. But as I studied the faces of everyone around me and thought about the things I did have—a boyfriend who loved me; my family; a loveable, cuddly dog who was ever faithful; a best friend who was by my side through even the strangest of times; and of course, my health—I realized there was nothing else for me to want.

Sure, my life was weird and had been filled with obstacles and challenges not even the most skilled fortune teller could predict. But through all the ups and downs that were thrown at me, it was still *my life*, and I didn't think I'd really want to trade places with anyone, no matter what they had that might seem appealing for a fleeting moment.

No, at the end of the day, I wouldn't change a thing.